DARK STREETS

BOOK ONE:

AGENTS OF FEAR

DARK STREETS

BOOK ONE:

AGENTS OF FEAR

ALEX JAMES

Novels by Alex James:

AMAZON SEVEN
VOLUME ONE
Book One: Mission Queen
Book Two: Queen Renegade
Book Three: Intergalactic Ingenue (Pre-order)
Book Four: Princess Executor (Pre-order)

SAGA OF THE URBAN SORCERERS:
Book One: The Summoning of Barker Moon
Book Two: The Reckoning of Emerald Tarragon
Book Three: The Shaping of Cheryl Equiniox (Pre-order)

THE CHRONICLES OF THE TERRAGUARD:
Book One: Maker of Rules

THE ASCENSION SEQUENCE:
VOLUME ONE
The Pandora Sequence
VOLUME TWO
Book One: The Pandora Inheritance
Book Two: The Pandora Arcana (Pre-order)
Book Three: The Daughters of Pandora (Pre-order)

DARK STREETS:
Book One: Agents of Fear
Book Two: Avatars of Wrath (Pre-Order)

www.GalexyTales.com

(or search "GALEXY TALES" at Amazon!)

Dark Streets – Book One: Agents of Fear

Copyright © 2015 Alex James

Cover Illustration Copyright © 2015 by Galexy Tales
Cover design by Michal Dutkiewicz and Alex James
Cover Art & Illustrations © 2015 Michal Dutkiewicz

Book production by Ingram Spark
Editor: Melissa Sheldrick
Editorial Consultant: Gretel Newman-Sugrue
Text layout: Adam Dutkiewicz

Galexy Edition 1.2 (Edited from the original ebook)

Dedication

This book is dedicated to Clive Barker
(especially for *Weaveworld*)

ONE: BEG

I

The kid thought that he was ten years old, although he could not have told anyone that, let alone himself, for sure.

He was begging, he thought. He remembered that word, sometimes. But he did not think of the word, not as a going concern. He was not doing that. He was not doing anything.

He was not ten. He was not begging.

He just was.

Without guardians to remind him, he had lost the need to remember how long his life had been. He had barely experienced enough time to know what life was, or that being on the street was what his life had become, before he'd realized that his life wasn't going to last.

The kid knew that there was less of him now. He was thin, but he hadn't always been. Not thin like this. His features were hollowed with malnutrition, his body was pale, but he remembered that he had, a long time ago, played. With other kids and a ball. Kicking it or something. It seemed silly now. Like a silly dream maybe. A dream he'd had a long time ago, when he'd been able to sleep deeply enough to have dreams.

He felt frail, and weak, and that was normal enough for him, so that he did not think of himself as that any more.

He hadn't washed for days, maybe weeks.

He was starting to the think that the dirt on his skin kept him a little bit warmer at night.

He sat on the filthy cement, against a rough concrete wall that was layered with faded, shredded posters. The concerts they advertised had all long-since been cancelled, and the paper on which they had been printed was now frayed and peeling like the sunburned skin of a dying senior.

He'd sung, once upon a time.

It seemed like ages ago.

Yet because he possessed a premature wisdom, a perspective a boy his age gained only from an early succession of painful events, he also knew it could not have been very long ago. Because although he did not recall his age exactly, whether he was actually ten yet, or still nine, or if everything going past in a grey daze had taken him up to eleven, he knew that none of those numbers were high, or large, and that he was not very old.

He had sung for his supper, like a beggar boy.

He was a beggar boy, after all.

So he heard, as people passed him by, reminding him of that word, what he was doing.

He had a little white coffee cup today.

Starve-a-foam, he'd heard someone say. He didn't like these ones, they broke too easily when the men with the clean trousers and polished shoes, and the women with the smooth legs and high heels, went out of their way to tread on his cup.

But it was all he'd been able to find last night.

The kid always expected the people to steal the money, whatever few silver coins he'd managed to collect (hardly ever the precious gold, and never plastic) but they never did. They just crushed or kicked whatever container he had, and sometimes kicked him. Cracked a rib once, the junkie nurse from the back of the club had said.

When he'd eaten well, and his thinking seemed to work better, he felt some pain there and wondered if the rib might not still be cracked.

Did these things fix themselves?

Nothing else seemed to.

He didn't sing any more. He just sat and hoped.

Although, he wouldn't have called it hope.

When the car pulled up he knew it was the end.

The car was long and low and shining black. From where he was sitting it blotted out all of the streetlights, and the sounds of the city; the drunks and cars, and took with it the last of his ability to think, to evaluate, and to properly consider self-preservation. The rear car door clicked open and swung out toward him. He couldn't see inside. He knew that his mind had ceased to work properly, as it had done a few times before, because the car seemed to be right in front of him, despite the fact that it was at least six or seven paces to the side of the road.

He didn't remember standing up, and taking the six or seven paces, but the seat was so soft and the air inside so warm that the end didn't seem so bad now. The fight had gone out of him.

The end could take as long as it liked.

It could stay forever, if it felt like this.

II

The driver adjusted his rear vision mirror and watched the kid. He was leaving marks on the leather. Dirt, or crap? You never knew how far gone these kids would be. Dancer liked them at least to be semi-aware. You could usually tell, after they'd had a wash and a decent feed, whether or not they could tell what was happening. This one was watching him, seemed to recognize that he had entered some other realm.

So, still vaguely self-aware.

But he was hopeless, and would succumb.

Everyone did, eventually.

III

The kid watched out of the car window until the city neon passed away, then the white of the ordinary street lights took over as buildings passed by. Then there were houses and eventually trees, until it was almost completely dark outside and the driver pulled up somewhere and let the engine idle. They were a long way out of the city. Good. The city was bad. It was nothing but trouble. The driver's window lowered and he spoke into a security panel.

'Weekend package.'

The window slid back up and the car moved on.

The driver looked into the kid's eyes through the mirror.

'Yeah, that's right kid. Real people on security. Lucky he's so rich, or we'd be replaced by automatons and programs.'

The kid knew what he meant, but didn't answer.

They parked in an enclosed garage and the driver stepped out and opened the back door for him. The kid stepped out and was ushered through a series of doors into a house, up some stairs, then across a landing toward a wide corridor. Half way down the corridor, the kid almost curled up to sleep on the plush white carpet. It was so thick, he could feel it beneath the worn soles of his sneakers.

But the driver opened another door to reveal a glorious white marble bathroom.

The kid took pause but the driver touched him for the first and only time by placing his hand in the centre of his back and shoving him forward, across the marble floor.

Then he closed and locked the door, leaving the kid alone.

The expensive soaps looked like lollies.

He sniffed them; powerful fruit smells. He considered eating them. Before he could, the driver returned with some clean white towels, placed them by the bath, and exited again.

Under the towels were some new clothes, all white.

He turned the hot water on.

IV

The bath had been like a dream until he had woken, almost drowning in the bubbles, and leapt out.

Nobody came. Eventually he got back in, with memories from somewhere, long ago, of getting into the shit with a grownup who took care of him, for getting the bathroom floor wet.

After a while he felt too wet, too clammy. He got out and dried himself, surprised that he remembered how. Then he dressed in the clothes the driver had left for him. As soon as he had, the driver returned and led him away to a big room in which everything seemed to be made entirely of dark stained wood, where he was seated at the end of a huge dark-chocolate dining table.

A place had been set, so he sat and waited.

He felt squeaky clean now, and new, even though the white kid-size suit was too big for him and he had to roll up the jacket sleeves to properly touch anything. The driver returned again with a plate of food that the kid had smelled at least two minutes before it arrived; a huge steak, with peas and carrots and gravy, and a bowl of fries. The driver snapped open a can of Coke and poured it into a wine glass. The kid could not believe his eyes as he dug in, rolling up his sleeves to use the glistening silver knife and fork.

He now knew that he had died on the street and been taken to Heaven.

It was God watching from the security cameras that kept whirring in and out of focus on the walls around him.

God was good, after all.

The driver led the kid down another hall. He was very tired now, sleepy-eyed even as he walked through the last door, into a wood paneled study, as the driver closed the door behind him. The kid stood there alone a while, listening to the old round clock steadily tick-tocking on the mantle. He couldn't tell time from a clock without numbers. It was getting late now, though. Then he looked around. A long white wig, and a hammer and gavel were placed proudly on the large wooden desk. Thick books lined the many book shelves.

From somewhere he remembered that these were the tools of a judge.

He remembered someone telling him, when he first got onto the street; the old judges used to let you do what you want, so long as you didn't hurt anyone else. But since the change, all the new judges did was hurt people for not doing as they were told.

Another door opened beside him and he was startled to see a thin old man walk into the room. Was this God? God was the final judge, after all.

'I like to see a young man clean and washed.'

The kid did not respond.

The judge stared momentarily, examining the kid.

'A very pretty young man.'

He was old. Did this mean he was good? An uncomfortable feeling dawned on the kid and showed in his eyes, which the thin judge seemed to like. But the kid was too tired to speak. He would let it happen. This was God, after all. God, in the form of an old judge, who might be one of the good ones.

'So much evil in the world,' God spoke. 'How does such beauty remain uncorrupted?'

God walked up to the kid, took him by the chin and angled his face up so he could gaze down. His hands were warm, as though they had just been washed, and scrubbed. The man looked ancient. The kid stared up with his tired, puppy-dog eyes. God released him.

'Through there,' God pointed, indicating an interior door. The kid walked up to it.

He still couldn't think well. He opened it.

Would it be Heaven?

There was a huge four-post bed, like in fairy tales. It was covered in weird tools, the kind he'd seen in hospitals, plus some leather straps and many colorful plastic toys. At first, he didn't know what to make of them. But once it occurred to him that they could quite easily be used for hurting, his eyes did not linger there and he realized for the first time what it meant to be where he was.

He turned back to God, absolute terror dawning in his eyes.

He was surprised to see the terror reflected back in God's eyes, and was utterly stunned at the reason.

A tall girl was standing behind God. She held a knife at his throat. Already a trickle of blood was staining God's crisp, white shirt collar.

'Open the safe, Dancer.'

The way the woman spoke, she would have seemed tough with or without the knife. Suddenly more alert than he had been for weeks, perhaps months, the kid realized that this man was not God. He was just a man called Dancer. He looked into the eyes of the woman with the knife at Dancer's throat. She stared back at him, cold. She had long black hair and mean brown eyes. She wore a tight black suit, like the ones the men and women in the city wore, but the jacket was buttoned up really tight, with no shirt underneath, so he could see the edges of her bosoms, squeezed together.

But she was not a business woman.

The suit looked older than any other suit he'd seen, like maybe she'd worn it every day for a long time. Something about that, about her, made him feel protected.

The kid heard a noise from behind him, in the bedroom, and spun about.

Another girl stood there.

The kid didn't know what to do.

This one was thinner, paler. She had straight red hair with gold streaks that went down past her shoulders. She looked a bit younger than the other, but when she turned her head, to look behind her, the light changed and suddenly she looked older. She might have been an elf warrior then, from some game he used to play, in another world before he'd been thrown to the wolves.

She was so fierce looking, right then. Sharp-faced, like… one of those wild orange dogs… that raided the bins everywhere, and bred, more and more, after everything went bad and his Daddy had...

His brain switched back to the girl. The woman.

Somewhere in between.

Her clothes were not for business; she wore a gray wool waistcoat over a pale, frayed orange shirt, with a long deep-crimson coat, brown pants and Doc Marten boots.

One look at each and he could tell they were not outsiders, from the bush.

They were from the streets too.

'Open the safe you perverted bastard.' The mean one practically hissed the demand. She was angry. 'Or my companion will rip the combination from your mind. Like taking candy from a baby.'

The kid felt something on his shoulder, from behind, and realized that the elf one had placed her hand there. He couldn't help but flinch. But when he twisted around a bit to look up at her, she wasn't looking back down at him. She was staring at Dancer, icy cold.

'You'll be caught.' Dancer was afraid. The kid could hear it. 'They'll bring back hanging.'

The mean one shifted the knife sideways.

'They already did.'

More blood trickled onto Dancer's white collar. A red stain was spreading.

'Besides...' She smiled. '...you don't know who we are.'

'You must have some sort of record. To get past my security you must have done something like this before.'

The two women exchanged a short, sharp smile.

'You've got it backwards, mate. It's us who know that you've done this before.'

'You'll never –'

The two women suddenly spoke together.

' – never get away with this.'

Dancer was truly terrified now.

'You can't be more than eighteen years old, either of you...'

The kid could hear the fear rise in Dancer's voice. 'I can find a place for you… you're young, you can start again, I can –'

'The safe!' The mean one snapped the demand as though she had been gravely insulted.

Dancer sneered and spat his words. 'Find it yourself.'

'Okay. Do it, Cass.'

'Cass!' Dancer was momentarily gleeful. 'Now I have a name!'

'It won't matter…' The mean one smiled. 'We don't care that you know she's Cass, or that I'm Shylee.'

Cass moved forward, past the kid, the dark-crimson coat brushing softly against him. He looked up and saw concern on her features.

Whatever she was about to do, she didn't want to.

But it wouldn't stop her.

She regarded Dancer shortly then closed her eyes to concentrate. Dancer's eyes began to glow from within, with a hurtful red light. He screamed like an animal and fell to his knees.

At least, he did once Shylee let him.

Cass went to a painting behind Dancer's desk, lifted it from a hook and rested it against the bureau beneath. The painting was small, a blur of yellow and orange flowers. There was a small safe in the wall behind it.

Shylee groaned. 'You're kidding! I could have guessed that!'

'I don't think he ever…' Cass paused. 'He never expected anyone to be in here. It was…' She shrugged. '…hiding the safe is just tradition. A joke.'

Shylee grunted disapprovingly as she faced the flat palm of her open hand at the safe, as though she might somehow open it from across the room. Then she gritted her teeth and tensed. The lights flickered, then the door to the safe glowed momentarily bright orange, then simply slid down the wall in a steaming molten mess.

The kid couldn't believe his eyes. Dripping blobs of it almost set the carpet on fire, until Cass stamped out the edges with her Docs.

Dancer gaped at the sight. Tears flooded his yellowed eyes, and streamed down his hollow cheeks.

'Jesus, Shylee,' Cass sighed. 'I could have... I took the combination from his mind as well as the location!'

Shylee just smiled a crooked, satisfied grin and went to the safe.

'Relax. It wasn't enough of a disruption to alert –' She glanced at the kid. ' – the media.'

Shylee's smile vanished as she removed some small, transparent money bags from the wall cavity. The kid came over to see. The bags were filled with children's teeth.

Shylee spun around to Dancer.

Cass spoke with soft horror.

'They might not be... they could be his grandchildren's – ?'

The kid could see that Shylee was really, bitterly angry now. He flinched at the tone of her voice. '…yes. They could.'

Suddenly she had a gun in her hand, whipped up from the side pocket of her suit jacket, then a silencer from the other pocket. The silencer was attached before the kid knew what either of the objects were. Now she was pointing the gun between Dancer's eyes, his old man's eyes, which were overflowing with tears. Then he was bawling.

'You can't! I'm a powerful man! This is my house! You can't catch me here!'

'Wrong.'

'This is an execution!'

'Right.'

Cass grabbed the kid, lifted him quickly and pressed his face against her breast. It was soft, and warm.

He heard a click, then a strange, brutal sound, then he heard Dancer fall straight to the floor, crumpling with one shot.

Looking up with one eye, the kid could see that Cass was watching Shylee. He heard Shylee move back to the safe.

'How much?'

'Give me a minute.'

'Shylee. The kid.'

Still pressed against her, the kid felt her nod down at Dancer's body.

The kid tried to peek, but Cass pushed his head deeper into her breast. But he could still see. Out of the side of his eye, under her arm, he saw Shylee reach in and remove several cash bricks from the ruined safe, then place them in a plastic shopping bag she pulled from her pants pocket.

'Bloody hell. There's a shitload.'

'There's ten,' Cass counted quickly.

There was also a small velvet purse, for precious jewels, or something like that. Like his Mum had used to keep her rings in. Before his Daddy had sold them to the men from the big casino.

Shylee placed the bag in under her jacket lapel, tight into her bosoms.

Cass nodded. 'Let's go.'

She turned, and the kid saw Shylee scatter the remaining contents of the safe over the desk.

'Shriveled bits of murdered children, in small bags.'

'Shylee – bloody hell! The kid!'

'He's been watching the whole time under your arm, Cass. He's been out there, he knows the score.'

Cass grasped him tighter, speaking into his ear.

'Hold on tight.'

Then she readdressed Shylee, more curtly.

'Coming?'

'You go.'

Cass sighed.

The kid felt dizzy for a second… then they were gone.

Somewhere else.

And for the first time in years, he remembered what it was like to feel safe.

TWO: HOUND

Shylee watched as Cass closed her eyes, and seemed to shimmer. Then the lights in the study flickered, and Cass and the kid vanished. She remembered when they had taken chances, doing that, without line-of-sight.

Now it was easy.

Good. It was easy, and they were gone.

The flickering lights would make the security guys nervous, but she knew full-well none of them would dare interrupt him, the dead judge at her feet, during what she had heard him refer a little earlier to as his 'charity work'.

She looked around.

He had a screen and a connection. A collection of discs. Hard drives. There was a personal cell phone on the desk. All of these things, once simple, now meant that he was wealthy, and important.

They would set the dogs after them now, her and Cass. They would breed new dogs, specifically to hunt them down.

Good, again. Bring them on. She and Cass would catch them, retrain them and send them back to rip out the throats of their masters.

Fantasy.

They'd be dead soon. One of them, then the other in quick succession.

They were dependent on each other now.

Couldn't live…

Shylee swallowed hard.

This was the right thing. It was what she had been born into, made for. Something was guiding her to this, even if it was her own sense of…

Focus.

Don't drift.

Hungry.

Should have stolen some food, eaten before. But the kid. They'd been watching the kid. They saw the limo.

This little office of Dancer's, just a room in the middle of a giant mansion, must have cost more than where she had lived, before all this. And she'd lived okay. She went and took a look inside the bedroom. It wasn't the judge's real bedroom of course. This was his play room. But there was a wardrobe, where he stored his old coats. Everyone in the city needed a coat now, at night. Almost every night, if you went out, no matter how hot the day had been. And Shylee was almost nothing but out at night now.

Still, two coats would change their lives.

They'd be warm for sure as winter came in.

She could take four, six. They could stash two sets.

Pedo coats.

She'd never be able to get it out of her mind.

Fruit of the poisoned tree.

Shylee looked again at the desk, at the disgusting evidence, then crossed to the study door. On the way she caught her own reflection in a mirror above the closed fireplace. This had probably been the butler's room, during the early years of colonization. The place was old enough for that. She knew this, because she'd read quite a bit, at one stage. When it seemed like things were turning bad, and the older student she'd been with had wanted to know why, had wanted her to know why.

He'd been older, a third year.

She'd just started, hadn't even decided on her major.

He'd said that she could move in, after the censorship purge had frightened everyone. He was keeping books Central Security said promoted terror. Before then, she'd been okay, helping a friend run one of the last bookstores the internet hadn't killed. But the list of banned… no, disapproved books, they were called, had been so long, so very, impossibly long, that there had been little choice but for the owner to close it.

Man. Did that feel like another life now, or what?

Actually, it felt like another world; a fantasy world, a movie she'd seen too many times, a long time ago, obsessed over in her teens.

How old was she now, anyway?

She'd been eighteen in her first year of university.

What an idiot she'd been.

Still, Cass kept track of dates.

Shylee wondered; did she even, really, know what year it was anymore?

Thirteen, fourteen, fifteen, sixteen?

Eighteen?

Was she eighteen, in two thousand and eighteen?

No. That wasn't it. That wasn't her reality. But the rest of it had been real.

She had lost that job and soon after there had been no more book stores, no more jobs, and no more welfare to fall back on.

She looked at herself, hard in the mirror.

How old was she now?

What had their names been? The book store owner? The third year who'd gotten her to read about history? About all the people the World Wars had killed, then the Soviets, and the Chinese, and all the other batshit-crazy dictators?

What had all their names been?

Her surname… could she remember it?

Her eyes, staring back from the mirror. Her black hair unwashed. Just black. Still thick, lush even. Still looked okay, even unwashed. She and Cass trimmed each other's hair, straight, Shylee to her shoulder tops, Cass to her shoulder blades. Every full moon. They menstruated together on the half. And they killed together. Whoever deserved it. Whenever they could catch up with them.

Her eyes looked darker. All black now. All pupil.

She still could see herself though. Her old self.

Under what she had become. What she had grown into.

Maybe she was twenty-one by now? Or twenty-two? Then again… had she even turned twenty? In this moment, in this mirror, she had no idea.

She'd always been a type, she knew that. Not everyone's type. A strong Italian-Anglo mix; thick eyebrows and black eyes, a strong Roman nose and big rosy lips, but darker skin than the average Aussie-Anglo. Hers was a strong woman's face, striking. She'd been ignored and passed over by men she found attractive, she'd been called beautiful by men who were nice enough, but did nothing to excite her. She was too much, generally, for the pathetic, androgynous boys that the pop-music world had started to demand, that all the female hormones and secret chemicals in the water had started to create, before the music industry had all but vanished overnight. And she had been way too much for most of the Aussie-Italian Stallion wannabes that had existed within her cultural circle, who wanted to be fucked every night by someone who knew what they were doing, but still lived with their sainted virgin mothers.

She wasn't a housekeeper. She was an oath-keeper. Never, never, nothing like her own mother.

No, she had always been too tall to blend in with the other Euro-party girls, and not heavy enough for the Euro-curve boys. Even when she had, on occasion, tried to look pretty, she'd always looked like she had tried to look pretty. And she was too smart, too sarcastic, to either enjoy the company of, or being treated like either of those types. But she had always looked naturally like a girl you would not fuck with. Even when she did, on occasion, allow someone to fuck her. Especially, then.

What Shylee could do, consequently, was look cool. Like a proper rock chick. She could do dark, she could do angry, and she could do demure, in infinitely variable degrees. But what she did best was business. When she smoked, she looked like she had been born with a cigarette in her hand. She could smolder. When she picked up a cigar, she looked like the mob boss's daughter.

Like she meant business.

By the time she left high school, she'd gradually figured it all out. Her look was always some kind of variation on some kind of darker image. A response to what was emerging then, as it always had, as it had after the pale pastel posers of the eighties, and now, again, or at least, *just then*, as a response to the ridiculous metrosexual, hipster men of the new millennium. The effeminate men at the end of each generational turning. They had just been coming in, when everything had gone to hell, and she had been forced to run.

Then all of her kind had learned; dress like you are who you are.

You can get about, but be careful and stick to the shadows, the corners, the alcoves and underpasses. Don't be homeless; be ghosts, be trolls, be lost, but above all be *dangerous*. But do not be seen. Do not *truly* be seen.

If you do it right, people will not see you because they will be too scared to admit to themselves that you are real.

Cass knew all about it.

Cass had heard.

She'd kept clean, though. Physically. They both had. It wasn't hard if you wanted to. If you still cared. It meant something, to be clean, and they still recognized the importance of that.

They had water.

That was hard to come by, clean water.

But they'd found some.

What had that guy's name been? Third year, two years older. Rich parents paying for his apartment. She'd still had a part-scholarship, a place in her course and a right to be there, but she'd been penniless. No endowment, no student loan. No such thing anymore. Two or three years older, and that had seemed like twenty years to her, when she had been eighteen, in her first year of…

So she *had* been eighteen.

With that boy, that man.

For a second then, she thought that his face was manifesting in the mirror, and that she was mentally ill after all. That her life now, life on the streets, hiding and using her powers, was a fantasy, a delusion of her schizophrenic mind. And that this was a shard of light, of sanity; she was bearing witness to a true vision, a genuine hallucination. Her true mind, desperately trying to wake her up from the nightmare reality…

But, no. The boy, or the young man, in the mirror… he was one of them.

With the powers.

The Wr… roh… *roh*…

He was good-looking. Same age as her, maybe. Before The Censorship, before The Purge, there had been an actor, like this kid; androgynous when he was young, but he'd carried off a hard male awakening, of the man that had always been lurking, just underneath. What the hell had his name been?

God, everyone knew him.

Everyone had, anyway.

Dean Capri? Leon… Cappuccini? Looked a bit like this guy… Probably in prison by now. Or had he been one of the actors they'd made reform, and do the public service announcements? Shit, maybe this guy *was him*? Maybe Deano Caprice had manifested the powers, and now…?

But no. This wasn't him. Too young. Just a poor kid with dark blonde adult sexuality emerging out of androgynous handsomeness, living on the streets. Another doomed hyper. Looked a bit like that famous movie star did, when he was – what? Twenty one? Two? Who knew? Who cared? It didn't matter. Their minds were connecting or something. He could see her too. He looked shocked at her. Jesus, was she that horrible?

Then she caught it.

His thought, about her, and her lips.

What they'd feel like if she were –

Jesus!

Her hand went to her throat and their connection was gone.

That had actually *shocked her*!

But… she'd been acceptably progressive, in her time, about that sort of thing. Living with a guy, sharing his apartment… it hadn't just been about the books, and him encouraging her, treating her like an adult, like someone who could be educated…

Sure, that had helped. But it had all been part of it.

They'd done… *everything*.

But it had been so long ago.

Now…

It was just her and Cass.

Had been…

…for so long now.

She gulped.

Wow.

Someone could still look at her and think of her like… *that*.

But… the Robbie La Caprice look alike was gone.

They'd never meet.

Their lingering connection suggested he wasn't from here.

One of their kind, who had fled here, for the myth.

Probably N'American.

Her eyes glazed over the desk calendar.

It was July 2015.

The Censorship had been three years ago, The Purge more recent.

She'd run… what?

Six months after The Censorship?

She had seen The Purge, the bitterness of December 2012, from a distance.

More than two years she'd been out here.

That was all it had taken. Forgetting the name of the famous actor. Of any famous person. The name of her boyfriend.

Her own surname.

She snapped.

She opened the office door and shouted down the corridor in as deep and masculine a voice as she could muster.

'Oh Jesus! The kid's escaped! He's loose!'

She stepped back into the room, into the corner behind the desk, where she would not be seen, and waited a second. Then she saw the cigar box. Right there. Her mouth watered.

Could she?

Pedo cigars?

She made two quick steps out of ambush position to the desk, flipped the box open, and smelt the aroma almost instantly.

Christ, oh, Christ that was amazing.

Cubans.

My God.

It's full of Cubans.

She didn't even know if they made them anymore.

If Cuba was a real place any more…

She grabbed a handful and stepped back into the corner again.

She could hear footsteps, running on the carpet.

Then she stepped forward again, to the box, flipped the lid, put them back, closed it again.

If she couldn't take the coat…

Then she picked up the whole box, and tucked it under her arm.

She looked down at the floor, at the old man with this brains splattered on the wall behind him.

'Fuck you, demon pedo. Your fucking wraiths will only steal them.'

The driver appeared at the door.

The accomplice.

'Where'd he – ?'

Shylee shot him in the head with the silencer.

It was survival.

Survival.

Of course she should have taken the *god damn* coats.

And now it was *too late.*

She stepped over the driver's body, and his open-mouthed expression of shock. Then she advanced out into the corridor, trying not to disturb the blood splatter pattern. A bullet hit the door frame by her head, splintering wood. She spun about and fired back at the security guy, hitting him in the chest with three shots.

They always took pause when they saw her.

She cut a striking figure.

Shylee bellowed.

'Any more of you *wraiths* in this *moral vacuum?*'

She couldn't help it. She wanted to stay, to kill them all. But she couldn't. She had to go. They'd all be killed anyway, in the cover up. The staff, who all knew, would be killed. The cops who came, and all knew, and covered it up, would then be killed.

'What the fuck?'

She turned around. It was a chef.

'Who are you? Where's the kid? If he gets out we all go to fucking prison!'

Shylee stared down the corridor at him.

'Where's your gun?'

'I – I left it in the kitchen! How'd he get out? The old man usually had them strung up by now!'

'Leonardo DiCaprio.'

'*What?*'

'And Stray.'

'Stray? What the fuck does that mean? I know the kid's a stray! They're always strays! Who the fuck are you?'

'Stray, Shylee Stray.'

She shot him three times as well.

'That was my name.'

There. That was two things remembered.

And another thing too.

That there was nobody else out here, nobody else, doing anything like she was.

Like she was, like Cass was.

And if she got herself killed out here, killing people who were dead anyway, Cass would give up.

Then there really would be nobody. Nobody to remind her of what it had been like before The Censorship, or what her name had been, or what boys were like, when they touched you like they meant it.

She threw her head back and cried out, a guttural scream from the bottom of her lungs.

It felt good, she needed it.

Then, she realized that she couldn't stop.

She closed her eyes and visualized the place where they'd watched the limo drive in, where Cass would be waiting for her. Then the power came up from the base of her spine, and down from the top of her head, and in from her shoulders and across from her hips, all like a six pointed cross that connected in her diaphragm, and she paused her breath, like she'd been taught, let the scream go a second, and rushed herself there, shimmering and vanishing, just like Cass had, as the lights of the old, huge, dark house flickered and blew.

One day, before they finally caught and killed her, she was going to look into a mirror, and keep her eyes open, and vanish, *rush*, to somewhere where there was also a mirror, just to see what the hell it looked like when she did this.

She opened her eyes. She could see the shimmering from this side, when she did open her eyes, like everything was being distorted by a heatwave over a desert plane. She saw stars, wobbling.

She was still crying out, it had kept going, and she still had her head back. She had no idea what had come over her, no idea how long her cry was going to last. If she could even stop it at all.

It was… a cry of righteous disgust, Shylee decided, as it finally faded.

She was pleased about that, that it faded; but she felt a lot better.

Down the street, outside the high stone walls of the gardens of the house of the notorious pedo, Cass was still holding the kid in her arms.

Shylee stood for a while, panting with anger after her scream, vapor pluming in front of her face.

Cass came up to her. Shylee hoped that Cass hadn't already become too attached to the kid. Cass was cool, but she was too soft.

And the kid had to go.

III

Shylee didn't like to go inside the monastery gates.

For some reason, it didn't feel right.

She lit one of the Cubans, and sure enough the Mother Superior saw and started up the gravel driveway.

Then Shylee walked down, and met the big nun half way. Shylee was feeling pretty pleased with herself, but she was worn out and hungry, and she didn't want to walk any more than she had to. Still, it only seemed fair.

Behind her, just outside the gates, Cass still held the kid. The kid hadn't looked up since they'd rushed, and she was starting to wonder if she would have to crowbar him off her.

Mother Superior smiled tightly, but warmly, as their feet simultaneously crunched to a halt in the middle of the drive. Shylee immediately handed her the plastic bag of cash bricks.

'You know…' Mother Superior whispered, deeply. '…I've said, it's not a matter of money…'

Shylee exhaled a smoky halo around the nun's head, heavy in the cold of the night. She'd practiced that, and was again pleased with herself that she'd pulled it off.

'And I've told you, sister. It's no good to us. This is for the kid. You put it in an account for him. For his education. For his future. For his therapy.'

Mother Superior eyed Shylee carefully.

'Every time, a damaged child. And all this money.'

Shylee nodded. 'You've always been good enough not to ask.'

'If I find out who you are, you'll stop bringing the children to us? To safety?'

Shylee grinned, sharp. 'Sister, even we don't know who we are. And as for finding us… good luck.'

'You're just too cool for school, aren't you young lady? But I'm grateful, and I thank you.'

'I used to go to school, sister. I used to read. That's how I know.'

'What's that now, that you think you know?'

Shylee gave her a bitter, lop-sided smile.

'That everything that's happened, that's happening, is about as bad and wrong and unholy as it gets.'

Mother Superior returned the crooked, unhappy smile, despite herself, unable to disagree.

Shylee beckoned Cass forward.

She walked to them, her Docs crunching on the tiny white stones, into the light.

It was a shock. Shylee didn't get to mirrors much, and until tonight hadn't seen herself in quite a while. Now, in contrast, here was Cass. She saw her now, in the light, as she had seen herself in the study mirror. There was just one street light on the country road, to the side of the stone wall gates at the end of the gravel drive. There was starlight, too. Strong out here. And the soft glow from the orphanage. Illuminated from all that, from all different angles and sources as she came forward, Cass looked so pale; like a ghost, an actual ghost. Her hair, centrally parted and cut straight at her shoulder-blades by Shylee herself, was shining like amber, like sunlight on honey, from that weird fire and yellow she'd dyed it, somehow, without saying. Shylee had been so shocked that morning, when Cass's hair had gone honey, but she'd not said anything. She still hadn't, and now it was too late; the moment had passed.

But Cass was just as weird, in a good way, and just as striking with the way she was unusually beautiful as Shylee was; as anyone was. She was fully white, but her eyes were genuinely that almond shape people talked about, that almost nobody had; wide, actually shaped like leaves, and hazel. Through and around this, her lashes were thick and black, and the line of her upper eyelid, and the line between her lower lid and cheek, were also very sharply defined, so as to form, in effect, two more sharp black lines. Now, here, it was like watching the white-shrouded spirit of an Egyptian princess walk toward her, bizarrely dressed like a chimney sweep.

As though to accentuate this, Cass's head was angled down, her chin on the boy's shoulder, but her eyes were angled up. She looked quite frightening; a mix of threat and sheer cool. Her nose, her lips, her chin were all pronounced; pointed, pursed and sharp, lending her the aspect of a fox, a fox that was somehow manifested as human, a wily trickster shapeshifter who'd transformed into a beautiful, pale white, fire-haired assassin,

or assassin's helper. Sleek and nimble, for a flash she looked about as cunning, as threatening, even Luciferian, as any woman Shylee had ever seen.

Then she moved a few more steps forward and the light shifted from her hair, and she looked up; and there, instead of the devilish fox, was Cass again, pale and waifish and angelic.

'The fox and the hound…'

Mother Superior's whisper made Shylee snap her gaze back.

Was she…? Had she…?

'Well, when you're done…'

The Mother looked at Shylee, with a lifetime of knowing.
'…when you're done, daughter, you know where to come.'

THREE: FOX

I

Cass had grinned just a little, to herself, as she'd listened.

Shylee had called the woman 'sister' not in a religious or even feminist sense. Rather, she said it as John Wayne would say it. Almost with the accent. Sas-tarr.

The kid's hold on her tightened. She wouldn't let go until she was certain. The kid whispered to her.

'Did she kill him?'

Cass didn't respond.

'She killed him, didn't she?' The kid demanded, albeit softly. 'The horrible man. Dancer. Because he was going to kill me?'

Cass whispered back. 'He was already dead. He was dead inside. How can you...?' She paused, reconsidered, then realized what she was trying to say. '...you can't kill something that's already dead. Can you?'

She knew the kid was still pondering this, as Shylee beckoned them forward with a sharp wave.

'I want him in the orphanage tomorrow...' Shylee was demanding.

'The others have all gone to good homes.' The nun had a kind face. Her features were cross-hatched with what looked like a century of concern. 'The money will be disguised as a donation, a gift, until they are old enough to be told... of their great expectations, shall we say?'

'By that time,' Shylee smirked, 'we won't care what fiction you create for them.'

Cass wondered what the old nun had said to Shylee, to make her suddenly so snappish and defensive. Usually, these two got along. What had the nun seen in her tonight?

Cass tried to put the kid down, but he was like a cat with his claws in.

Mother Superior spoke sweetly but firmly.

'Come with me child.'

The kid looked out at the nun, then up at Cass.

'You need to go with her,' Cass spoke calmly, but nicely. 'You'll be safe.'

The kid assessed the nun again, then reburied his head in Cass's chest.

She was tired. Fuck. She was really tired. And the night was nowhere near over. It was time to go.

'This is one of the old churches…' The nun was stating things very clearly. You couldn't help believe her. Cass guessed it was well-practiced. The art of making people believe things that weren't necessarily so. 'Like they're supposed to be. Not like the city ones.'

The kid looked up and stared at Cass again, deep into her eyes this time.

'You can sleep here. I promise. A real bed. As long as you like.'

The kid seemed to understand.

Cass felt his grip loosen. He was just as tired as she was. More. Slowly he slid down her front, dragging her coat and waistcoat down, forcing her to bend. Then his feet touched the ground, and he was walking, crunching, toward sanctuary. When he reached Shylee, he ran past her and leaped into the giant arms of the massive nun. The nun lifted him, as Cass had, and he gripped her like a koala. It was as though the rediscovery of maternal comfort was something he could no longer bear to be without, and he buried himself deep in her robes.

Cass thought she might cry.

She pushed it down.

She always felt like she would cry.

But she never did; she always pushed it down.

One day, she'd pay for that.

The nun looked down and the kid looked up at her.

Their eyes met.

The nun would have looked up, back at them then, to thank them one more time.

But they weren't there anymore.

They could see her, though. The orphanage, or monastery, or whatever it was called; this place where nuns lived… it was visible, from the rooftop of the church next door, where they'd rushed to.

They were good at this now, they barely had to point.

To another roof, and gone. Then the next, and the next.

Then they were out, further into the country, heading home.

II

The dirt path was wide, and the road open.

It was a familiar landmark to them now, and when they reached it, they simply walked on.

Shylee puffed smoke as they moved.

Cass sighed.

'You killed them all, didn't you?'

Shylee shrugged. 'Those that came running.'

They walked on until Cass sighed again.

She didn't mind. She just…

She just didn't want Shylee to start liking it or anything. She had a name for it now, almost a spiritual thing. Shylee was getting more spiritual. It wasn't a concern, but Cass just hoped… it wasn't anything, like, crazy-making.

Cass didn't get all that spiritual stuff.

'We can't keep going like this.'

'We have to keep going.'

'We'll get caught.'

'We'll never get caught.'

They walked on in silence after that.

The kid watched over the big black and white woman's shoulder as she walked him into the massive old hotel.

He was okay, he knew.

For now.

Maybe for now and forever.

Who knew?

Safe, until someone came for the ladies here.

That was bound to happen.

Sooner or later.

Nothing lasted forever.

Especially not the people who tried to be good.

At the end of the drive, the air shimmered. Smoke appeared, then a figure materialized in the shadows. He was dressed in a long grey coat, and a black fur top hat, and he was looking up.

The kid followed his gaze as the door to the giant hotel closed behind him.

Shylee and Cass were up on the church roof, watching him as he was taken into safety.

He loved them. They were and always would be his angels, who'd saved him from The Devil.

He watched as the new person… a man, he thought, took a long, intense drag on his cigarette.

Then Shylee and Cass were gone.

And then, so was the smoke.

FOUR: TEXAS

I

Davy Worth hugged his theatrical black-wool cape around him as he assessed the hundred-plus hot women and handsome men that were lined up outside the club.

Or were they cute girls and nice boys?

There was barely any distinction any more. These days it was all about how you looked…

Huh. No, not these days. It had always been about that.

It had always been about what you could carry, project, and maintain.

But it was different now.

That was all still so, but in another way.

He supposed that age laws still existed, and restrictions like that. Back home in NUSA, there had always been rules set in stone, to do with age restriction and alcohol and drugs and statutory age limits, defined by people with the best interests of mental health and the community in mind, protecting innocence against predation.

He supposed that those laws existed in Australia as well.

They had pretty much existed in almost every western-style democracy.

He supposed they could still be found in the books, those laws, the set-in-stone books, and that technically, those laws still existed. Technically, they were still laws. But like a lot of things that used to be set in stone, nobody knew or cared about them anymore; nobody anywhere, apparently. Certainly nobody cared about laws to do with age restrictions, let alone enough to enforce them.

Davy sighed at his thoughts, hugged his cloak a little tighter, and listened to the beat of the club from across the street. The adjacent shop entrance alcove had been a sandwich bar that had, until fairly recently, serviced the staff in the local unemployment office. When that whole department had been absorbed into the newly-formed

Department of Employment, and relocated into one of the three Central towers in the center of the city, the little sandwich bar had closed down too.

Unlike the club.

The dulled beat of the dance music pumped through the walls of the nightclub and out onto the street, perpetually. Again, technically it was a nightclub, but it never closed, genuinely earning the standard abbreviation 'club'.

The line was always there. Alive with people, and constant, even if it was just a trickle in the early hours, and just a few comings and goings closer to dawn and dusk. An immortal creature, with its own biorhythms, its flesh and blood ever-replenished.

And spirit?

He was thinking too much. He never used to think at all.

He used to just go into clubs and zero in on the hottest three chicks, then play them off. He'd keep 'em in the air, bang the sluttiest one in the bathroom, the moodiest in the alley, and the cutest one back at her place, all in time to be home for momma to cook him breakfast. Just keep poppin' those pills, Davy. Poppin' the sex pills, all night long, just like that guy there was doin'. And that guy, and that guy…

He couldn't even get turned on now, watching these girls. Or, maybe he could, if he tried. If he wanted to. Maybe he just didn't want to. Maybe he was getting turned on, just thinking about how he couldn't have them, how these tramps were just not part of his life any more. How he couldn't have them now, even if did want to… and that made him suddenly want them again, even more. Even more than last night, or the night before, or…

He shivered.

Knock it off, Davy.

Holy Jesus.

He shivered again; the chill breeze kept coming.

This city was supposed to be nice. His parents had been here once, for a few days. Before he'd been born. He figured that the whole climate thing must have happened by now; the big change, the major shift, because the city seemed like a desert city now. But he never heard anybody talk about it. That was, when he did hear people talk. And nothing about it was never mentioned in any of the newspapers.

But the weather here was like the weather in Vegas. Kind of. He was pretty sure that hadn't always been the case, though. It was like Vegas, or somewhere like that, in that it was freezing cold on winter nights, with bitter winds, and still hot in the day, with baking sunshine. Desert weather. All seasons, day and night, merciless. Living rough here, you had to keep two sets of clothes, and swap out twice a day, at least, because there were still days, every now and then, for no rhyme or reason, where it seemed like some other season. Mild and okay. But that never lasted long. About as long as it took you to adjust; then freezing or boiling again. Mad.

The alcove was diagonal to the club, which was on the corner of a T junction, near the end of the so-called nightclub precinct. He could stay there, unseen, looking diagonally across at the door, at the line, all night if he wanted. Then he would see the people come out the side of the club, up on the other side of the corner, onto the T-stalk. Five minutes later, five hours later. He'd haunted this stretch enough times now to know that this one was the alcove where the music vibrations from the club carried the clearest, the one where you had a chance to actually guess what song it was.

Hours of amusement.

They still played some of the tracks he knew from back home, a couple of years old now, sometimes more. But it wasn't the kind of club that played, like, retro or anything. In another year, if he and Kelli lasted that long hiding here, he wouldn't know any of the tracks they played, other than in their muffled, vibrated form.

Another freezing western wind blasted up the street.

It wasn't near dawn yet, but the final hours were starting.

The brick would be here soon.

Davy watched another hour as the line grew, then as it slowly diminished until one by one all the beautifuls, handsomes, cutes and nices, in whatever shape or form or standard, were regurgitated, inebriated, coupled off or grouped together, and vanished into the early morning. Many of them, like him, were on their own.

Davy had played the counting game along with the bouncers all night, picked and chosen with them as to which and how many of the most beautiful would be allowed entry when the numbers inside were high, and kept count of the ratio of men to women. He had a hard-on for a while, keeping them in mind, watching them and remembering them; their hair, their dress, color and length, and knew then for sure that it was still possible, but it was all under control.

It was always.

Under control.

Then, when the club had gone quiet, he had come up two short; two girls. Brunette pink micro dress, blonde yellow tube top. He hoped they were okay. There were still people going into the club at this time of night, but they were older, and weirder. Desperados, they used to call them, he and his buddies, when they'd been leaving last and watching them come in. Older, late twenties usually, but past forty some of them; heavier drinkers, more experienced but more blasé. Losers, losing their looks, losing the plot. Stayed at the party too long, nobody left to go home with.

'If you know what I mean…' Davy uttered, barely aloud.

At least, that's what it had seemed like at the time, in Austin, where drinking wasn't such a big deal, and everyone had activated their requisite alcoholic gene to some degree. No such thing as a latent alcoholic gene in Texas, they'd joked. The weather was too hot, and so too were the ladies. But now he saw these late-coming stragglers for what they were. Just folks. Sad, sad folks, some of them not much older than he was, looking for someone to… some contact. Just human contact.

The two main bouncers went inside and an older, harder looking guy, leaner and calmer with less to prove, took their place.

The older you got, the weirder you got. Couldn't help it.

It was actually a good thing, Davy was starting to realize.

Mostly.

A bit later, the two original bouncers departed from the back, and the two girls he'd kept count of, pink micro and yellow tube, emerged with them. Dragged like rag dolls, laughing like drunks.

One bouncer got into a car, and pink micro leaped like a kitten onto the passenger seat, with her head in his lap practically before he'd sat. The car was almost facing him directly. He'd known that. He'd known that car was the big Kiwi bouncer's car. He couldn't really see the look he had on his face, right now, but he could have guessed; triumph. Was that why he'd stayed so late? To see this? Again? The other bouncer was banging yellow tube on the trunk, her ankles locked around his shoulders.

Then there was a flurry, as though by some prearranged signal, and both couples stopped. Then the second duo were in the back of the car, and it was gone, swinging past his alcove, the intense headlights flashing in, just in time to miss spotlighting his voyeur's vantage.

He let go a deep breath. He'd folded himself back, into his cape, into the alcove, pulled down the hood, without knowing.

Now, only he remained from the start of the night.

He flipped the hood back up from his face. Even though there was neon and flouro and plain old white electric light all up and down the long street, it did seem darker now, just before the dawn. Then it started to rain.

Davy pulled further back into shelter.

He knew that he could see himself in the reflection of the empty service café if he turned around. He'd managed not to do that, all night. But now, as he was closer to the glass, against his better judgment, he turned and assessed himself.

There he was; there was Davy Worth.

He looked a lot older now, but he was getting used to that. Two years were worth ten, when you could never relax, never sleep. Not well, anyway. Not longer than a few hours, max. He wasn't so shocked any more that he'd aged prematurely, aged as much as this.

This was him now.

It had happened, no turning back.

Not any of it; the clock, Kelli, any of it.

What did shock him, just for a second, what always shocked him, was the fact that he looked so damn disheveled. He still expected to look into his reflection as see the fine

young man he had been back in Austin; that guy, looking back from his own ensuite, attached to his massive bedroom, in his parents' massive house, in fine old West Lake Hills.

Whenever he looked now, he needed a shave, and to wash his hair. He needed… Lord, just a *shower*. The cut that had been so stylish not so long ago was now overlong, way overgrown, even though Kelli had for months done her best to keep it the same. He tied it back now, with one of her hair-ties. Rat's Tails, they used to call them. He had a *Rat's Tail* now.

Davy knew that his jeans were dirty, and that his socks smelled. His tee was frayed, his sweater had holes… but his leather jacket, that was still good. Built to be worn every day. Built to last. He'd never felt the cold much, so three layers did him okay. But even so… Kelli had been right about the cape. The cape worked, for whatever reason.

Three nights out in the cold, way back at the start, freezing on the hard ground, and something had happened to her. Kelli had worked it out. Thought through…

Who they were.

Who they'd been, and who they were now.

She'd found a way, out there, thinking, for them to survive.

Kelli needed more though.

More layers, but…

Just, more.

But he'd fix it for her.

Dammit, he would.

The short scarf, beneath the cape, tight around his muscular neck, made him look like something out of a British Historical, the kind of soap opera melodrama set hundreds of years ago, or during one of those old fashioned wars, that his parents had made him and Kelli watch on Sunday nights on the local PBS.

He'd started to kinda like them, in the end.

They were kinda… addictive.

At least, before PBS had been shut down. That had been the start.

His papa had warned him.

'Son, America's been fractured for too long, and the rifts are too wide, too well-established to repair now. America is like an old house these days, in that respect. And you know what they say about old houses, son? If you really love the Old Girl, you can keep some of the ol' foundations, see? An', well, that's what America is like now; some of the basic infrastructure? That can stay. But the rest…?'

Then he'd smiled, like he couldn't help it.

Davy always found it strange that the further this had developed, the idea that America would break apart into smaller countries, the more pronounced his papa's Texan accent had become. Davy's momma had raised him to speak naturally, and pronounce things in a more generic Trans-American accent. Like actors learned to do on television. Like Kelli had been learning to do. Her teachers had been pleased that she was already so well-advanced in that department, while many of her contemporaries had required one-on-one elocution lessons. All the wealthy mommas wanted that for their daughters; film, theatre, or country. Even a beauty queen, devoted to charity, would do. His papa had gone along with it, all of it. He owned TV stations, he understood.

He'd spoken appropriately, until then.

Until Texas had started taking steps.

'Well, son, in that case, it's like this; the rest, well it's just got to go. Those parts of her have just got to be torn down and rebuilt from scratch. And, well, this part of the country, we can't afford any liberals no more. If Texas is gonna survive, as its own country, like, well… one of them fancy European corporate-countries…' His papa had shrugged and spread his arms. All he needed was the ten gallon hat. '…then some things have just got to be allowed to… pass away, I s'pose.'

Some things, it turned out, had required a little more encouragement.

And some things, he supposed, had sprung up to take their place…

Then, Davy's mind did one of those things.

He'd known it was going to; he'd felt it coming, letting his mind wander, into the past, thinking about all that… crap. All that crap he'd left behind. He hated it when this happened. It always came outa nowhere, always freaked the crap out of him.

His reflection changed.

Crap.

He knew what it was; somewhere close, right now, another one of them, another one of *his kind*, was looking into a reflective surface and checking themselves out. Letting their mind wander, too.

It was a girl. Maybe a woman. No, somewhere in between. Scary. Dark hair and harsh black eyes, a face like a spoiled rich girl from some nighttime soap, but, man, if she cleaned up she could be… with her tits jammed together like that, under the black jacket like that. God All Mighty. He could just imagine those hot, wet lips, wrapping real tight around his –

She jolted, then; she got that. Heard it from his mind. Her hand went up to her bare throat, as though she'd been shocked to receive that thought. She sneered, her fat lips curving meanly, and turned away. Then she was gone from the reflection, and he was face to face with himself again. Suddenly, the lust in his eyes, right there.

Dickensian Davy. The Giant Dick.

There was a thud behind him and the brick skidded into the edge of the alcove. He stepped out, into the rain, in his hacked-up Nikes.

Thomas God Damn Crapper.

They were going to fall apart soon.

Steal. They needed to steal again.

He felt tight around his neck, angry for no reason. That was the closest he'd felt to anyone, like that, for… forever it seemed. And she'd known, she'd known he was there, known he'd been hot for her, in just that moment…

But; wait. Did that mean – she had seen him, too? Was she staring into a mirror somewhere and seeing – him? As he had seen her? That hadn't happened before. He'd seen other faces but they had never known. There had never been any kind of *recognition.* Mutual – recognition.

He shook himself out of it; what good was thinking all that fucked up crap?

The newspaper delivery truck had passed by. *Without him noticing.* All night here waiting for it and… never mind. He needed to stay alert. He was drifting, daydreaming, fantasizing. Too many distractions. Too many micro-skirts, too much cleavage. And black jackets. Shining dark hair and full, mean, soap opera lips. There couldn't be any of that, he couldn't afford it.

He probably needed to eat, too.

He grabbed the twine cord and picked up the brick of newspapers, lifting them easily out of the rain.

On the top copy, the headline read:
HIGH COURT JUDGE MURDERED IN HOME
Then he left the alcove, the same way he'd come.

II

From the lobby of the abandoned thirty floor office building, Davy made his way up the stairs at his regular, steady pace, carrying the newspaper brick in both arms before him.

He had not read a newspaper in many years until he had fled his home, had not even been aware that newspapers still existed. When his father had finally bought a tablet and cancelled their paper-subscription to *The Statesman*, *The Business Journal*, *The Hollywood Reporter* and *Variety* on the same day, it had surprised Davy no end. Soon after that, when the paper had stopped landing on their front lawn every morning, he had naturally assumed that this was the fabled 'death of print', or something close to it. So Davy had been somewhat surprised to arrive here, more than a year later, to discover that printed newspapers did still exist, even if it was on the other side of the world, in a city that seemed at least three years behind Austin. A remnant, he had supposed, that would not last much longer. Then he'd heard, and realized why.

NUSA Central Planning had blocked all the phones, and partitioned the internet, right across all the new American countries. All those things that the government had threatened to do in the interests of security, which the internet experts said could never be done… well, Central Planning Security had done them, and the rest of the western world had followed suit.

Phones, the internet, satellites… the whole world he'd grown up with.

Only for the elites now.

Only for Central Government, Central Management or Central Panning, or those with special privileges.

Bureau 88.

That kind of thing.

'You didn't need to take away the guns, after all…' Kelli had said. 'You just take away their phones, and they lose the will to live. They don't care about their guns anymore.'

Davy had heard that gun deaths had shot up after the 2012 Crash and the Phone Purge that Easter. Self-inflicted gun deaths, that was; when they'd killed or commandeered all the satellite towers, people had killed themselves.

Forced to talk face to face for the first time in years.

That's what he'd heard, anyway.

III

Despite food being harder and harder to come by, Davy kept fit. He still had principles, and discipline. He'd been fit as a race horse, back in the old life. He'd worked out regularly, a total junkie. Scored there too, all the time.

Played.

So every time he came home, he calmly but diligently climbed the stairs all the way to the twenty eighth floor.

No hurry, a reasonable pace. Heart rate strong and steady.

Reaching home, he made his way down the long corridor to what had once been some kind of executive office suite, although there was hardly anything left of that now. But it was okay. The pale cream walls needed dusting for cobwebs, and a good scrub in places, but they would do. The concrete floors still bore the marks where the carpet had long ago been stripped, but that was okay too. The large offices, which were located on either side of the enormous office suite they resided within, were totally empty, and almost all the walls were glass, so visibility was excellent. And noises reverberated up through the dead elevator shafts and stairwells so clearly, that he had started to be able to tell the difference between rats, cats, possums, foxes and… whatever else.

But Davy and Kelli Worth had hidden, and made temporary

accommodation, in worse places.

Much worse.

Two weeks back, a feral cat had made its way up to them, but once it had seen them it had never returned. They heard it running, all the way down, and couldn't help laugh at the receding sound of its scrambling claws around each stairwell corner. It had been the best laugh they'd had in ages.

Davy knew that when he walked in, Kelli would be sitting behind the desk they'd found when they'd arrived.

Broken and abandoned.

'That's the only qualification anything or anyone needs to get employed here these days,' Kelli had quipped.

The desk was one of the few things that had remained, up here on the executive floor, from the previous occupants. There had been a few other items scattered down the stairs, as though people had fled in a hurry, taking everything they had been able to carry, and leaving whatever they dropped on the way down before the doors were locked forever. On the tenth floor landing there had been a beer keg. Empty, but Davy had a good eye, an eye for dimension. He'd done a loose measurement then pushed it all the way back up, floor by floor. He'd been so hungry afterwards. That had been more than three weeks ago, on the night they'd arrived.

The last time they'd risked stealing hot food.

They were really no damn good at stealing.

Not either of 'em, any damn good.

But they'd needed it.

A celebration, or a Last Supper, depending.

They just didn't have the talent, and couldn't seem to get the hang of it. They hailed from a good family after all, and damn it, they'd never even had to think about this kind of life, about stealing, about these kinds of things, going cold and hungry, hiding from the cops. Never. Why the hell would they?

Davy smiled at his little sister. Sure enough, she was sitting behind the large and slightly battered desk, its legless corner propped up with the empty beer keg. Close enough to an exact fit. He was proud of that, somehow. Just a little thing, but, Lord Almighty, at least something he had tried to do had worked out right.

The walls around them were all tinted glass; they could see out, but nobody could see in. Maybe a spotlight from a helicopter, but that was unlikely. Bureau 88 had a strong presence here in Australia, and Central's buildings dominated the city skyline, but it seemed to be only administrative; not to the extent of power they had back home, where they could command the military. Although… you weren't supposed to even think that, let alone say it.

Framing Kelli was a prominent view of those triple office buildings; new government buildings, only three years old, he'd been told.

Post-crash, post '07.

Australian Central Government, Planning and Security. The central one was slightly higher than the two flanking it, although they didn't really know which was which. Kelli said the biggest one would be Government. They had the ego. But everyone knew that the real power was in Planning.

This, their most recent temporary home, was also one of the tallest buildings in the city. But it was located in the old sector, and the neon night-skyline of the active and occupied new sector, where Davy had just been, was spread out before and beneath them. Behind the city, over the hills that led out to the high desert plane, the half-full moon was rising late, into the burgeoning sunrise, and would be crossing the blazing blue sky all day.

Kelli loved her chair.

They'd found it, one wheel missing, on the fifth floor stairwell. Kelli had been sure that someone had broken it on the way down, trying to take it with them, and that the wheel must still have been in the building somewhere. Piecing it together, one evening with nothing better to do, like every other evening now, they had figured that the company, whatever it had been (absolutely no sign of branding remained) had gone under in the crash. Maybe not before the Global Crash in '07, but certainly before the Purge in '12. The staff had been told they were fired, and to get their things and leave. Someone had brought up a beer keg. Then, somewhere along the line, a bunch of drunk, disgruntled staff, probably all newly broke, with all their assets frozen, had tried to make off with whatever they could. The most keen had tried for chairs and maybe even the boss's desk, which was how and why the leg had been broken off.

At some point, much later, the liquidation squad had come through for the carpets, and even the glass in some of the office windows along the executive corridor. They'd taken light fittings, copper wire from the walls, everything. But they hadn't run amok; it had all been very careful and professional. As though, one day, the infrastructure might be used again. The strangest thing was though; they'd taken all the stairwell doors, and set the elevators so they remained open. The cage was at the top, and in the middle of each wide open and empty open-space floor below them was an exposed elevator shaft.

'They threw stuff down there; metal to be scrapped,' Davy had guessed. 'Took the doors off, so what they had to carry… they didn't want to have to keep opening and jamming them I suppose. Maybe they were metal? Good scrap, too?'

At first when Davy and Kelli had found the building, they had not been able to believe their luck. There was no power connected, and no security cameras.

The whole building was locked up, and completely dead.

They'd been directed there by another of their kind, someone they'd met on the way out. The boy had said he'd been watching the building but wasn't sure. Maybe it was safe. Maybe it was a trap. A Bureau 88 trap.

'They do that now?'

'They're gonna start, mate…' The kid had been no more than thirteen. '…youse can fucken bet on that.'

Even so, he'd said, if he hadn't had to go, he'd be there now.

But they could have it, no worries. He wasn't coming back to Adelaide. They could fucken keep it. He was going north, to Darwin.

'They pay us up there. The Asians. They don't wanna hunt us down an' kill us. They wanna use us. Take us to their business meetings, tell 'em if their partners are bullshitting 'em.'

Davy and Kelli had heard that before.

'I want to talk to someone who's come back…' Kelli had responded.

So far, so far as they knew, nobody had come back. But why would they?

They would either be dead, or employed by Asian businessmen and safe.

Davy had let that go. They were safe enough here, for the time being.

Maybe the kid would actually come back?

Tell them it was all bullshit.

Show them the way home.

IV

Here, at first, Davy hadn't slept for two nights.

Kelli had slept like a baby, in her cape, on the desk. Then Kelli had offered to do the same for him. Now they'd been here almost a month. The longest they'd been anywhere, other than the *Head Clear*.

Kelli was huddled in the chair, its upholstery almost new, wrapped in her cape, and an old blanket, reading a book. She was small enough to do that, like a giant family pet that had her own chair. Although he'd never actually say it, Davy could'a sworn, for serious, back in Austin… he'd seen Great Danes and Old English Sheep Dogs that were bigger than Kelli.

She must have heard the upward echoes of his coming all this time, carrying the brick, but she looked up immediately and seemed relieved to see him. He used to get a little peeved at that, like it were a little too passive-aggressive, a little too much like a damn girlfriend or somethin'… but then he realized she was relieved to see that he was okay. To look into his eyes and see that he'd held it together another night. He supposed, when he thought about it, that he was the same whenever she went out. Not that she did much, not anymore.

Kelli had looked for that little fourth wheel for a whole day before she'd finally found it, in the furthest corner of the lobby, under the security desk. Since then, she'd barely gotten out of that chair. At least it sure seemed that way, some days. Davy supposed; really, she could have been doin' anything back here while he was out all night.

For a while, Kelli too had attempted to partially maintain her clean-cut college-kid look; the bland sharpness that would have been expected of them at home. Davy had even tried to cut her hair, once, a few weeks back. He'd tried, but afterwards she'd gone quiet, and kept out of his way all afternoon, until night. Even then, she hadn't spoken to him at all, until sunrise.

It had been that morning she'd found the missing chair wheel.

The tension between them had been okay, after that.

Now her fringe was past her chin again, and the back of her hair down to her shoulder blades. She kept it in place with a dirty white beanie at night, and a generic black baseball cap during the day. Wearing hats inside. Their parents would not have approved at all. Still, she kept 'em on. Almost always. When she didn't wear a hat, you could see the sandier but still light-blonde of her real hair, down to her ears almost. Maybe that was why? Didn't matter; all that did, was that she was still here to wear the damn silly things.

Every night since he'd realized that newspapers still existed, or had come back into style, or necessity, maybe both, and that the newspaper truck still delivered to the closed-down café, Davy had gone out there. And every night, he'd come back with a newspaper brick.

They were doing better for it.

To begin with it had just been extra weight up the stairs, although in the back of his mind he knew that homeless people stuffed the lining between their clothes with newspapers to keep warm. He hadn't really wanted to face that. The fact that he was now homeless, in a city that was freezing cold at night, and that he was about to practice something homeless people practiced.

It might have been safe up here, relatively, but God Damn it was cold, thirty-odd floors high with no air-con. Even so, once he'd brought the papers up, he hadn't done that; the stuffing his clothes with newspapers like a homeless person thing…

Some remnant of pride, despite the lack of self-preservation, which he had held onto all this time, had stopped him again.

It had been Kelli who had suggested that the paper bricks were actually quite a find; that they shouldn't cut the twine. That they should not sleep *with* it, that they should sleep *on* it.

After all, they were both well aware, at this point, that even one night on the freezing concrete floor might kill them. They'd quickly realized things that people in their position realized… well, pretty damn quick. Realized, or died. Like, when you were sleeping rough, that if you only had one layer, one blanket, it was more often than not better to sleep on top of that layer, one layer removed from the freezing earth, than to have it over you, or even better, fold it like a bag.

They'd remembered that one from school camps.

And, don't set up in a cave, unless you're positive nothing already lives there.

That was another one Davy always remembered, for some reason.

And then, don't set up in a dry creek bed; flash floods kill people all the time.

That was another.

Then they'd realized, even more quickly, that it was better to stay indoors, even if they were risking getting caught. Stay indoors, find more blankets.

It had taken a few nights for the shock to wear off, for them to start thinking straight, accepting what they were, what they'd become, and… to deal.

Eventually, they had.

Kelli had seen to that.

Kelli had snapped out of it, back to it, first.

Up here, before the bricks, she had always taken the chair, and he had always taken the desk. But the desk had been hard. Kelli had told him that the office chair was uncomfortable too, but the way she curled up in it… he let her have it. He was more than happy to.

He placed the paper brick with the others.

Twenty one now.

Kelli was so small she could sleep in the office chair and make it look like a throne. So small, or, petite, he was supposed to call it, being tiny, she could sleep on two rows by five of the newspaper bricks. And tonight, he would be okay, finally, with two rows of five and one at the end. Tonight would be the first time his feet didn't stick out, over the edge. Off the floor, with blankets, the newspaper bricks had made a huge difference.

They slept beside each other, with the two brick beds about a meter apart, but never huddled close. It was too weird. They'd never been that kind of family. The hugging, touchy-feely kind. They'd tried to share a blanket on the desk, that first night when it was all they had, and they'd eaten well, and he'd been more tired than usual from bringing up the keg. But they were both uncomfortable cuddling, and he'd fallen off a couple of times, trying to find enough space, facing away from her. In the end, after having those first few crucial moments of falling asleep totally broken several times, his mind hadn't been able to get back there. So he'd stayed awake for forty eight hours, on guard.

Deep down, but not deep enough that he couldn't admit it to himself, he was afraid. His sister was cute. You'd have to be blind.

All his buddies had said so at one time or another. Producers had wanted her for TV. For real. And she had been too soft when they cuddled. He might have dreamed. Had dreamed, every night, about women. He would dream again, he knew. Especially if he kept going to the club, and watching the beautiful people.

That would not be good, spooning his sister.

He wasn't made for this.

He was made to be out and about.

Far and wide.

Twenty one bricks.

Three weeks.

He hadn't even *touched* a girl in more than a year.

They were doing okay, though. They were doing okay.

But the signs of wear and tear were becoming all too apparent. He had not realized until this morning, until he had become reabsorbed in his reflection, what a parody of their old lives their 'look' had now become.

Davy attempted a grin as he turned to her.

'You look like the CEO of Street People Inc.'

'You're late again.'

'I had to take the stairs. The elevator isn't working.'

'You've been to that club again.'

'Really, darling, next you'll be checking for lipstick on my collar!'

They'd tried to do more and more exaggerated posh British accents as they went, but they were both terrible at British. Even Kelli's drama teacher, who'd loved her more than any of her other students, had said she would have trouble playing British. They laughed a bit at everything to do with the exchange, then Davy sat on the desk and looked out, out past her chair. He saw Kelli stare down at the newspaper brick, at the new headline. There were other headlines like it, on the preceding bricks.

'Five hours to get the paper...' Kelli uttered. 'We have the longest driveway...'

'It's something to do,' Davy shrugged. 'Until we get a place that will take a dog.'

'You could always read one.'

'Read a dog?'

She smirked. 'Read a paper!'

He guffawed. 'That would unbalance your bed. It would be like the princess and the pea. One newspaper lower, and oh, I can't sleep!'

'Well, thank you brother…' Kelli stood, the chair rolling back behind her, and gestured broadly with both arms, opening her cape and curtseying to reveal her the collar of her own frayed t-shirt and torn wooly jumper beneath. '…for at least recognizing that I still have the sensibility of a princess, even though I could never be recognized as one!'

Davy smiled warmly.

God, she was pretty. Small, and pretty, and… well, she had been well-regarded.

Davy kept the smile going. 'Princess of the Kingdom of Street People.'

Kelli bowed. 'Fake Street People, I shall have you know. Squire!'

She'd pronounced it 'Skwy-orr!' and he laughed again.

She was okay, his kid sister.

Making the most of it. Keeping positive. That kind of thing.

Even though he had always loved her, and protected her, he was coming to realize now that, back then, really, he'd hardly known her. And now it didn't matter. Now, all they had was each other, and who they had become.

Kelli smirked. 'You know, in order to read a paper, you'd have to learn to read, and what'd be the point in that?'

Davy rolled his eyes. 'I used to read. You know that.' Davy pointed at her. 'We're like those prisoners of war who faked being crazy to get sent home, then ended up doing it so well, they started to believe it themselves.'

'And really went crazy.'

He clicked his fingers triumphantly. 'See? If I didn't read, how'd I know something like that, huh?'

Kelli sighed. But she smiled. Davy liked it when they were good with each other. When he could make her all chirpy, and sarcastic again.

'I saw that too, Davy. It was one of this PBS series they used to make us watch, that one in the German prison camp. You didn't read it, you watched it.'

'Watching those old British things was like reading.'

Kelli laughed. 'I guess so. I could have used some subtitles, before I developed my ear. *Such as it is, darling*. Hey. That actually sounded good that time. Damn! I'm finally getting it and there's nothing to use it for!'

Davy jumped off the desk and walked closer to the window, suddenly pensive and irritated.

'I used to read…'

'Sure. Maxim. FHM. You know, the classics.'

'No…' He turned back to her. 'Really. You know I did. Maybe not great literature, but it wasn't all crap. You really think they don't let people read any more?'

He knew that Kelli was more aware of what was happening in the world than he was. She talked to people sometimes, when she could. Even normal people. After all, she could pretend. If things hadn't finished for them in the real world, she would have pretended for a living, and she would have been good. If not great. Probably great. He decided not to think about that. In any case, Kelli could talk to the normals, and she could talk to the others, the others like them, too.

They didn't meet any of the others very often. It was too dangerous. But when they did, Davy almost couldn't stand being near them. The guys especially. The other people who were like them… they were almost *too much* like them, and that was way too intense. Unless they were like Zara, or the dark haired girl he'd seen in the reflection.

Then it was a different story, a different *intense*.

But Kelli talked to them, when she saw them, as long as she

dared. They swapped information.

It was what they were doing here.

That kid.

Talking to him.

It had led them here.

Kelli smiled. She looked at him, and he could see that she was going to try and reassure him. But then something else happened; something with which he was becoming increasingly familiar. The corners of her mouth tightened suddenly, her eyes narrowed, and she looked all of a sudden like she had caught glare from somewhere. She frowned, deeply.

'I do…' Kelli said. 'I do think they've stopped people reading. Everything but the paper, and selected websites.'

It had been their mother who had insisted upon calling Kelli 'petite'. Not short, or tiny, or small. She was five one, 'five three in heels', and classically pretty. But if you really looked at her, she was tiny. When she frowned, seriously frowned, it looked a little cute, but it also somehow possessed an unnerving gravity. Perhaps because her forehead was so neat, so small, that there was almost something childlike about her; the scale of her. A creature who looked so innocent should not seem so genuinely upset, should not be having thoughts that formed a frown like that, a frown that came from somewhere that could not be anything but haunted, and dark.

Davy grumbled. 'You know, I remember Papa saying, that after Reagan was killed, Mama said that if the Russians could make centralized government work, and the Chinese could make centralized government work, then why couldn't America?'

They looked at each other. They did that, every now and then, usually when they were talking about how their parents had been.

'That was when I started to worry.'

'America's not a communist country, Davy. It's not even really socialist. It's a corporate dictatorship now. It's six or seven different countries run by a handful of corporate boards who pretend Washington is still something to do with democracy.'

'New-Ess-Ay…' Davy uttered scornfully. 'New–Ess-Ay! New–Ess-Ay!'

He remembered a lot of people chanting that. He might have chanted it himself, once or twice. Tried it out, as all his buddies had. Banged one of the suits once, who'd come to see the game. She'd given him a kit, and told him to come see her in Houston.

Was Texas Mexico now? Or Mexico Texas?

New Texas? Nexas? Nexus?

He'd heard it called a lot of names, as they'd gotten further away, but it was basically still one thing. It was Southern Oil using illegal Mexicans as the new slave class, just like California pretended they didn't. With Texas and Mexico and – he really didn't know which other states had gone along with forming one of the five new countries… or was it six? Kelli had suggested it was maybe seven now…?

– anyway, with all that, who could keep track?

He remembered his Dad talking about it, with his friends. When they realized that it was not just going to happen, that it was *happening*; that the United States was breaking up and reforming.

They'd talked, the Big Men. They said; there were brands everyone knew, iconic American cities and states that you could build a message around, an idea, a concept, an ethos.

A way of life.

A franchise, an empire, a fortune.

Texas was one, of course.

New York, L.A, Chicago, Washington, Vegas… these names resonated globally.

Few others did as strongly.

Seattle maybe? Atlanta, Miami? New Orleans… Utah…? Denver maybe?

Then you were really stretching. States; many with the same names, but California would probably hold. There were plenty of others that made mild traction, Oklahoma, for instance, but so far as these men were concerned, the names of the states were essentially interchangeable, and disposable.

Did anyone, other than the inconsequential people who actually lived there, really know the difference between Nebraska and Idaho anymore? Kentucky and Kansas?

Still, it had emerged after a while, there was Alaska, and Hawaii. People seemed to know and like them. Cold and hot, snow and lava. And in the end... couldn't Disneyland actually have its own Corporate Magical Kingdom? McDonalds? Coke? Maybe it was it worth forming new states, or new counties, around, say, Yellowstone, or the Grand Canyon, or The Rockies? Hollywood, even?

With surprising speed, openly corporate-controlled power blocs, formed out of various pre-existing economic entities, had gelled. One from New York, Washington, Philly and Boston to the east; another from California and San Francisco to the west, then Texas and its surrounding states, and a chunk of Mexico, whose border had become meaningless in the south; the fourth out of Utah and some of the better-faring post-crash flyover states, with many of the northern and Midwestern flyer-overs all-but abandoned, becoming Canadian in all but name. Finally, the grand new country of Atlanta, incorporating Miami, and New Orleans, had confirmed it for all time, by claiming independence. The dissolution of the United States had happened not with a bang, not with a Second Civil War, but with a resigned whimper, and the formation of their own new country in a loose new Union, based upon Europe. The New America, or New United States of America, had been birthed.

Somewhere along the line, it had clearly been decided that 'America' and 'United States' were brands worth maintaining.

And then, Illinois. Except it was all just 'Chicago' now, following Atlanta's lead; the country of Chicago, because nobody, only one in fifty, had even heard of the States that surrounded it, couldn't even name them. Wisconsin, and Michigan, and Ohio, all the states surrounding Illinois were all just the country of Chicago now.

At least, he'd heard.

They'd both heard.

They'd both heard different, too.

But that was the picture that seemed the most likely, given everything.

NUSA, or N'America, was basically just a collection of corporate states, each with their own private armed forces, and private police, and all that came with that.

Nobody really knew where the nukes had gone.

'We had no idea then, remember? How many people they'd killed, between them, in the twentieth century. The Soviets and the Maoists. We only found out about it later. But there was talk; people I knew, they knew.'

Davy stared at her. He really hadn't known her at all.

'What happens when a power structure that encourages the most charismatic and intelligent of the sociopaths to rise to the top, suddenly realizes that it has enough power to seize the satellite towers?'

'The New United States.' Davy had answered that question before.

'California had the world's sixth largest economy. It had the most progressive left wing government on Earth. Most of the rest of the country loved guns for their own sake. You can't blame California…'

'It's nothing to do with us any more, Kelli…'

'I know.'

They were still looking at each other.

The first glow of morning was back-lighting the hills.

Where the hell were they?

Adelaide?

Where the hell was that?

'I'm sorry Kelli.'

'What for?' Kelli shrugged. Then she sighed.

He was sorry for… just, everything.

'I know. You don't need to be.'

'We'll make it north. Darwin is real. It has to be.'

Kelli sighed. 'I know. History…' She made that disgruntled face again. '…there's always a place. A place where they let things go on. There has to be, there has to be a free city. Nothing works, the big lie doesn't work without one. It's like pressure valve.'

Davy kind of understood that. She meant, like Hong Kong had gone on, even though China had been a Communist dictatorship. Like the Russians had traded contraband with Alaska. What the hell had happened to Alaska, anyway? Had it become a country? A brand? Nobody ever mentioned that place anymore.

Maybe they should have headed there?

'How much longer are we going to stay here?' Kelli asked suddenly. 'I mean, do you even want to stay?'

Davy kept staring out at the three office towers, across the dry and frigid night.

'You know what those back-packers said. We need to head north before the wet season.' Then he shook his head. 'Wet season.'

It seemed ridiculous.

Kelli examined the paper on the top of the brick, running her fingers over the date.

May 23rd, 2021.

'God Davy…' Kellie uttered. '…do you know what day it is?'

'Day? I don't even really know if it's summer or winter.'

Kelli glanced out. 'Summer's just started…'

'…so winter just started at home.' Davy shrugged. 'It's been two years. Jesus… has it really been?'

'Two years…' Kelli spoke softly. 'We've lived in the woods, become thieves, fugitives, walked across America and sailed the Pacific to Australia… and I barely remember any of it.'

Davy squeezed his eyes shut. 'I don't want to think about it. I just want to… think ahead.'

Kelli smiled sadly. 'A whole two years and you're still my chaperone... all those things I've forgotten, but I still remember that night.'

He opened his eyes and saw that she was staring at him.

'Me too.'

It was why they were here, after all.

'He's probably still in a coma...' Davy uttered.

Kelli walked over to him.

'Don't…'

They could see their reflections in the glow of the approaching sunrise.

'Wow…' Kelli uttered. '…if Mama and Papa could see us now…'

'If Jed and Mary-Beth could see us now...' Davy turned and looked down at his little sister. He met her upturned gaze squarely. 'They'd turn us in.'

There was silence between them again for a while as they looked back out, trying not to catch each other's eye in the reflection. The clouds over the hills, behind the city, were glowing. The city was visible.

Night was gone.

'Wet season starts in October…' Kelli told him. He already knew. 'They said we needed to be well across the interior by then, or we could get stuck. If there really is an underground railroad across the desert, do you think…?'

She trailed off and Davy didn't answer. There was a railroad. A real railroad, sure. Two days, total luxury. Or a plane that took three and a half hours. A few hundred bucks, once upon a time. Now it would cost a small fortune. Now, stealing a car was like stealing a train. And driving anywhere…

They had no ID.

They looked awful.

They would have to trust just about anyone would told them

they were with the underground.

'Did you try that little shop?' Kelli asked finally. 'The one where you got the chocolate last week?'

Davy grunted. 'The one down the road from that one closed, now they've got twice as many customers.' He smirked. 'I guess Central Planning thought the one down the road was inefficient...'

'Or surplus.'

They stared at the three buildings.

'I was worried that you took too much last time...'

'Maybe I did. But I won't go back. If I rush in I'll be seen, if I walk in, they'll call the cops.'

He knew what Kelli was thinking. Rush in, rush out. What was the big deal? But they both knew; neither were up to that. Dark streets were one thing, crowded stores were quite another.

'It won't be as bad in Darwin.'

Davy kissed her on the top of her head, then went to his newspaper brick mattress. It was okay, once you got used to the twine. If you were tired enough.

Kelli took out the top paper.

'The princess does this every day. If she didn't, only then would the royal bed feel uneven.'

She started to read the front page article as Davy closed his eyes. Immediately he sensed; it didn't feel like he was getting to sleep any time, like, quick smart.

Tense.

Way too tense.

'...local authorities are baffled...' Kelli uttered. '...several murders of 'high profile' Australians in recent months... Central Security to take over investigation.'

She paused. He didn't look.

'...some believe the execution-style murders to be a string of contract killings by the world's leading assassin, known only as The Black Dog.'

Davy laughed bitterly.

'Dad was always on at me to read the paper. You need to know the world son, he used to say, if you expect to make your way in it.'

Kelli continued to read. 'Community groups... what does that all mean, anyway? Authorities and community groups? It means the spin, and the suspicion, that's what it means.'

Davy made a grumble, signifying his agreement.

'...community groups have linked the murders to a long-suspected *pedophile ring*...' Kelli winced. 'Oh! Oh dear Jesus in Heaven! How can people...?' She gulped and shook her head, as though she had been forced to swallow something rancid and toxic. Then she went on. '...but; police are denying the existence of both that ring and the Black Dog. Police claim that the murders are the work of a high-I.Q. serial killer, who is targeting wealthy phil - philanthropists. Security around the city has been ... increased.'

'What does that mean? Some maniac's going around knocking off rich assholes?'

'You know better than that.'

Davy half-rolled and twisted his neck up to see Kelli. She was staring right at him, over the top of the paper, in a way he hadn't seen before. He didn't want to hear this. He rolled back over again and closed his eyes.

'Whoever is killing these people, Davy, has the power, the Wrath.'

Davy opened his eyes and stared at his reflection, across the room. It was half-light outside, but he could still see himself, stretched out on the brick-bed, staring back.

'Perhaps...' Kelli continued, nervous, '...if we can track them down, we could... band together?'

He rolled over and propped himself back up.

'It's bad enough that you and me travel together. But hooking up with psychos? And don't you remember what happened last time 'people like us' tried to take action? Have you forgotten why we're on the run? It's what I said before – you know what would happen if Jed and Mary-Beth were here.'

'You said. They'd turn us in.'

'No. You know what would happen. If they were here...'

He paused, thinking twice, then lay down and turned over again.

'I know.' He knew Kelli had tears in her eyes. 'If Mama and Papa were here...' He heard her gulp. 'We'd have no choice. We'd have to kill them.'

Davy was silent.

FIVE: DEFENSE

I

Kelli knew that Davy had been staring at the girls, across the road from the club.

She'd followed him one night, and seen it.

Davy, just standing there, all night, in the same place, staring.

And he wasn't just staring because that had once been his world, the one he'd left behind, lost forever. Well, maybe he was, a bit. Maybe that was part of it. And he wasn't staring at the boys, wishing he could be drinking with them, drugging with them, joking and roughhousing; in envy maybe, but that wasn't it, either.

It was the girls.

It was lust.

Davy had always been a player.

At high school, and then in college, there had always been a big pool for him to fish from. And Davy being Davy, with his so-called All-American good looks, it was more like him having a barrel to shoot into. If that was even the appropriate term. Kelli didn't know. She didn't know boys talk or sex talk, or whatever else there was. She liked boys, she liked fantasizing, she liked orgasms.

Just, not crude.

Not all that primitive stuff.

And not with… just anyone, not with, 'whoever'. She simply didn't think like that. Her body didn't work like that; her heart didn't skip, her juices didn't flow, just for that. There had to be something. It had to be someone who… who fit the lock. Who was right, and turned the key. Who she not only liked, but who… well, she guessed, turned her on. And that was hard for her. That had proved very difficult to find, no matter how hard she tried, how wide she searched, or how much she wanted to find it. And how hard she wanted to find that boy, that man, that… someone, didn't seem to matter either.

She had found one, just once, and he had gone.

Off to college, across the country, somewhere else.

Tears and heartache and, well, be very careful about falling again.

Still, Kelli had long ago gotten past the idea of thinking of her brother's unrestrained sexuality in a negative way, and dealing with the fact that he was… well, a sexual animal. A pig, really. Someone she would despise, if she didn't love him so much.

Long ago, one of the girls in her class, she'd forgotten which now, it was all so long ago, had told her about this boy she'd been dating. Not the way Kelli would use the word, meaning actual dating, going out to movies, going out to eat, and hanging out on the couch, getting to know each other, and at least until the third date before… anything. Anything at all. And usually, before she decided, no. Not this one. Sorry, but, you're not it.

This girl had meant dating, meaning; fucking.

Kelli knew that not all the girls were like her. Most of them thought of her, she was sure, as a 'good girl'. But she knew some of the naughty girls, and the bad girls, and she didn't judge. Just, that whole thing, as many dicks as possible before settling, or choosing, or, whatever the theory was, it just wasn't her. It didn't appeal.

But this girl, she was new, and she wouldn't shut up.

She was okay, but; just… she wouldn't stop talking about all the guys she wanted to bang, or to bang her, or… whatever. Eventually she'd found one who would, which wouldn't have been difficult because she was so damn willing and, well, *damn cute* on the face of it. And so, she'd been telling Kelli all about this boy.

Kelli had listened, out of politeness really. It was okay, she supposed, hearing sex talk. In a lot of ways she would rather hear that kind of talk than a lot of mean-spirited back-stabbing and bitching. Kelli had been that girl, she now realized, who was represented from time to time in movies and on TV as 'the nice girl'. Not the 'good girl' meaning the prude or the Christian or the repressive. The *nice girl*, who likes boys, but who yearns. She seems to like everyone, and sees everyone's best side, and everyone kind of likes her, too. Even the ones who said they didn't really did. Except they psychos, and they hated everyone indiscriminately. She was, according to her corresponding pop culture archetype, the 'everybody's friend girl', who waits for the right one, or, the right ones even, as they come along, and in the end, gets the man she's been waiting for.

Just… it hadn't turned out that way.

The man she'd been waiting for, turned out to be the man who told her, in no uncertain terms, that she was not going to get what she'd been waiting for. Instead, she was going to get what was *coming to her…*

But that was another story.

That was back in N'America, in the last days of America, before Obama's assassination.

Anyway, this new slutty cute girl, she had been going on and on…

She was a transferred sophomore, and Kelli was a junior, a year older. But Kelli was going to be a TV actress, it seemed, whether she really wanted that or not, and all the cute girls came to her eventually, just to check her out.

She was always nice, always accommodating, always supportive and encouraging. She didn't try, she'd once told her Mama, who'd been fishing to see how genuine she was. It just came 'all natural like', she told her. She wanted other people to be happy, and she liked to try and help to see that happen.

End of, Mama.

Mama.

So anyway, as the cute slutty girl… Cherise! That was her name. So as Cherise went on and on, Kelli couldn't help herself. She couldn't help but think; how do you think this makes you seem to everyone? That you've been here in Austin four weeks and already you're going on about this stud, this stud and his big cock, and how he keeps drillin' an' drillin', and he don't stop until it's all done, and how he tastes like pineapple, and how it's huge, like ten inches, even bigger maybe, but he's so gentle as he gliiiides it down yer throat, don't choke yer or nothin', and so generous with his mouth, and his humpin', and how pink the shaft is, and how beautiful purple-violet the head is, like a dolphin, how long and streamline, prettiest penis she ever did see…?

How do you think that makes you sound?

'All the girls say so, at least the ones hot enough for him to wanna do them…'

Of course, Kelli realized, it, the slutty talk, made her sound like half the other girls. And the fact that she had banged this stud gained her total acceptance with them the very next week; immediate all access pass into the cute and slutty clique.

And Kelli didn't judge.

Again, she liked sex. In some ways she wished she had that facility, to have a lot, and for it not to matter.

'…cause, he's like, soooo, oh, so hot, and how his muscles ripple when he's fucken', like his abs, they're like the skin of a drum, like war drums, ripplin' and poundin'…

Kelli had to admit, she got worked up.

So apparently, this guy, this stud, kept goin' every time, until she was done and she was happy, and it was a point of pride with him.

'Came like a fire hose, splishin' and a splashin'!'

Cherise's smile was a mile wide, remembering. Like she was remembering a puppy playing under a garden sprinkler or something. Not some stud, doing… well, whatever. All over.

'And he always said the cutest things when he was done. Funny little phrases, like. Never take leave of a beautiful lady who ain't pleased to have made your acquaintance…' She smiled, remembering fondly. '…that was one of 'em…'

Kelli's heart dropped into her guts at that moment.

'…so a girl never felt cheap when he had to go rush of to do all his sports or whatever…'

That was when she knew it was Davy.

That had been one of Papa's expressions… Davy had liked to copy Papa's expressions, but not around the family. Just when he thought nobody would know.

She remembered asking, although she hadn't wanted to know, what this big stud's name was. The girl hadn't remembered. They'd done it, like, *fifteen times in three weeks* and she *couldn't remember his name?*

Good Lord Jesus Almighty!

All she could remember was that it started with a 'D'.

D for Dick!

'Ah dunno, sweetie…' Cherise had said, as they'd eaten their lunch in the library that day. 'Some big dumb athlete whose Daddy is some kind of TV station billionaire, or somethin'. Ain't that somethin'? And his Daddy's all pals with all the ol' money boys and oil billionaires, he owns like five local stations across Texas and Oklahoma, and Kansas too, I think. I looked him up on the internet and all. And *sure*, I mean, that's all well and good, sure it is, but hot God damn girl, whoever lands that boy's gonna have a hell of a time keepin' him happy!'

Kelli had been sick, after lunch.

'Ain't no goin' into that lion's cage without no pre-nup girl, that's all I'm sayin'…'

Kelli hadn't spoken to Davy for a week after that. Nothing rude, just keeping out of his way. She could barely look at him, without thinking…

Cherise on the other hand had apologized a week later and they had maintained an amicable relationship, right up to Prom Night.

'Hey sis', how's it goin'? Feel like I haven't seen yer all week!'

They'd always been friendly. But not nosy, or particularly interested. Just; hope it's all cool with you, let me know if yer need anything!

He'd punched a guy once for talking trash about her. She knew, from the guy's sister, who'd been pissed. Then again, about a year later, held a guy's head down in the mud on the practice field until he'd admitted that no, his sister had not blown him under the bleachers. Then a third guy, who had claimed she'd let him cop a feel in the back of the movies while they'd made out. She'd had to tell Davy, that one was true. But it was the first time, and she was glad he'd held him by his feet upside down from the science building third floor, because he'd broken his promise not to tell.

Guys kind'a stopped hitting on her after all that; she was pretty much relieved.

So she decided to get to know her big brother a little more. She remembered, it was kind of like; well, if he's gonna be my champion, and be all, like, super-protective, I'd better try and get to the bottom of it, so I can, like, maybe try and train him a little. Just to make certain he didn't get it wrong again, or come on too strong if anything did happen. She didn't want him to, like, *completely* frighten them off or nothin'. Just… take out the trash. Quietly, and effectively, but so nobody really got hurt. Nobody who didn't deserve it. And even then, not too bad.

So they started talking, and Davy started telling her that, yeah, he wasn't a good boy. Not like that, anyway. Not where girls were concerned. But he, like, knew that *she* was a good girl.

She was not a good girl necessarily, she corrected.

She was 'the nice girl', like in the movies.

Point taken. Davy wasn't no fool or nothing, quite the reverse at it happened. But he knew how bad, how dirty, how fucked up, let's put it plainly, some of these naughty girls could be. And, like, that was just how they were. In Davy's view of things, some of them were built that way, some of them had chosen to be that way, and some of them, it had to be said, were just plain screwed up. But whether they just liked fucking naturally, or, wanted to experiment, or, were tryin' to get back at an ex, or their papa, or their mama, or whatever, they were like that, and that's the way they were. It was kind of, unspoken, but that was that. You gave 'em what they wanted. Everyone got what they wanted. Everyone was, like, if not totally happy, like, in an entire world view kind of fashion, at least they were satisfied, for a time.

On the other hand, Kelli gradually came to realize, if a girl wasn't like that, and didn't want to be treated like that, or seen to be like that, or talked about in that way, then she'd better not act like that; she'd better stay out of it and not go there. The ones that didn't, Davy considered, and considered this very strongly, should not be spoken about in that way, because, sex was great. Sex was awesome and wild and sometimes dirty and bad but mostly awesome and fun. But if you weren't made for it, like that, like sport, like animals, then you were made different. You were made for something, Davy considered, more pure. Like, real love. Not just, settling down and makin' babies with the one you like fuckin' the best. Or the best one left, after the dust had settled. Real, true, you really only ever have the hots for that one person (or two, or three) lurrrrv.

'Doesn't have to be just one,' Davy had told her. 'I know you were with that guy, last year, and he went away. And that's why you were cryin' for a week. But; you didn't chase him, and you're still… lookin'. I can tell. You're still looking for the next special one, to see if he's the stayer special one.'

She'd supposed, she considered him to be right. And she'd smiled. Big, broad and happier than heck to have found this new level of connection with her big brother. They'd never really talked about this kind of thing before, and it felt good.

'But, just the special ones, right sis? And the most special is, hopefully, the one you end up with.'

She'd shrugged. 'Hopefully…'

'It's like the Holy Grail. It's like those knights. They held themselves up, right? They said, we're gonna go for this… *Grail*, right? And that's, like, God, or at least, tryin' to figure God out? That's his, like… quest, or something? If ya, like, wanna know him better? So if you say, like, to the world, through your behavior, and your… like, posture? The way you carry yourself? Walk and talk and project? Right? And the way you… kind of smile at everyone, but not fake, for real, like you wanna get to know them and see the best in them; and how, for most people, that brings out, at least, a little of the best in them? Then, you're like, not better than us, or…too good. Nothin' like that. But you sacrifice the satisfaction that comes from being bad, from being mean and dirty or even, yeah, sometimes cruel, or nasty, you sacrifice the satisfaction that comes from having that on demand. And that's something, that sacrifice. That's something that deserves to be treated different. Like I said, not better, necessarily, just; you don't have to put up with people sayin' they *had* yer, when they didn't. Because, your… mission parameters? They're not the same. Your bound'ries are different. It's a different standard. Not better. Just different. And it takes… spirit, I suppose. And spirit, that kind of spirit, should be rewarded, and respected. And all us who live in the now, with the sex and the beer and the weed and whatever, we just need to recognize that. And because I know that, and they know that, even if they need a little reminding sometimes, and because you're my sister, my little sister who I love, if they don't respect that, well…'

His face went all red.

She got the idea.

Somewhere along the line, although he could never quite articulate it, he'd become the defender of her honor. She wasn't entirely sure how she felt about that; whether she even needed it. But she was okay with it. It was their thing; it was family.

But that was then.

Waiting for him every night though, now, in the empty office block, had become very difficult.

She was concerned about what he might do.

Whether or not it was safe to let him out every night.

She knew he didn't like to… manage things himself. It just didn't work for him; it didn't with these 'animal' types. But she didn't know how he hadn't gone mad. They'd been on the run, on the road, on the street now for two years. She'd thought maybe more; she'd genuinely lost track after the first year, until tonight. Had always been too tired to look at the date on one of the newspapers, and make the simple calculation. Too scared, maybe.

But seeing it, tonight, the two year anniversary date…

Davy had probably made it with three women before the prom had been half way through…

How had he not gone crazy, up 'til now?

Even she had needed to… manage herself, once or twice, out here on the road; just waking up from a dream sometimes, a lovely, sexy dream, and finding it unbearable, not to grab the opportunity, and maintain the fantasy, before grimmest reality set in again.

She was almost certain though, that Davy had abstained.

For a long time.

She was worried he was going to go mad. Maybe kill someone. A woman. Maybe… hurt her first.

She didn't like to think about him like that, her defender.

But she wondered.

She couldn't stop herself thinking; maybe when it came to it, maybe he wouldn't be able to stop himself.

She remembered Zara.

She'd been a few years older. Kelli herself was, what? Nineteen by now? But sometimes, she still thought of herself as sixteen, seventeen; as someone to whom another woman in their twenties, even early twenties, seemed as adult and grown up as her fortysomething parents had seemed.

Zara had been traveling with her brother in law, Kingston. Zara was one of their kind, with the Wrath. So was Kingston. But, just like Davy and Kelli, they had it in different ways.

Zara had told her all sorts of things, but one of them was that she 'took care of Kingston', without him knowing. She'd said that Kingston was an animal kind, like Davy. She'd met a few of them, with the Wrath. They had the Wrath deep, these 'animal magnetismos' (Zara had called them).

They were like pit bulls for the Wrath.

Accordingly, you had to master them.

Otherwise, they attracted… the things.

The things, they all knew.

They'd all seen them.

The things… they had a name… Kelli knew, but she couldn't think… and they appeared. When things got bad. Just *appeared*. Slowly, but inevitably. They shifted into this reality, from somewhere else, when all this… stuff, this running and hiding and constant anxiety, the fight or flight, every second, always adrenalized, always tired, until you got to new levels of anxiety and weariness, until *that* got the better of you.

There were the smaller ones, the ones they all knew.

Like… slugs.

A foot long.

Feelers and mandibles and claws and tentacles.

They came out of the walls, or the floor, or…

She didn't like to think.

She'd seen one in a bath once.

Lord, it made her feel sick.

But then, Zara said, there was another kind of those things. The other kind were worse, and they had wanted Zara's brother-in-law Kingston, and they would want Davy. They came though, she said, when Kingston was at his most pent up and angry, frustrated and total-complete-shit grumpy, having nightmares and snarling in his sleep.

And you could see; they wanted him.

They wanted a fight, a match.

They wanted his blood.

She could see them, black and squirming, in the glass.

Sometimes even in the concrete.

And she knew; her brother-in-law needed to come.

This had shocked Kelli. And she had been surprised at how shocked she had been. The very idea…

Kingston didn't even really *need* to get laid; he just needed to blow off some steam. Or, rather, have someone do it for him. But apparently, Kingston couldn't do that for himself. He'd never been able to, Zara told her.

Kelli remembered then, Davy had told her once; to him, that was dirty, and depraved. Not having sex with a different quartet of revolving women every lunar cycle, like a sex-beast werewolf. No, that wasn't dirty. But, masturbation? That was the thing that was 'wrong', that was the thing that made him feel sick. That was the debased thing, he'd told her; that was retarded. Like, monkeys throwing poo, or something.

Kelli couldn't see it. Zara couldn't see it. Or, at least, they couldn't really understand. Not fully. But that was Kingston. And that was Davy.

And they both had the Wrath. The Wrath, like attack dogs…

Kelli had thought about that. About the way Davy had it. And the way she had it. Like they were… complimentary.

IV

Zara and Kingston had brought them in.

They'd fled Austin in the night. Bureau 88 had been massive there, and backed by the Church. They'd have been killed, for sure, for what had gone down at the Prom. The day before, they probably would have agreed with it.

Davy had seemed to know what he was doing. He'd thought it through, she'd later realized, many times; and she had known what to do, when he hadn't.

By the time they were safe, they had come across others with the Wrath. They had realized that there was a strange sensation, when there were others around. You could feel, with your mind, if it was okay to approach. Zara had approached them when they had been tired and hungry, and offered to share food. She and Kingston had found an abandoned warehouse on the outskirts of Detroit, and had been living there a few weeks.

'Why, look at you…'

Zara had looked Kelli up and down. Mostly down, but not in a mean way. Kelli was short, there was no gettin' round that. Zara was tall; ain't no avoidin' that neither.

'Raggedy southerners, messy children…'

Kelli had to look right up at her. But her smile was amazing, so wide and engaging, automatically mesmerizing, she didn't care.

'Child, you are just like one of those tiny little things out of Hollywood, aren't you?'

'I'm from Austin.'

'Well, you don't sound like an Austin girl! Where's your yee-haw, cowgal? No, you're just like one of those tiny little things who looks all giant and enormous when they're on the big screen but when you see them in real life they ain't nothin' but a little pixie thing. Are you a pixie, child?'

It turned out she was talking like her momma had, which she did when she got excited.

'Little girls like you, grown women the size of a teenage child… I always look at your kind and I say; where do they keep everything? All those innards? Lungs, kidneys, all those miles of intestines…? There ain't the room! Not in that tiny little figure!'

Kelli had laughed. Then Davy had laughed.

Lord, it had felt good.

Zara and Kingston could have mugged or killed or just robbed them at that point, they were so disarmed by her full-on charm.

But it had been earnest; they were all in it together. Although they had all learned by then not to stay together too long, they had all learned, finally, that it was good when they stayed together for a short while. When one with the Wrath met another, whether loners or partners, so long as they didn't, like, rub you the wrong way, or their company didn't give you a migraine, then you could spend a night or two… and it was okay.

It made the life on the run worth living a few days more.

Before the… *things* showed up again.

Zara and Kingston had been in the warehouse, but they were going to move on. They didn't think they had been found, not by the Bureau anyway, but the *things* were gathering in the corners, and it was time.

They'd had a good night. Neither of them were couples, of course, but it kind of felt like they were. Like they were visiting people they'd met on holiday, who'd meant it when they said 'you must come and stay'.

They had talked the first night until dawn, then slept. Then they had talked again, the next night, and Kelli and Davy had offered to stay awake, to give their hosts extra sleeping time. Zara and Phil had been grateful and each had slept an amazing twelve hours each.

She'd thought, maybe, that Zara had attended to Davy, at one point, when they'd gone off together. Nothing was said when they came back. They hadn't even pretended that they'd been doing something else; they just pretended that they hadn't even been gone. For more than an hour.

In the meantime, Kelli had sat and talked with Kingston. He'd known, he'd seen, perhaps there had even been some exchange between the brutes; better for Kingston not to try anything with Kelli. Whatever; there hadn't even been the slightest hint.

But Zara and Davy had done it, she was sure, thinking again, thinking now.

Zara had done it, just as a favor.

She'd said to her, not long before they'd gone their separate ways again…

'You know, we can do things. Some of us can do different things, some of us, the same things, some of us are better than others at those things. But it's a normal scale, you know? Like, whatever instrument you play. You're going to get better if you practice, you're probably unlucky if you have the urge but you truly suck, but most likely of all, you'll be okay. Just okay, somewhere in the big middle ground, if you have the spark to start with, and practice, right? Well, Kingston gets all worked up. Gets Wrath Rage, right?'

Wrath Rage…

'So, once a month, I just steal a bottle, we find a warehouse somewhere, and we just go at it. And then, next day…'

She waved her hand.

'Mind trick. Never happened. Just wipe it away. I can do that. I'm… really good at that.'

Kelli had a terrible thought.

'Oh, child! Of course you'd think that; we have to live without trust most of the time, but sweetie, no; I haven't done it to you, or your brother. No, I mean, I don't want Kingston remembering something like that! He still thinks he's getting back to Grand Rapids someday, to see my sister! His wife, my sister, who turned him the fuck in, to Bureau 88! Low bitch. No sister of mine no longer. Too gutless to turn me in, her own sister, but she told me; that was her plan all along. Get rid of us both; both in one hit. She knew. She knew I'd run. She knew I wouldn't leave Kingston, I'm too good for this world she said. So she got rid of us both, didn't she? Last I heard, flown to the damn New Knighted Kingdom and shacked up with a lily white toy boy – and on all the benefits!'

Zara had told her a lot.

That after the Obama assassination, there had been riots in all the black urban neighborhoods across the northern states and the mid-west. Complete chaos. Although it was part of the country of New York now, the state of Maryland was a demilitarized zone, all but abandoned except for, some said, a kind of impromptu fort that had erected around central D.C and the White House. Marshall Law had been declared almost everywhere, and the private police forces had been activated in virtually every old state of the old union. Corporate Cops and Unconstitutional Curfews.

Then, after that, the blacks had started to disappear. They'd been born and raised in Detroit, Zara and her sister, but they'd moved to Grand Rapids when she was a teenager. Her aunt had gone to London for work, but really because they had a grandmother there who said they could claim benefits, if they got there in time and accepted some personal tech that was inserted, painlessly injected, under the skin of their right arm.

'Marshal Law has never been revoked…' Kingston had said, when Kelli had asked him if he knew anything more.

'That was all around the time…' Kelli gulped. '…the time we ran.'

Kingston nodded.

'I understand. A person loses track.'

He hadn't spoken much during their forty eight hours together, but around the fire while their sibling and significant Wrath-others were doing their thing, he'd opened up a bit.

'Before the breakdown, corporate police, under the aegis of the Emergency Federal Government, targeted black neighborhoods for what they called urban terror cells. Now the six countries… seven if Alaska is still there, I suppose, are all building more of those new hi-tech maximum security prisons, the ones with the work programs, and points and incentive programs that, somehow, you can never pay off. My brother's in one, they got him into one of the first ones, him and his two grown kids. Don't know what became of the little ones. Most of my nephews and nieces are in there too; there's one in Portland. Enormous. Like a mini-city now. Practically the whole city. Three hundred thousand prisoners. None of them would talk to me when I called; I used a fake name, fake ID, zapped the system a bit; they took the call, knew I had the Wrath. Said it was from Satan. That the Church says it's better if I die. It was only a matter of time before… my wife..'

'Zara told me.'

'Maybe one day…' Kingston had nodded to himself. '…when all this said and done, and people come to their senses…'

They were quiet for a little while after that. She thought Kingston was trying to hide his tears. She didn't bother. Then he didn't either.

After a while, Kingston spoke again. Softly.

'Marshal Law in every N'American country. Next generation will be born into it. Central Security's wiping out all the history, rewriting it… the next batch of kids won't know the difference. My people, black people, have been rounded up and segregated and put into those work cities… and the Emergency Federal Government, the EFG, is still in control.'

'But how does that work? I thought… they were… all different counties now?' Kelli asked. 'Texas, Chicago, New York, California…?'

'It don't matter. They just redistributed the power under a new fascist regime. Same people, different names. The EFG are the people that staged the coup. Wait 'til they all go to war. Follow the money, ain't that what they used to say? Everyone answers to EFG Central Planning now… and Bureau 88.'

'What… what does the President say? If there's still an Emergency Federal Government, is the… is there still a…?'

She knew this was idiotic. As soon as she said it. She looked across at him, across the barren warehouse. He was handsome. And angry. Davy was angry, and emotional, but he wasn't broken yet.

'I'm sorry. That was a stupid question.'

'No…' Kingston had uttered. 'It's the right question.'

Kingston was silent again. Then he spoke, low and slowly.

'We let go of the safeguards. We stopped believing that it could happen; every time the organized sociopaths took control, and started the killing again, they did it in a civilized country, where the general population, the intellectuals, began to think that cold-hearted people don't exist. Or that they can be made to see differently. That the emotionless maniacs don't disguise themselves as empathic humans, and operate in secret, learning to camouflage by mimicking; that's a myth, that psychology isn't even real; that there are no such things as conspiracies, and that things made in labs and factories are the same things that have evolved with us over millennia. These are all the things that are good for them, to make us believe. And contrary to popular belief, the intellectuals who say that there are no evil people, and no conspiracies, those people aren't necessarily the first to go. The people who say it can't happen, then, it's not going to happen, then finally, it's not happening, they are right there until the end. The intellectual who denies the existence of the sociopath, or the psychopaths; the fascists and the sadists, the Machiavellians without empathy, there is nothing more valuable to them. There is nothing more valuable to a brilliant killer than an elite who denies him, by saying; he is too brilliant to be a killer.'

Kelli stared at him. He was looking down at the concrete.

She knew what he was saying was right… but it scared her.

'Bureau 88…' Kelli uttered, as quiet as Kingston had been. '… they'll get us all, in the end.'

Kingston looked up, across the barren warehouse floor.

'Nobody knows if there is a Federal Government still. Don't seem to be no resistance to what's happened. No… Second Civil War. Against the Six Countries and Central Planning that rules 'em all from the shadows. If there is a President, even a sham President, I don't even know his name. Or her name. Don't know that anybody does. I started hearing people say, a while back, that EFG doesn't even stand for Emergency Federal Government anymore.'

'But… what else can it stand for?'

'They didn't say. Just… it didn't stand for that no more.'

'No. I suppose it doesn't… not anymore.'

v

It stuck with her.

Kingston's stuff about black prison camps.

Zara's stuff, about milking her brother in law, to keep the monsters at bay.

Being able to wipe his memory; anyone's memory, presumably, if you had the knack, the ability, within your particular set of skills…

The fact that the monsters wanted him.

His pent up force.

But mostly, it was the idea of rounding people up. Finding an excuse, and rounding them up. What was it about these people? They kept turning up in history, again and again. Just a small number, finding the worst of the people, and manipulating the worst in them. Empowering themselves, then their ghouls.

And then, the rounding up.

Prisons, mass murders, then wholesale slaughter…

She was right; nobody wanted it.

Nobody ever wanted it.

But still, it happened. Time and again. Whether it was temples or factories or wars or disease; they managed. And nobody ever said anything, in the thousands of years of the history of all this; and if they did, it was never enough, or it was always too late.

Everyone was just too damn…

Oh.

Right…

That was what those *things* were called.

Those shifting, crawling, tentacle things, that wanted sadness and despair and anxiety, and even rage.

That's what their name was.

The Fear.

They were called; *The Fear*.

SIX: PSYCH

Rutger Ink was doing what he could to get the kids.

But they were smart. They weren't making it easy.

Still, he knew where most of them were, and most of them were here in Australia. Right where they were supposed to be, where the bait of a Darwin Shangri La had led them.

City by city, the Bureau would find them.

The Bureau had to; there was nobody else, and there was too much at stake.

Ink's long fingers slid the newspaper back and forth over the hardwood surface, then spun it in windmill fashion a few times until the bold headline was facing him again.

HIGH COURT JUDGE MURDERED IN HOME

He couldn't believe society had gone all the way back to paper. News. Papers.

But it wasn't paper, he knew. It wasn't from trees, anyway. Some kind of plastic that felt like paper. They couldn't even get tradition right. All they could get right was artifice. They were exceptionally good at that.

Ink kept staring at the headline, then assessed a few more he had lying about on the desk.

HEART SURGEON'S DEATH 'SUSPICIOUS'

TV STAR FOUND HANGED

SENATOR DEAD - HOME INVASION

Now. I wonder what they did to deserve that.

He felt Tamara Chant approach, deep in his bones, long before he heard her heels impact softly with the carpeted corridor outside, and long before she entered his office.

He had begun to grind his molars the second she set foot within the very outer radius of his personal space. And Ink knew that he was not a man without personal space issues. He was a big man, with a strong sense of himself. He worked out, did yoga, and meditated. His aura extended to a significant circumference and if anyone broke its radius, he knew. When it was Tamara Chant, it was like someone had thrown a rock through his living room window.

Part of his annoyance, if he were to be honest with himself, almost certainly came from her appearance. Tamara Chant carried herself like a model of high fashion, with the flashy wardrobe, striking bone structure, bulimic figure and overt projection of cold, aloof sexuality to back it up. But she wasn't. She wasn't a vapid catwalker.

She was the most dangerous woman he knew.

And he'd known some dangerous women in his time.

Despite the fact that she looked twenty five, Tamara Chant could carry herself with the gravitas of an elder statesman if she so chose. Although her records remained sealed and unavailable to him as a condition of his appointment, Ink had it on good authority that was thirty two years old. After all, she had run the Bureau herself for four years. Ink had no idea what, or who, she had done to get that job. He did not want to imagine what had driven her to the position of what amounted to, back then, The Prime Inquisitor.

Just born to it, Ink suspected.

Born to exterminate.

'Nothing.'

Tamara's opening statement was as routinely blunt as it was openly arrogant, however it was delivered with all the light-weight energy and superficial positivity of an experienced real estate agent. It was as though the rock through the window had alerted him to, and suddenly amplified, a distant car alarm that had been wailing away in the background for some time.

Everything about Tamara Chant's brand of super-positive bullshit annoyed the hell out of Ink. But it was all just the tip of the iceberg, as to the enormous weight of things that he detested about this woman.

'Nothing?' Ink responded.

'Rutger, I am sorry to say that there are absolutely no leads at all. Nor any real motive, so far as we can tell. They just killed that poor man. Barbarians, naturally. It's… what we've come to expect at the Bureau, over the years. There is something about their, well, let's say *enhanced* mental state that renders them without conscience. Just like psychopaths, although that title is way too good for them. At least psychopaths create competition and growth. All these evil children can manage is destruction and the meaningless executions of great and noble members of the new society.'

Dancer had been a card carrying member of the old society, albeit in the worst way.

Still, now he knew how Tamara Chant's team would spin the murder.

Rutger Ink stood.

Tamara Chant was tall and slender, but then again, so was he. Her file, what he could see of it, said five six for height. Ink was six one, and standing before him today she seemed almost his height. She always had; she had worn five inch heels since the first day of his appointment. But he did not want to give her the satisfaction of looking; she would know, and he would know that she knew, and it would simply add to the bizarre equation of intense, just-under-the-surface, mutually hateful competition that was always there, like a black pit between them.

'Miss Chant. What is your purpose here?'

Tamara Chant looked around.

Ink's office was huge, according to his station. But it was empty apart from the desk, which sat in a seemingly random position three quarters back and two thirds across, diagonally facing the other towers. Ink had placed only the last week of newspapers upon it, and set a high, deep office chair before it, in which he sometimes slept but more often used for meditation. Other than that, the giant office was just a plushly carpeted executive office space, essentially empty, high in the center of the northern tower of Central Security.

'Could my purpose possibly involve finding you the ideal interior decorator that, quite clearly, has so far and so gratingly eluded you, Mister Ink?'

She smiled. She had long legs, a long neck, big hair and a big mouth. Her big mouth was wide too, with an enormous smile that was almost shocking. At least it had been,

the first time she'd employed it upon him. She was currently wielding it to about half maximum wattage.

Ink allowed himself a tight smile in return.

'Allow me to rephrase the question, Miss Chant. What is the purpose of this organization? Exactly.'

'Mister Ink?'

'Mister Ink, now? You're sticking with that?'

She laughed. 'Rutger.' Then she smiled again. 'I'm sorry, I am forever forgetting exactly what footing we're on. My friends in Central Security never seem that sure, either. One day soon they might make up their minds, I think.'

She'd come with the job. He'd had no choice.

Then, suddenly she acquiesced.

'Bureau 88 is responsible for tracking down genuine psychics, sir. People with high-functioning mental abilities.'

Ink looked at her. The trouble with these types was that they did whatever it was you least expected; sometimes that was what you did expect, sometimes it was a triple play, and sometimes it was all simply to get along. Whichever, her ultimate intent was to confuse and confound.

'So, Miss Chant…?'

She smiled again. '…a needle pulling thread, sir?'

He could see it. He really could. How she must have been able to charm the old bureaucrats. She'd been allowed to keep half of her security force in the current team, and if his information was correct, had remained in constant contact with, and most likely in command of, those she had been forced to, pretend to, retire.

Exactly half.

Regardless, they were all loyal to her. Word was, she picked and chose from them, like a harem, on a weekly basis. Sometimes bi-weekly, he'd been informed, if Ink was really pissing her off. Trouble was, with a real, highly intelligent, genuinely sadistic

Machiavellian sociopath, especially one with homicidal tendencies like Tamara, you could never really know what it was that had pissed them off. They were so alien, such game players, always in their head, always watching and analyzing everything you did for an advantage, something they could exploit, computing and storing it all for later, weaponizing your relationship, that… well, who the hell could keep track of all that? These sociopaths were born with this ability; it was like being autistic, being a maths genius, or being a hyperpsychic. Some said they were interspecies predators, some that they'd been progressed by natural selection to motivate the species. Whatever, they could always simply play you, and they could never stop. They didn't know how. And Tamara Chant was one of the worst, or best, depending, that he'd ever come across.

She was just so *determined*.

'So, can you tell me what's so damned special about this current target?'

Tamara looked at him again, employing a slight forward movement of her head that politely, and yet quite aggressively, suggested, huh? It was an amazing gesture if you could perfect it. It also carried with it the clear suggestion that you were a fucking idiot. Just a simple jutting of the neck, which he would dearly love to wring, and a slight arching of the eyebrows to indicate lack of understanding. But it was the flicker, the side of her massive mouth, which he would dearly love to punch, that she damn well knew that he would dearly like to punch; that was the kicker. That was the thing that simultaneously said; fuck you; I beg your pardon; are you going to ask that again, you massive fucking idiot?

Oh yes, she was good.

Her giant hair was parted at the side today; still a rich, strawberry blonde. The part to her right was straight but the curls began at her shoulders and continued right down to her bust. He did not look, because that was the idea. The line of the curls drew your eye there.

'Bureau 88 made plenty of kills before I arrived, Tamara. Why can't your people simply *catch* this one?'

Tamara still had no response.

'Very well. What do you think is different about this case?'

Tamara spoke now. 'Perhaps our agents, sir?'

Clearly, from her tone, that should have been obvious.

Ink shrugged. 'I've no reason to disbelieve that our agents are possessed with every ability to execute their mission.'

'Perhaps if Directive Midwich was restored, they might regain their...'

'Ability?'

'Enthusiasm, sir.'

Ink paused there. She'd never made the divide between them so clear. She must have been pretty sure that he was reaching the end of his tenure.

'You still think Bureau 88 should continue hunting and killing them? Murdering the hyperpsychics?'

Tamara shrugged. 'The hyperpsychics are a dangerous breed – in fact, a genetic defect.'

'They are people, Miss Chant. They are human...'

'Barely human. But part of them, some small part, is still human. And like humans, some are smarter than others. Perhaps that is what's different? Maybe these freaks are just smarter than the other freaks?'

'Some say the same about psychopaths. Even sociopaths, although I understand it's considered borderline offensive to raise such subjects in today's corridors of power.'

'It is. Just as it is considered offensive to make disparaging remarks about how one might use one's natural skill-set to advance within government; these ideas of the past that one should not employ all the elements one possesses to exploit, to one's advantage, are now quite rightly seen as naïve and ludicrous.'

'Nepotism, bribery, sexual favors…?'

She laughed again, but he could tell that he had touched a nerve. Her wide mouth flashed her enormous white teeth but he could see, clearly, that her nostrils simultaneously flared in anger.

He'd learned; that was her tell.

Her nose was flat, but it was large. Her nostrils were invisible, until she was mad. Then they flared up, were circular and black, and wide. Just like her eyes; narrow most of the time, but when she wanted she could open her gaze and destroy a person with her crystal blue irises. Distract them, misdirect them, or simply attract them. Her black mascara and long, pitch-black eyelashes were always in place, but she had wisely chosen to keep her eyebrows, immaculately crafted, the same soft but lustrous strawberry blonde that was her natural hair color, beneath the brighter blonde, and whatever color hair extensions she had mixed and matched that day. Today she was pink; solid, bright but not shocking, with black accessories. Huge circular gold earrings with black bases, and jet-black extensions down her back, with black rings and gold bangles, and ebony jewels adorning her slender, pink-nailed hands. The pale pink shirt collar, beneath her tight fuchsia business suit, was high and tight, no hint of anything more today, just the swift arc of her lean, exposed neck. To compensate, the business skirt was very high on her thigh, with black stockings highlighting the incredible line of her slender…

Jesus. Fuck.

…there would be a suspender belt…

Stop.

Pink pumps, five inch heels, exactly the color of her lipstick.

Stop! Fuck!

When he looked up again, in the period of microseconds it had taken for him to take all that in, factor its design and the way she had put herself together, the trick had worked and he was focused back on her lips. In those microseconds she had licked them; they were moist.

She opened her mouth.

She had a wide tongue that was apparent, would be apparent to anyone, when she opened her mouth at length.

'Ahhhh-ummmm…?'

That was the thing with her mouth; she had a strong, V-shaped protruding jaw, to accommodate the giant smile; a crocodile jaw, somehow to go with the reptilian glint in her eye, and her bite.

'…are you truly that retrograde? A woman should *not* step into her power? She should be *fair*? To… the *males*? Who have suppressed her sex and oppressed her sensuality for two thousand years?'

Ink nodded. 'You understand; they make the same arguments for sociopaths now. And yet, the advantages of the hyperpsychics are…?'

'A level of advantage for which the world is totally unprepared.'

'A distraction from the manipulations of the sadistic Machiapaths who have infiltrated almost every western-style democratic government? Effectively staging a worldwide coup de tat that can, probably…'

'Machiapaths?'

'I'm offering it up, as new word.'

'Meaning, Machiavellian sociopaths?'

'…a worldwide coup d'état that can probably never be reversed, at least not without a massive, bloody revolution? That should make a lot of weapons manufacturers, and drug manufacturers, and hardware and software manufacturers, very, very wealthy. Or, is it the unfair competition, or tendency to conspire that worries you all so? Yes, Tamara, that's exactly what I thought you might say.'

Tamara's nostrils blew in and out like shark gills, but her smile remained; her teeth were clenched and tight now, her pink lips… it wasn't that they were full, just that they were so wide…

Had that gone too far?

'You have three friends in high places.' She spoke softly and clearly.

No smile.

Yes, he had gone too far with that.

'I have many friends in slightly lower places, sir.'

'I am aware.'

'You have brought me, and my team, here, to this pissant city. You have my job. A position I earned, after ten years in the Bureau. Giving old men hand jobs, and lap dances to withered old lesbians.'

'Are there no young men in the EFG?'

She stared at him, almost furious. Then she seemed to assess him, make a decision, an instinctive choice, and flick a switch in her mind. It all happened so quickly. Ink was trained to see these things, but anybody else would be utterly confounded. She simply turned into a completely different version of herself, instantly, right before his eyes. She relaxed, huffed, shrugged and smiled at him. He almost believed the smile; it almost wiped the slate clean, although he knew there was no such chance. Not after he had actually managed to push one of her buttons. They were near impossible to find, and she would make him pay. But for now she had decided the most disarming thing to do would be to deploy an alternate persona, presumably always available to her, of candid nonchalance.

'Young men, yes. Not many young women, but that is changing now that the new acceptance of sexual politics has finally come about. Men have been...' She huffed again. '...I like it. It's a fringe benefit. Fuck anyone you like. If they can't resist you, and you gain something from it, that's hardly your fault. If they can't resist seduction, it's their issue, their weakness. Handle your emotions, handle your career.' She smiled, straight, cool. 'But I want my old job back, Rutger. My mission is to exterminate the hyperpsychics. I will do that. They may appear again, through

the genetic lines of evolution and natural selection, and should
it be that I am still here, still alive in the next generation, I will
wipe them out again. Perhaps, then, after that, should there be
nobody remaining in the world who shares my desire to see them
exterminated, or is willing to do the job, or nobody remaining
who deems it necessary… then the world will be ready for them.
Until that day, which my advisors assure me is many generations
away, many hundreds of years… I will employ whatever means
I must, in order to attain reinstatement…' She looked around
with a beaming smile. '…and employ an experienced interior
decorator.'

Ink said nothing. He thought it wise.

'You know, Rutger, there are those who believe this is not a
conscious statement of focus, of dedication. But an unconscious
statement that you now realize you are into something major,
that is way over your head, and that you do not expect to be
around long.' She shrugged, her hands suddenly shifting about
before her, softly animated. 'People do talk, you know. People *do*
speculate.'

Her blue eyes turned suddenly high beam.

Was she a cunning teenage mind in the body of a woman?
Or a demon in the body of something in between? It wasn't
right that he should acknowledge, hormonally, that she was a
powerfully sexually attractive creature, yet hate her so intensely,
with every…

Her smile had shifted.

*She knows exactly what I'm thinking… she knows exactly what
she's going for, with each exchange, like a chess master, and she can see
the response she wants when she gets it.*

'You're a very bright woman, Tamara. I'm sure you will give
yourself every chance possible to attain your goals. But not while
I am here. And my three friends are not going anywhere, anytime
soon.'

'I don't need to kill them, Rutger. Just scare them.'

He was stunned at this. That was the desired effect. He tried to think like her; accepted her candid, cutthroat authority and responded quickly.

'Indeed, you didn't kill all your targets when you ran the Bureau, did you?'

'Is that so?'

It worked, he'd volleyed.

'After all, there are still psychics, unaccounted for, who were active in the nineties.'

'It's true. Several stories of first generation hyperpsychics have gained a certain degree of notoriety. There is one I recall. A few years back. Sometime before your tenure, Rutger. Sir. Bureau 88 apprehended an American hyperpsychic, Henry Aldrich, who'd been listed as a terrorist during the Clinton administration.'

'I recall the report.'

Tamara smiled. 'Aldrich had come all the way out to Australia to hide. Many Americans do, still. For some reason they're always heading north. Something about a… hyperpsychic Shangri-La? In *Darwin?*' She laughed. It was almost genuine, he determined. 'Darwin! I mean, can you *imagine?*'

'Yes…' Ink grumbled. '…it's a useful myth.' And she should know. She'd started it, after all. 'Henry Aldrich was found and killed on a commune near Alice Springs. You led the execution squad personally. There were others, harboring him, but as a hyperpsychic he was alone.'

'So much for Shangri-La.'

'But there are others, still unaccounted for… most notably… now, what was her name?'

'Do you mean… Amy May, sir?'

The very mention of the name had caused several muscles in Tamara's neck and shoulders to tense uncontrollably.

But she held her poise, Ink noticed.

She had played a very risky hand here; she had spoken the name of the woman who, by all accounts, she hated more than anyone.

And that was something.
Tamara Chant was completely, perfectly sociopathic.
She generally had no time for hate.

SEVEN: FIGHT

'Amy May,' Tamara restated. 'An Alpha-psychic infamous for her covert attempts to lobby the Australian government for protection in the early years of the new millennium. She is rumored to be still at large.'

Tamara had felt her neck pinch again, a deep tendon, but she had contained it that time.

Amy May.

She had not uttered that name for almost a decade. Speaking it made bile rise in her gullet. She could taste it, acid. The flavor of her breakfast smoothie.

'But…' She could tell Ink's smile was completely forced, smug. 'Amy May is a myth, surely? Like…people seeing Elvis after he died? Or people saying that Bob Dylan still did concerts even after he joined the Church. Amy May is dead.'

She'd kill him if she could.

Just give the order, and he would be gone.

Never found.

'Dead?' The idiot asked.

Like so many orders she had given.

The lonely old country church had been somewhere out in the middle of nowhere, country New South Wales, she remembered.

The name of Amy May had irrevocably summoned the image of the solid stone structure, surrounded and shaded by tall gums. Gravel pathway to the side entrance. The doors locked from within. She had not believed that they had gathered in one place. So stupid. Incredible.

She remembered standing several meters from the entrance, backed up by a dozen of her men; Bureau bounty hunters, well-armed, all dressed in military-style casuals, the way she liked. It didn't matter who was in them. It was the uniform she liked.

'Yes. Amy May being alive is almost certainly a myth, Rutger. I remember the incident. At the time, Bureau 88 took part in a mission to quell a gathering of hyperpsychics at the Church of St Peter, about a day's drive from anywhere.' She sighed. 'That interminable drive. Trees everywhere, hills, rocks… miles from civilization. Driving into some kind of eucalyptus forest… then through it, on all dirt roads. Appalling.'

Tamara recalled May's determined stance as they had faced off, as May had stepped from the side door of the church.

May had thought they were negotiating.

They were a cult.

A cult of low-brained freaks.

Bureau 88 did not negotiate, not with anyone, let alone cults.

Let alone a cult of hyperpsychics.

They were here to destroy cults and cleanse hyperpsychics from the gene pool. That was part of the reason she could not abide Ink.

It was nothing personal.

It never had been.

Never was.

She could not understand people who took things personally. She understood that there was a personal dimension, like that, for many people. She had an intellectual grasp of what that was; she could play that, mimic it. But she did not have it. That was not the problem, though. Given that she understood what it was, she could not comprehend why people brought that emotional dimension into their business practices. Into their career path, their ambition. There was no place for it. She knew it could be switched off; she had seen people switch it off. Be cold, be practical, pragmatic. It was the credo of the business practitioner; it was *nothing personal*. It was always about the growth. Fiscal growth, political growth, professional growth. It was always about progression, and numbers on the board, on the sheet, on the screen, or even in the mind. As she had intimated earlier, if you could not control your emotional state, then what were you doing, in business, in competition for power? Please move on, this is not pleasant for any of us, kindly shut the door on your way out.

It was like playing with an amateur.

There was no challenge.

'We offered them a peaceful solution...'

A blatant lie, but an established one within the narrative that had taken hold, in her favor.

Back then, the way May had believed her promises... as though one could ever negotiate in good faith with a *cult*. The way she had led her people from the church...

'...but they swarmed on us.'

The way the cult had fallen to the bullets...

But her bullet, the first, had missed May at the front of the group. Instead, it had taken off the side of the head off of the woman behind her.

The way her hyper-grey-matter had sprayed, along with the shrapnel of her skull fragments, and brain blood, backwards onto the stone church wall... it had been like a crimson firework. Tamara had found that fascinating. Engaging. She had developed a taste for it, at that moment. The juxtaposition of factors in her killing, the sheer contrast of the woman's freak life, and the physical process of her death; that was something she could appreciate. She had reacted, in a positive way, to her hand in it. In some way, she found that she finally understood artistry. True artistry. Its facility and spontaneity, for the first time.

She had been born, or born again, in some way, in that moment.

The way they had all fled back into the church, leaving their fallen behind them before her men could get to the rear and bar the church doors. She had shot, and had given the order to shoot, way too early. She had been too keen to see the hyper-freaks forever dispatched.

The way the church doors had slammed, the knowledge that they would use their hyperpsychic abilities now, without remorse or fear of reprisal.

Abandoning the sense that the church represented anything.

Anything.

It was, and always had been, a building that symbolized insanity to all but those who participated in the collective delusion. It was a fantasy respite from the primal fear of death; the thing that ultimately rendered the non-existence of human consciousness.

Obvious to anyone who wanted to see it.

The doors closing, the final look into May's eyes as their gazes locked.

Either gaze would have shattered glass.

Tamara knew hate when she saw it.

Knew defeat when she felt it.

She would like to have seen Amy May naked in that moment. She was beautiful, and had by all accounts a beautiful body. The full tension in her body, just then, would have been something she could have appreciated. She had always appreciated such things. Physicality, tension; biological expressions of peak sensations. It powered her, in a sense. It was one of the things she had hunted, and had continued to track, as her life had proceeded.

Yes. She had been born again, outside the church, in the moment that she had killed for the first time.

Tamara Chant.

Raised in that moment, when she had locked eyes with Amy May. Raised high, in the understanding. Not just of what she would, from now on, pursue. But also of what hatred truly meant.

The notion that she could combine the hunt, and murder, and art, and hatred, delicious hatred, as one, had not yet occurred to her.

But... she had been raised high enough in that moment to see it from there.

The glint of sunlight off of the bright amber ring May was wearing as the doors swung closed.

The order she had given, to set fire to the church.

'Somehow...'

They might just have blown it up.

'…things escalated. As they can, when tensions are running high…'

But she had wanted them to burn.

She knew most of them, from their files; she wanted to see… could she attribute their screams, correctly from one to another? How would she know, in the end? But she knew; she would know.

Tamara Chant had not spoken for some succession of long seconds, and became aware that her recall had almost caused her to zone out, right in front of Ink. That did not happen often. She did not often have cause to recall the day of one of her most favorite, and favored triumphs. The moment of her rebirth.

His face was impassive however, as he continued to examine her. He thought he had seen something, found a weakness. He hadn't. She didn't have any, not like the ones Ink was searching for. Didn't he realize; she'd read all the same books? She knew what his kind thought of her kind. The theories and profiles. She broke out a smile of self-satisfaction, to make him think that she had taken some kind of gleeful, sadistic pleasure in it.

Gave him what he wanted to see; a standard villainess.

Ink was good though; he saw more than most. He was almost on the brink of realizing the truth about her sociopathic personality. That there wasn't really anything to find; that she was interested in things, intensely sometimes, and that chasing them gave her…

He would call it pleasure.

But it wasn't pleasure as the non-sociopathic population, which she privately called motes… it wasn't what the *motes* would call pleasure. It was sharper, more intense, less filtered, less contaminated, less compromised by the emotions, or morality, or the thing they called empathy. She'd heard the mote expression that anticipation was nine tenths of pleasure. It had been one of the first expressions she had heard that had allowed her to understand the motes more clearly; they were scared, so they waited, and imagined, and yearned. Almost all of them never carried through, never *did*.

But Tamara Chant *did*.

Unhindered, and whenever she had the opportunity. Because there was always more. She always wanted more. More escalated, and more intense. That was all there was. More.

'There was a fire fight. They had guns. That wasn't in our intelligence. Something inside caught fire. Or, maybe one of the branches over the roof caught fire. A powder spark? We're not sure; it was very confusing. We had intended to take them alive and interrogate them. The bodies were almost all burned beyond recognition, but two were certainly identified as female.'

Tamara allowed herself to linger again on a mental image. The charred bodies being carried out on stretchers from the blackened, smoking, stone ruins of the church. Her moment of triumph as she had thrown the blanket aside.

'Amy May...' She swallowed smoothie acid again. '...was off the grid, and had been for years. There were no records of her that she hadn't wiped, no DNA to match the body with. But I was able to positively identify her body. Our informant had told us that she wore a distinctive ring, an amber jewel, that had been given to her in adolescence. She had worn it so long that she was unable to remove it. I personally identified that ring on the corpse.'

The way the burned hand had shriveled like a talon, and the bright amber jewel had remained, even as the metal of the ring and setting had melded into the charred ring finger.

'Permanent as ever...'

Ink was still staring at her.

She wondered what she would do with him, sometimes. She had almost seduced him. She would have been able; there was a part of this man that enjoyed his self-loathing a little too much. He was obviously fighting a strong sexual attraction toward her. It would have been so bittersweet, so melancholic, so intense for him, to have been seduced by her. But her sexual response was so strong, and the part of the sociopathic female mind which created that lost all inhibition as she reached orgasm, with matching strength. It was common in sociopaths, and psychopaths, to have a high libido, which she did, and unusually intense but fast orgasms, which she certainly did. In the heat of

passion, as he tried to hate-fuck her to death, she might demand him to choke her. He hated her so much, he would do it. Maybe he would do it too well.

Or maybe he would simply ask her a question, and she would answer.

'Do your background,' Ink ordered her, suddenly sharp.

Good; he had seen that. That she had fantasized about him. That would keep him awake tonight. It was simple to rob these motes of sleep, make them weak and unreasoning. Malleable.

'Sir?' She scoffed, borderline satirical. 'Are you suggesting I haven't?'

'The television presenter was a serial rapist of underage girls. The surgeon had ties to heroin importers and the international slave trade...'

'They are no different to any of the new elite. It is not our task to police them.'

'I'm not saying it is.'

'You're not suggesting that we buy into this preposterous urban myth? A hyperpsychic serial killer targeting a pedophile ring?'

'Dancer was a murdering pedophile. A homicidal sadist.'

'Alleged.'

'My point being, Miss Chant, that seeing as the evidence; molten safes, no point of enforced entry, local power fluctuations...' Ink stopped there. She watched his expressions; he must have known that there was no point in reading the entire list. It was boring even him, with his tedious dedication to some kind of self-created moral system. '...it all, clearly, points to hyperpsychics behind these Black Dog killings. And to the fact that that they need to be found and stopped, service to humanity notwithstanding.'

God, what a bore.

How much longer?

It was almost intolerable.

Now she had to pretend to be professional, to be his arch enemy.

As though he had any chance of getting away with this.

How would she kill him?

Would she make him choke her first?

Choke her, while he was inside her, and just when he started to think he was really going to go through with it… stab him in the neck? Have two of her men come in, from nowhere, and string him up? Or fake him out; make him think he had killed her somehow, and revel in his remorse? Maybe even carry it on; an affair. On again, off again, until she had him as her self-loathing little puppet? Could she make him useful? Surely she could. See him promoted, up through the ranks, as her glove puppet?

'It is my feeling, sir, that since the cancellation of Directive Midwich…'

He was angry now.

'Directive Midwich is over!'

It was a cliché but he was handsome… well, more handsome, when he was angry.

'For the last time, Tamara! There is no longer sanction from within Bureau 88 for the murder of hyperpsychics. How do I get that to sink in? Bureau 88 is no longer a cover for your psychotic, psychic-phobic vigilante squad! Nor is it the current policy of… what's left of the Australian government to hunt and kill hyperpsychics!'

She spent more time coordinating her outfits each morning than she did thinking about Ink. But when she did, she thought hard. He had power. Of course he did. But was the seduction the fastest route to his undoing? Maybe he would fold; maybe he would be one of those men who just required a decent spanking once a week, and then whatever Mommy says goes. But no; he hadn't reached this position, one of the most powerful in the country, and achieved this ridiculous Drum Directive, that had

the ability to change the way hyperpsychics were dealt with
everywhere, by possessing a weakness that was so easily discovered
and exploited. She would seduce him, he would fold, and then he
would introduce some tedious element of double-bluff into it…
but maybe that could be stimulating? A real battle? What would
he do with her, if he had her alone?

Truly. Alone.

What would she do with him? Neither would truly know
until…

'The new Directive, Directive Drum, states clearly that you find
them and bring them in alive. It will be enforced. By you Tamara,
or you and your pack of animals will have no legal sanction to
provide cover, even for your hunts. Do you understand?'

'Of course I do. Sir.'

'Then go! Bring 'em back – *alive!*'

She took a last look at him.

Ten years her senior. Clear skin, clear eyes, clear intent.
Intelligent but transparent. Not even trying to hide his agenda
from her. He thinks because he's in charge, he's actually in change.
But his suits were crisp, always. Fitted. Olive, navy, clay, rotated.
Military colors. Weird wavy hair. Not a redhead, not a blonde,
not brown. That strange beige hair. But the side part, the crest;
he combed it like that, but it went there naturally. Puffy eyes, a
long nose and a cruel, low mouth. Long grooves, down each side,
that never formed a smile. High cheek bones and hollow cheeks.
Tense neck and a matching tie that was as immaculately tight,
and buttoned down, as the rest of him. Clean, shined, lace-up
shoes. Actual shiny leather shoes. Excellent teeth; he tended to
flash them as he spoke, articulated.

'Tamara.'

'Sir?'

'Please. Go.'

She turned and departed. She'd known it had been there, the
chemical attraction. But he'd pushed a button in her, and the
unexpected had occurred. Rather than make her want to stab

him to death, she now found that she would not settle until she had screwed him to death. Hard, over and over, until he was dead.

Or she was dead.

She'd heard about his. It was said that narcissistic sociopaths, and psychopaths, suddenly became bored. Changed their goals. She'd been killing these freaks for a decade nearly. If Ink killed her, so be it. She'd grown weary of it all. But she was going there. She was definitely going there. It presented too much of a hunt, and far too much of a potential adrenalin charge, not to go after him like that.

She was suddenly bored with all this… bureaucratic shit.

Men and guns.

And the fucking hyper fucking psychics.

As Tamara departed the office, Chambers was there waiting. He immediately fell in step, one behind her.

If he killed her…

…that was it.

She felt a lecture coming on.

'Chambers…'

'Ma'am?'

They strode along the carpeted corridor.

'You asked me the other day…'

'I did ma'am?'

'Wait until I tell you Chambers.'

'Ma'am.'

She let him wait a second or two.

'You asked me the other day…'

'What did I ask ma'am?'

'*Chambers.*'

'Sorry ma'am.'

'Chambers, you asked me, *if you recall*, why don't they, they hypers, all just appear…'

At her office door Ackerman was providing sentry. They walked in, past him and he stood to attention, just a little tighter as she passed.

'Enter Ackerman. Close the door.'

Ackerman was concerned. She had demanded cunnilingus of him this morning. He'd never performed as such for her, and she hadn't remarked in the afterglow. He wasn't sure if he'd liked it, if she'd liked it, if he'd performed to her satisfaction, or even properly. The truth was, she didn't care. She was easily pleased in that regard. But this was good; now he needed to prove himself some other way.

'Ma'am; I remember now, I asked, why don't the freaks just appear in here? Zap in? Like they do? And just… kill us all?'

Tamara nodded.

'That's right Chambers, you did. And I don't think I answered you, did I?'

'No ma'am. In fact yer told me ter shut the fuck up, ma'am.'

She was dialing him out again, even now.

Rushing.

She knew that's what the hyperpsychics were calling it. That they had named their mental ability to teleport. From torture, and observation, but mostly torture, they had ascertained that most of the hypers required line of sight to achieve this; at least they did in an emergency. Anxiety interfered with their powers, their focus, their wavelengths; whatever screwed up mutated brain chemistry these freaks possessed.

Ink was right; they had caught some, prior to Directive Drum. Tortured them into disorientation, so they couldn't use their powers. Discovered drugs that dulled their powers; anti-depressants, and anti-bipolar medication came in handy. Large doses of processed sugar. She knew they had telekinesis, a few of them, and almost all of them had telepathy. One of these current serial killers, it seemed, could burn things, and used sound waves to disorientate. But that kind was rare; she was rare. So was her partner, who could dig around and take memories. Some of them could even wipe memories, she'd heard. It didn't matter. They would all be slaughtered in time and once the last Bureau member died, nobody would ever know they'd existed.

They almost had them now. Only a few dozen left, and most of them here, in this godforsaken desert country, headed for this backwater that the Bureau had chosen as its hidden headquarters, when most people thought it was Houston.

She, and the Bureau had also worked out, over the years, that the hyper's abilities caused fluctuations in the local power grid. Studying what footage they could find, they had discovered that, while in effect, the appearance of a hyper flickered the lights. It also pulled in power from not only the local electrical grid but also, she'd been informed, from the Earth's own magnetic field. She didn't care enough to understand what that meant, but she knew that the upshot was that they had the potential, if they ever got their act together, to be very, very powerful. If they could draw strength, fuel their hyperpsychic powers from the natural energy grids of the Earth itself, as some had suggested they might…

Then…

Well, that would be it.

They would win.

They would conquer.

So they had to be stopped.

Regardless, if they came here, if they entered any major building, or shopping precinct; mall or quadrant or tower, the warning system would know. There were programs now that detected their shadow images seconds after they dropped in, almost anywhere now, to shoplift, within the digital security network. What had been webcams, and the internet, was now only available to the elite. But the infrastructure remained everywhere, and was primarily used to kill hyperpsychics.

Oh. The humanity.

Mandatory installation for all businesses.

Forget it's there.

Let us worry about what it's for.

The latest upgrades had just come online.

In the days of Midwich, it would have been the end of them all. The brother and sister in the tower would have been dead, weeks ago. But Ink just let them stay there. Sleeping, reading, and stalking club girls.

'Because maybe they would kill a few of us, but we would certainly kill them. And they don't want to die, Chambers. It's their flaw. They could kill me, kill Ink, kill all of you. But they are not prepared to risk everything to do it. Let alone lay down their lives.'

'Cowards…' Ackerman uttered.

'These two, who are killing all the old bastards, are among a handful of those we still haven't identified.' She huffed. 'But never mind. I suppose that in the end they really are doing the motes a favor. All those *disgusting old perverts.*' Then she sighed. Her business sigh. Bored at work already today, and it was only just sunrise.

'Just… something to consider…'

None of this was helping her find the first step toward seducing and killing Rutger Ink.

She looked at Chambers. He was young, and headstrong, and would do anything for her. This was what Tamara created; a cult of her own, a loyal troupe who would die for her. It wasn't difficult. All you had to do was to find the right ones.

Of course, they had to be male. Tamara did not hire women.

They had to possess the correct psychological profile; homicidally psychopathic, latent was okay, but also fetishistic, with a pseudo-military bent. They had to be too malleable to be decent mercenaries, and it helped if, unlike mercenaries, they weren't in it for the money. That they would do it anyway, given half a chance. After all, if worse came to worst, she might have to depend upon them whether they had been paid or not, whether they knew or not that there was no more money coming. They had to be devoted; doing it for her, or for the cause she represented, and made to believe that those two things were one and the same, indivisible. They had to be wound too tight to remain in standard security long; they had to feel that they were made for 'the life', yet did not fit through any of the conventional doors that they found down the strict military paths; army, police, security guards, even nightclub bouncers. They had to know that they did not belong anywhere there, so that when they found her, or she found them, they would realize; home.

But they also had to be from good stock. Able to be physically trained, and built up; ripped. They had to have poor parenting, so you could offer them discipline, and satisfaction, from the dual viewpoint of providing a paternal, masculine influence within the training and male bonding, but also a maternal, feminine force of influence, in that

her boys would be nourished with opportunities, allowed their free and violent reign and to never get caught, never to be punished. At least, no more than their fetishes demanded. In those regards, they had to be congratulated, rewarded, and allowed to feel pride, self-worth, from both father and mother.

'Ink is holding firm…' Tamara uttered. 'I thought he'd be more concerned by now. Perhaps, an ace…?'

Don Chambers had been a rebel without a conscience. His father had been weak and disinterested in anything but beer and sports, his mother a nagging shrew. In the meantime, right under their noses, Don had been killing the local feral cat population, to try and feel something other than ignored, and empty. After a house fire that little Donny had probably lit himself, he'd gone from foster home to foster home, tragically orphaned until Tamara had found him at fifteen, five years ago.

'His policies are pathetic,' Chambers sneered.

As with the children of any decent psychopathic parent, no phrase came from Chambers' mouth that he hadn't heard from her own lips first. Likewise, as she played the part of his psychopathic mother also, no thought entered Chambers' mind that had not been screened first by the filters that she had installed there.

'How long are you going to let him undermine Bureau 88's very function? Directive Midwich was the very reason for the Bureau's formation! It's been that way since 1988!'

He was like one of those marvelous parrots that just kept repeating anything they heard, if they heard it often enough. She had intended it so; it was one of the reasons she had made him her nominal personal assistant. He was so good at throwing things back at her that she could not afford to forget. Her own catchphrases, mental loops and mantras; Chambers, her own private echo chamber, broadcasting verbally. She smiled. Who said psychopaths, or sociopaths, or homicidal maniacs, whatever she was supposed to be this psycho-season, didn't have a sense of humor?

Ackerman.

Echo man.

Echo and Chambers.

Didn't... *quite* work.

But it was there, a symbol, and she felt satisfied that she had made it just for herself. In fact, she even had another boy in the wings. She had many, but this one's name would suit the joke as well.

'Ink is the most dangerous man in government right now!'

'Directive Drum...' Tamara mused. 'I'm sure it's from those idiotic books...' She sighed. '...they go on forever, and she kills all the good characters way too early.'

'...it means something?' Ackerman's propaganda playlist faltered. 'Does Midwich mean something? I thought they drew these names out of random generator?'

Tamara threw him a withering glance.

'He has them on his bookshelf, in his apartment. I used to watch him, before he realized his apartment was wired.'

Well, to be fair, he had realized that before he had set foot in his Central Planning assigned apartment. Central Security had him surveilled for his own safety, of course. Ink had instantly employed devices to prevent this, and argued their fair use against the Central Tribunal. He had dismantled the security systems immediately and installed his own, but then found that the first layer of Central surveillance was just dummy surveillance covering a much more comprehensive network that was capable of reading his micro expressions in the shower. Ink had dismantled this too, a clear violation of whatever privacy laws were left even to the elites, but appeared at first not to have noticed a third layer of pinhole security beneath that. A few days later, that had simply stopped working, and no attempt to get into his apartment had since proven effective. Ink was now, at least within his private domain in the executive government apartments on the eastern side of town, one of the few people in the city who remained, for the time each day that he stayed there, unsurveilled.

While she had watched him, however, she had noticed that he appeared to have no sexual release at all. No lover, no toys, no porn. She was sure that a man like that would need a lover. She could not understand that he did not. Or, did not appear to.

Where… *who* was she?

Tamara had always wondered.

Doug Ackerman stepped up.

Ackerman was a boy with a confused sexuality. His father had been rampantly homophobic, his mother simpering, pampering. His parents had made love as many times as it took for his mother to conceive two children, the elder of whom had joined the conventional army and of whom Ackerman's father was most proud. Mister Ackerman's psych profile showed that he was a closet homosexual. He had bullied his remaining son so that he would not 'become one' as well. This had confused Ackerman, who if he had been given the opportunity to explore his sexual identity, in a world that no longer existed and had not for at least a decade, would probably have self-identified essentially as a voyeuristic bisexual; he didn't care who was doing it, he just liked to watch. This was an excellent profile for Tamara, especially given that his father's tormenting, which had taken the form of a forced athletic career and an insanely tight chore and curfew schedule (lest he wander into 'sin') had led Doug Ackerman to believe that his father believed him to be a homo, or a sissy, or a fairy, or a pansy, or, whatever his tiny, repressed and tortured mind had thought of himself as, and so Doug could never do enough masculine activities to prove to his father that he was not any of those things. The army had spotted this and in a fearful climate of homophobia had turned down his application. Of course, Tamara had these psychological types flagged for her attention, and had taken it from there.

Poor Ackerman; he could simply not date rape enough boys or girls hard enough to prove to his father, and ultimately to himself, that he was not a sissy. Even though he would much rather just be watching someone else do it from a distance, one hand on his pecker, the other on his fourth generation Soviet night goggles.

'There are still enough of us, ma'am,' Chambers offered. 'Since Ink arrived and cleared the decks, you've managed to keep the best of us, the most loyal. And the others will come back too, ma'am. You just need to give the signal.'

'We can all be trusted, ma'am,' Ackerman insisted. 'You know that, without question. You fought to keep us, ma'am, because like you, we know the truth.'

'Indeed.'

She was getting turned on.

'And…' Tamara smiled. '…what might he truth be, Ackerman?'

He was ever-so keen to tell her.

'…that if the hyperpsychics are allowed to proceed, ma'am, to grow old and breed, then before long they will dominate humanity.'

'Ink has to be stopped!' Chambers insisted, sensing that Ackerman was gaining favor.

'Ink…' Ackerman completed the litany. '…and his bosses, the fools he represents, must be all stopped!'

Tamara nodded. 'That's right, my boys. So that we can be free again, to seek, locate and obliterate every last hyperpsychic in existence.'

They stood sharply to attention.

'Protocol 74,' Tamara ordered.

Instantly, Chambers and Ackerman began to wrestle each other.

They were her Spartans.

Her boys.

The winner got to sodomize the other, while she watched.

Her lovely, lovely boys.

EIGHT: REMEMBER

I

'She's Shursh, not Church.'

'What?'

Cassandra Casperelle was tired. She didn't want to hear any of Shylee's new thought spiritual bullshit tonight. That poor little kid had taken it out of her. The way he'd clung on, like a frightened animal.

How many slivers of her shattered heart did she have left?

How many remaining to part with?

How many more?

Before it, just... fucking, *broke*?

'Shursh. Some of the churches, that's what she meant, she said theirs is not like the ones in the city...'

To be fair, Shylee sounded thoroughly fucked as well. Still, Cass didn't need a reason, a philosophy or a spiritual system, not even a humanistic ethical code, not any of that, to know they were doing the world a favor, taking these fuckers out.

Wow, she was saying fuck a lot, in her mind lately.

That was new. She hardly ever said it out loud. But in her head... she used to frown upon harsh language when it was thrown about, like punctuation. She supposed that, within, she'd become a little less strict with herself, and a little more... well, fucked off.

They had rushed from outside the church, or the shursh, or whatever the fuck it was, across the rooftops, through the suburbs and finally, into the darkness of the woods. Then they had walked down the hill to the abandoned farmhouse. Homeless people would do that. Walk down from the woods. She was pretty sure they'd never been seen, even by farmers, even if there were any farmers left around here. But if they were seen, she would never have it said that whoever did see them would not automatically think – *hypers.*

Cass was tired, so very tired. She couldn't help thinking about how tired she was. And that was when you were really tired. When you couldn't stop thinking about how tired you were, or saying out loud;

'I'm so fucking tired.'

'I know Cass. Me too.'

There, she'd said fuck out loud.

Shylee had let her cigar go out. Keeping the rest for later. She had a whole box now, tucked under her arm. Good thing Cass liked the aroma.

'We need to get food.'

'I know.'

You had to eat, Cass knew. This thing… the Wrath, people seemed to call it, people like them. The *angry magic*, as she thought of it… if you didn't eat, it made you weak, and you slept all day and all night, and got weaker. Eventually, you just couldn't use it, couldn't psyche or rush or anything. She'd been there. Almost hadn't come back. Had, almost, not wanted to.

It was just, when she'd realized, remembered, in that terrible low… that she could scan, and go anywhere. Rush anywhere. She'd realized that she'd been using it to hide, to exist. Subsist, many would think. Really though, she could use it to… do anything.

But they had killed Hector, right in front of her.

How was she supposed to come back from that?

She had been dying. She had been sure. And then, something in her had turned over. Inexplicably, as she had realized that she would never get over Hector, she had started to come out of it. It was true; that was with her forever, and nothing would ever be the same. But that was her now, that was reality, as it had been shaped for her. All she could do was choose how to respond.

She could, at the last, maybe, make a difference.

Then, Shylee.

She'd met Shylee.

Shylee could use a gun.

When Shylee knew what they'd done, their targets, and known for sure, without doubt, Shylee just had that. Inside her. That ability to point, and click, and they were gone. Forever gone, forever punished, forever not going to destroy another person.

No question as to their guilt.

Cass could look inside.

Just look inside.

Cass had seem some things.

Shylee couldn't do that. She couldn't see in. Only Cass could do that, so far. Shylee could rush better though. Farther than anyone. She could go right through to the other side of the planet, to London, if she wanted. And she could get angry, and break things. Not, like, The Hulk. Not *smash*. Just like, *roar* at something and make it just… go away. Atomize, and blow to dust in the wind.

If she was angry enough.

And well-fed.

And they could talk, with their minds, secretly, if they wanted. They'd stopped doing that a while back though. It carried too much emotion with it. It was too hard, each of them feeling the resonance of how ruined the other was, how tapped out, how wrecked, how little there was between each of them keeping on doing this, and just breaking down and falling into madness and despair.

And, the last time, it was…

It had been just too intense.

What they meant to each other now.

How, without the other, each of them would simply…

Love was funny that way. It just came up, suddenly, and there was someone, someone you relied upon completely for everything, and could no longer do without. Someone who, if anything ever happened to them, you didn't know if you could go on.

But it had to remain unspoken.

Especially if it could not be expressed physically.

Lovers had that, that *way*, that alternative to words.

She and Shylee didn't.

What they did have, however, was a third way. With the Wrath, and the telepathy, it was *feelable*. They had discovered that, just like their clear thoughts, their stronger emotions were able to be exchanged as well, in a kind of… emotional telepathy, she supposed. Telempathy, if it really need a name.

She was sure the other hyperpsychics would have one by now; they seemed to want to name everything, something slick that sounded made-up from fiction. But there was nothing more real than this. Nothing Cass had ever experienced, more real than the emotion that had carried, under the surface, along with their recent telepathy.

The last one, that last exchange… it had floored her, devastated them both.

Maybe… those emotions were not ever really meant to be acknowledged like that. But they had been; they had been transmitted and received. Along with the desperation they both felt, and the way that anxiety was secretly simmering to the surface… there had been what they had really come to mean to each other.

And there had been no telepathy, no telempathy.

Not since then.

It had been too shocking, too powerful, to fully experience how interconnected your own needs and desperation, your survival urge and purpose for living, were interconnected with someone else's.

Maybe, if they kept going, one day, there would be more.

But for now… it was better to let it rest.

They could do without it.

They had done without it, dealing with Dancer.

Cass knew what needed to be done, though. They had found someone, long ago, who had taught them how to rush without making the noise. Once, rushing long distances had meant bringing with them a savage crack, like a thunderclap. The answer had been simple; pause your breathing. She had no idea why, but it had worked. So now, someone had to teach them how to telepathically communicate without the heart; without the screaming, aching heart, getting through, underneath the telepathic words.

'…they're worshipping the old nature deities, the underground movement, the underground church. The Divine Feminine is part of it. So they call them Shurshes. *Sh*, for She, I suppose. Shursh.'

The old farmhouse had been abandoned long ago as a living space, and converted into a storehouse. Cass had been sleeping on the old sacks of grain, Shylee on hay bales, both of them like cattle dogs. Most of the grain sacks were split and some of them were rotting, but they were stacked five or six high in places, and quite comfortable if you could get it right. It seemed clear nobody was coming to get them, and there weren't enough rats around to cause a problem, although they were clearly getting bolder with the cold weather.

Cass hated coming home at this time.

She had things to do before she bedded down, and by that time, in an hour or two, sunlight would start to enter through some of the slats between the boards across the windows. Cass remembered when staying up all night had been exciting. It had meant; coming home after partying all night, or that she'd maybe just made out with a boy, even gone back to his place. She hadn't done the one-nighter thing much, but when she had, she'd never brought the boy home. And she always preferred to sleep in her own bed, so the so-called 'walk of shame' had been made so infrequently that it had always felt exotic to her. Walk of triumph, really. Either she'd had a great night, or managed to find someone she actually wanted to have sex with. Usually both.

Win-win; Cassandra wins again!

Go Cassandra!

Now it meant trying to get to sleep, tense, anxious, with the sun up and her natural body rhythms working against her.

A swarm of rats vanished as they entered through the old kitchen, walking with increasingly more apparent exhaustion into the main room with the sacks. The boy was still there, sweating it out, like a junkie determined to get through cold turkey. She went immediately to him. They'd left the boy on the most comfortable section of grain sacks, but in the couple of hours they'd been gone he'd either shifted, or rolled and fallen to the floor and was now huddled in the corner where the sacks met the aging, hardwood floor boards. Maybe he had sensed it was cooler there. Who knew?

'I think he's...' Cass felt his forehead. He was cooling. '...he's almost there, Shy.'

'Almost where? Here with us? We're nowhere.'

Shylee's snark was welcome; it meant she was dealing.

'This was horrible,' Cass whispered. 'This part. Like, the worst alcohol poisoning ever. Do you remember this?'

'For me it actually was alcohol poisoning. I drank through it.'

Cass sighed. 'Oh yeah.' They'd talked about it, a long time ago it seemed now. When they'd first teamed up, and opened up. There had been alcohol involved then, too.

'Lots of vodka...' Shylee purred. 'I remember next to nothing. Poor kid. It looks like hell.'

'I think the migraines have stopped – that's a good sign.'

She looked back at Shylee, over her shoulder. Shylee was opening one of the last tins. She stared at the contents ruefully. Things hadn't gotten this bad in a while.

'This stuff has all sorts of suppressants in it...' Shylee shrugged. 'Maybe it would be good for him, if he can keep it down?'

'Nobody should be eating that *stuff*, Shy. Most of all *us*.'

Shylee sighed, staring down into the can. '…damn hungry.'

Then she put it down and started to unbutton her jacket. Cass kind of liked what she did with the black pant suit, when they went hunting, making herself all corporate bitch like that.

Shylee released one button and looked up at her, as though surprised.

'What are you going to tell him when he wakes up? Give him the usual rant?'

Then Cass realized that Shylee was looking just past her, over her shoulder. Cass turned back. The kid was sitting up, watching them. He looked about thirteen, into puberty, but he sounded younger.

'Where am I?'

Cass stood and took a few steps back, away from him, until she and Shylee stood together, looking down at him. Shylee smirked and dug a spoon into the can's contents. They'd removed all the labels one night, having both agreed that none of it tasted like what it was supposed to taste like, so it was better just to have a lucky dip and a surprise. A delicious, sloppy, sharply savory-sweet surprise, with chunks in it that dissolved under the slightest pressure.

Food, glorious food.

'You're nowhere,' Shylee uttered, staring at the spoon. With her top suit button released, her boobs were less tightly packed; a bit more exposed, a bit lower. Cass wasn't sure which was better or worse for a thirteen year old boy, the high perk or the low skin.

'My head hurts.'

'My stomach hurts…' Shylee countered. 'And I haven't even eaten this shit yet.'

Cass smiled at the boy as she looked him in the eyes. 'Do you remember your name?' The smile was meant to say; don't mind her, and bond them a bit.

He stared back.

'Kurt. Kurt Travis.'

Cass nodded. Then she adopted a voice, a bit like she remembered doctors did when they told you the results.

'So, what's happened is, your hyperpsychic powers have emerged, and you are close to the final stages of being fully operational. Do you follow me?'

'I… I think so. Yeah.'

She could tell that he did; he was becoming fearful in the right way. He was starting to wonder, what can I do? But at the same time, he was on the edge of panic. They imprisoned psychics, and killed hyperpsychics. Was he safe? Should be thinking about escape? Running? Dying, even?

'It's good that you're afraid. You don't need to be afraid of us, though.'

'But you need to be thinking, kid…' Shylee stated squarely. She turned her back to them both and fully unbuttoned the jacket, exposing her naked back. '…is this real?' She went to the window and grabbed a sports bra she kept there, with her warmer clothes, in a pile on top of an old cabinet. '…and I dreaming?' Cass watched the performance, tired but dryly amused. She hooped the sports bra over her head, and arms through, without either of them seeing anything even vaguely bosom-like, then turned around. The tight black cotton bra vanished instantly from view as she slid down a frayed grey T-shirt over the top of that. 'No kid, you're not. We're the real thing. If it was a dream, you might have seen my boobs just now.' She raised an eyebrow. 'Are we good?'

Cass smiled grimly at the kid, whose mouth was wide open.

'Unfortunately… you're sure your name is Kurt, right? You might be picking up random thoughts from anywhere right now…?'

Kurt stammered a second. 'Ye-yeah. I – I'm sure. It's Kurt.'

'Okay, so, unfortunately, Kurt… for reasons we don't understand, at first when it happens, it means high fever and crippling headaches.'

'The classic baptism of fire,' Shylee offered, sliding a black wooly jumper over the tee. It looked a bit moth-eaten, but Cass knew, it was warm as toast.

Kurt was a little thrown by that. 'What does she mean? Baptism? That's religious, isn't it? I'm not religious. I mean, my parents... they didn't – '

'Your parents?' Shylee unclipped her belt and pants, and slid them down. All Kurt could possibly glimpse were a pair or thermal tights. Even as she snatched up and kicked on her thick grey work jeans, Shylee maintained her scary, straight face for impact. 'When we turned up, Mummy and Daddy Travis had called the Bureau.' Under the hem of the huge jumper, her hands grappled to zip and button her jeans. '…because

the kind of fever little Kurt had come down with made things fly around the room when he sneezed.' She sat on a hay bale and grabbed a shoe. 'Do you recall that, kid?'

Kurt looked scared again; but not scared of them.

'Where are they?'

'Why do you care?' Shylee grabbed a second shoe, and pushed it on. Her job was almost done, her role almost played. 'They sold you out to Bureau 88.'

'Do you know what we're talking about?' Cass asked softly.

Kurt's shoulders sagged slightly. 'It's illegal to be psychic.'

'Yes.'

'And…' Kurt thought hard, then remembered. '…they execute hyperpsychics.' Cass waited. She'd done this a few times now. Seven times. It was better if they remembered it themselves.

'I remember…' Kurt continued, frowning a little. 'I remember… you two. I remember that you helped me. But I don't know where I am, and I don't know what's going to happen to me.'

Shylee was doing her laces.

'No-one knows what's going to happen to them, kid. Life's like that. That's part of the whole deal.'

Cass was surprised though, at what Kurt said next.

This was usually where they cried.

'Then, why do I feel like I *should* know?'

Cass looked to Shylee. Shylee shrugged, a bit sharply, then turned again to the window behind her. There was triple lane freeway about half a kilometer down the hill. Right through the old farm land. Express to wine country, and golf; to the adult playground towns that were now exclusive to the elites.

It had at first seemed apparent to them that the farmer had sold his land, and just walked away. At least, until they had taken a risk, after about a week, and gone to the newer farm house, further up along the tree line. After a while you got an instinct for an abandoned building, and sure enough, it looked like he had lived there alone, and just walked out one day, leaving everything. Like the *Marie Celeste*. But then they had found some bones that the foxes wouldn't touch, in the woods behind the house, which looked human. That was what you got, if you were alone, and held out too long against Central Planning. Foxes hated kerosene.

Anyway, Shylee was always worrying that they would be found, hiding here just out of plain sight, by someone who'd broken down, who'd come wandering up here to see if anyone could help make a call, or change a flat or something.

Whatever.

The freeway, through the slats, had become Shylee's TV now. She had loved TV, before this. Accordingly, her mind was filled with B-movie scenarios that she superimposed upon the freeway below. But Cass didn't try and stop her. Clichés were clichés for a reason. During the serial killer craze of an earlier decade, the media had always been running docudramas about how some the worst offenders of all time had been caught due to happenstance. She and Shylee were some of the worst offenders now. She didn't want to be listed, along with the above, on the next television documentary.

'Come with me.'

Cass stood, and so did Kurt. He was only a little shorter than her. He would be taller than her in a year, if he lasted. He was already good-looking; fresh faced, sweeping blonde hair that need a cut, but he was already haunted. Dark eyes. If she had been thirteen as well, she would have had a mad crush. It would have been her, making up all sorts of wild fantasy scenarios, about who he was and why he was so tortured, and if she could do anything…

To rescue him.

Now, she just felt sorry for herself at that age. And a little bit sorry for herself at this age; still the wheel turns. Our thoughts, desires, motivations and needs, they all came from somewhere.

We have to be *someone*.

The storehouse had three rooms, and the front door, such as it was, was boarded up beside the windows facing the freeway. There were two side-rooms, a bedroom at the front side and what remained of a kitchen facing the back. They had broken in through that door when they'd arrived and had been surprised to find it untouched. The homeless didn't come this far out from the city. It was too far to walk every day, and the average temperature was still a few degrees higher, even in these new desert nights.

Cass had been born and raised here, in Adelaide, the quietest big city in the world. It had been a mild weather city once. While her childhood summers had been Australian hot, she didn't remember them being this hot, and this dry, nor the nights this bitterly cold. The whole planet was changing. She had loved living here, had felt no calling for the bigger, wealthier, more cosmopolitan cities of the east coast.

But the truth was; the city she had loved fucking hated her now.

Still though, she was determined to stick it out, to make it work.

Even though the city she loved was abusing her.

Even though Bureau 88 had come here, and set up shop.

She could not face that.

So she was defending her abuser now, sure that she could change it.

The city she loved was making her one of those women.

One who would not leave, until it killed her.

III

The back door went out past an ancient outhouse, which still actually worked, somehow because it was connected to one of three old rain water tanks, two of which still held water. The tanks were such a rare find that she and Shylee were still thinking whether or not to spend the rest of the summer here because of them. There was enough water to get them through. Enough to make them break their own rules.

Two months they had been here now.

Their lair, where they rested, before they went out, to hunt and kill.

'See up there, that house?'

'Sure…'

She ushered him to the corner and pointed down at the freeway.

There was an abandoned petrol station and diner down there, the kind trucks and Greyhound buses used to stop at. They could still see the thin, crumbling remains of the exit and parking bay.

'That street is what used to be the main road, before progress paved the way for the elites.'

Cars roared gently by, cruising in the dawn light.

It felt like a Tuesday.

'We've been up the hill to the farmhouse, and it's in worse condition than this place. But no-one ever comes here. The tree-line down there, see?'

'Yeah.'

'It's closer to us, right? So we can see down to the freeway. But from the freeway, they can't really see us. You'd never know we were here. You'd have to want to stop and look. Behind us, over the hill, past the second farmhouse, there's just forest, and abandoned paddocks, all the way to the suburbs. Maybe one farm, miles away, where somebody lives. Nobody can see this place. It's half a kilometer from a freeway, but that line of trees means everyone's forgotten it.'

'Just like that?'

'We think the owner was murdered.'

'That's why...' Kurt uttered.

'Why what?'

Cass gave him a few seconds, but Kurt didn't answer.

'There's rain water here. From the tanks. That one is connected to the loo, and there's a kind of shower under it. It's cold, but you can have one, when the sun comes out. It's okay.'

Kurt looked up at the towers. They weren't huge, but the tree-line was enough to cover them from view. 'There used to be paddocks or something, where the freeway is, didn't there? And an old road. They sold the diner, but he wouldn't sell his land.' Kurt looked up at the water tanks again. 'He built these for cows or sheep or something?'

'We think so.'

'He lived here while he built the other house, didn't he?'

'It feels that way.'

Kurt knew what she meant. He looked around. Saw the water pipe to the house, to the outhouse.

'Cold water... septic tank. Is there water in the kitchen?'

'Cold. Very basic. But you can boil it. Make coffee. Wash.'

'What if someone sees the light?'

'The light?'

'From the fire.'

'We never light a fire. We have a hotplate that runs on solar batteries.'

'Okay.'

It was like this to begin with; your brain went at a thousand miles an hour. You thought of things you'd never think of usually.

'Remember, water tanks can be repaired. Batteries can be stolen. We'll teach you how to steal. Get stuff. Rain water can be sterilized. We steal chlorine tabs when we can. You need to find somewhere like this. Where there's water. That's the hardest thing, a water supply.'

His eyes widened suddenly, in fright. He was looking behind her. Cass wasn't scared though. Shylee walked forward and extended a glass bottle, filled with water.

'Three, three, three, kid.'

'What?' He accepted the water without thinking, and started to gulp it back.

Cass watched. He was thirsty in a way, and guzzling in a way, that only a teenage boy could be, and do. Totally without regard.

'It's a dumb rule of thumb; everyone's different. But if you're caught out in the high heat, or the ice cold, you're okay for three hours before you start dying. You can go without water for three days, and food for three weeks. Three, three, three. Maybe a bit shorter, maybe a bit longer. Everyone's different.'

Kurt gasped, half the bottle gone, nodded, then kept guzzling.

They just watched him. It was pretty cool, and not unamusing, in its way.

He stopped when the bottle was empty.

'I get it. No power. Natural water. Keep away from the elites. It's like the Middle Ages.'

Cass looked to Shylee. 'You educated?'

Kurt shrugged. 'Not 'specially. Just smart. I used to read what I could find. Whatever they didn't make us turn in. There's hardly anything left any more. Not that you're allowed to keep in the house. Kindles are illegal now.'

'Wow.' Cass was really taken aback.

Shylee frowned. 'We hadn't heard that one.'

'Last week. Dad said they don't want anyone looking at anything that isn't clearly labeled.' He handed the bottle back to Shylee. 'That thing you just did…?'

'It's called rushing.'

'That's how they got me. I was doing it, like, to check stuff out. What people do. Most people don't do anything when people aren't looking. They just watch TV. But some people…'

He screwed up his face. Clearly, he hadn't enjoyed what he'd seen.

Shylee let out a long sigh. 'So, you couldn't help spying one people, and the people you were spying on started to notice that the lights were flickering all the time, and the microwave was superheating everything, or everything in their fridge had frozen in between lunch and dinner, or even worse, their television reception suddenly needed retuning?'

Kurt nodded. 'I… maybe. That's *probably* what happened…?'

'Bureau 88 run commercials on the television to keep watch for things like that, Kurt…' Cass kept her voice low, and serious, concerned. '…you're going to have to be much more careful. Much smarter. If you are smart, you're going to have to learn to be smart all the time. Not just when you feel like it, or when trouble strikes. Okay?'

He nodded. 'Mm'kay…'

'You've got an accent, kid.' Shylee growled. 'Where you from?'

'Bellevue. Across from Seattle. What used to be Washington State.'

'Used to be?'

'Have you heard about what's happened to America?'

Cass shrugged. 'A little.'

Shylee nodded. 'Enough to know that if you're gonna hyper-down, you're better off to do it here.'

Kurt started breathing sharply through his nostrils, as though he were thinking, really hard.

'They tried to make it part of one of the new countries…'

'New countries? They really did that?'

'Yeah, sure they did.' Kurt was sounding less scared, and more invigorated, with each of his sharp breaths. 'Six counties. Seven if you count Alaska. I think. Mom and Pop could see it wasn't gonna work, they said. They sent me and my sister out here to be with my aunt, said they would be following on. But the Mormons wouldn't let 'em leave, Aunt Felicity said.'

'Morons?'

'Utah's a country now. The closest to Seattle, Bellevue, Portland… you know?'

'…okay.'

'Too many software people left Seattle and went north to Canada. Utah was tryin' to keep 'em. My uncle turned me in, not my Mom and Pop. I think Central Planning's gonna wanna keep 'em there. That's what I think.'

'Okay…'

Cass hadn't been around kids much. Were they all like this now? Super confident and speaking their mind at double time?

'I think Mom wanted to send me here because she knew. Before I even knew. She used to talk about hypers like they…' He huffed. '…like we were superheroes or somethin', cause she'd talk about, like, hypers, like they were evil, but she was, like, real excited about them. Knew way too much.'

'You think…' Cass asked softly. 'She really knew? She was… preparing you maybe?'

'She kept goin' on and on about how they were gonna all get to Darwin. All the hypers. For a while she heard it was Auckland, but it was always Darwin, really. Dad never said anything. Get to Darwin, and, like, all team up, against the forces of good. But I could tell, she didn't mean that. She mean the forces of evil. The hyperpsychic superhero army. I get it now; it was, like, she was tryin' to tell me. That's where I needed to go, after she sent me here.'

'Fighting the forces of evil…' Cass uttered.

'I guess she meant the Emergency Government. Though they don't call it that any more. I know it was dumb of me to go rushin' everywhere… but I couldn't help it. It was such a rush! Man, like, so rad. I couldn't help it!'

'Well done, kid,' Shylee laughed, low and short. 'Now look where you went and rushed off to.'

'Rush,' Kurt nodded. 'I get it. Like, you run, in a rush. You rush somewhere, to go quickly.'

Shylee stepped forward, vanished, then reappeared directly in front of him, in the blink of an eye. He staggered back a couple of steps, involuntary, and she slipped the empty bottle out of his hand.

'Rush,' Shylee told him. 'Practice. Learn to use it. See what you can do. Don't go near electricity. Electromagnetic fields, whatever the fuck.'

Kurt squinted. 'My head's hurting again.'

'You might even get to like it, kid. If you live long enough.'

'What does she mean?' Kurt looked to Cass. 'The headaches or the…?' Then he suddenly rubbed his eyes. Shylee turned and rushed back indoors. '…or the vanishing thing?'

Cass didn't answer, but she led him back inside as well.

Just walking.

'I get that I can't stay with you…' Kurt stated quietly. 'I get that… it's not right. Just two. Is that right?'

'Sorry.'

Shylee had gone right back to the window slats, staring out at the freeway.

'How do I know that?'

Cass shrugged. They sat beside each other on the sacks.

'We don't know. There's… just stuff we all know.'

'Well, how safe will I be when I'm out on my own?'

'You'll find someone, pair up. You'll be okay. It kind of just happens.'

Cass looked to Shylee. It's not like they hadn't talked about it. He was the youngest hyperpsychic they'd had to deal with, in this way at least. They weren't even sure, even at the risk of their own safety, whether it was the right thing to do, to make him go it alone, so soon. And yet, they had never met any other of their kind who didn't agree; solo, duo, fine.

A trio…

There was something about it that just begged for discovery, and death. Either from the Bureau, or from whatever those things were, that taunted from the shadows, and crawled under the concrete…

Three just seemed to be some kind of cursed critical mass.

'Listen…' Cass started. 'When you… I mean, if you… don't…' Christ. He was just a boy. Just hit puberty. He was quick, but he didn't know anything yet. 'If you keep to yourself, just for a while, you should be okay.'

'But…' Kurt couldn't quite put it together. '…you two live here, don't you? Together?'

Cass shrugged. 'We haven't always lived here. We used to move around a lot. And we haven't always been together. It's very dangerous to have more than two fully active hyperpsychics operating together for longer than a day or two. You'll understand. In fact, even a duo is very dangerous, unless the arrangement is for a specific reason.'

Kurt seemed a little more scared now.

'I know…' he nodded glumly. 'I know it, like… like you know it's bad to steal.'

His stomach grumbled. Then Shylee's did. Cass saw her opened can, still sitting on the window sill. She knew the contents had gone uneaten. She didn't blame her; it wasn't waste. It wasn't food. It was just… all they had.

'Is it Bureau 88?' Kurt asked gingerly. 'Is it because of them?'

'Look, it's okay. We'll teach you. Before you have to go. There's still time. A day or two. We know a thing or two about hiding from Bureau 88.'

Shylee added in a low tone. 'And being killed by Bureau 88.'

He stared at Shylee. Her expression offered him no respite, and Cass would expect nothing less. He was becoming increasingly more easily shocked now, and even more easily frightened. The bravado of his initial awakening had all but evaporated. But this was good; he had to know this. He had to be shocked.

'What does she mean, Cass?'

'I don't remember telling you my name.'

'I know both your names…' Kurt declared, again, as though that should have been obvious to them. 'Shylee Stray and Cassandra Casperelle. The same way I can see; what you're saying, you're telling the truth.'

'See we're telling the truth?'

'You know,' Kurt tapped the center of his forehead. 'Here. The colors.'

Shylee and Cass exchanged looks.

'We don't do that one. Cass can see memories, I can't. I can melt things, break things. Maybe that's your thing; seeing people's… truth.'

Cass sighed. 'Whatever it is, it's good. I means you're coming on fast…'

She flashed a look back at Shylee, just so she knew; *faster than anyone else I've ever seen.*

'So you've seen people… get killed?'

Cass hated this.

'I was with a man, for a few years…'

Cass smiled as she turned back to him.

'A man I loved.'

The smile she gave him was the kind you gave someone when you were telling them about something tragic, that had happened long ago, that almost tore you apart inside. Something that had, however, over time, now become something that was a kind of permanent but manageable sadness.

'They killed him.'

Shylee stepped up, blunt. 'It happened right in front of her.'

Cass understood. It was her way; she wanted him to remember this.

'You mean… you saw your… boyfriend…?'

'Don't look at that…' Cass warned him. 'If you can scan visually, don't.'

'I… I wouldn't,' Kurt scoffed. 'Why would I want to see that?'

It wasn't just that she wanted to protect him. Cass had no intention of ever going over that again. Permanent sadness was enough. She wasn't going to have the corpse dug up, and put it on display for another autopsy. Then she'd have to bury it away again. And it was much harder to repack than it was to unpack. Things like that never fit back into the box. The grave. The grief. Much harder, much more painful. One more time and the permanent would be worse. It might cripple her.

'Every one of us, every hyperpsychic living, anywhere, has their story. You have your story now, how your uncle dobbed you in.'

She looked back at Shylee. Her expression was dark; they both knew that if he survived the next week or two, after a year or so that would be the least of his stories. He would be lucky if he even remembered the name of the fucking arsehole uncle who'd shopped him to the Bureau in the first place.

'There's another thing…' Cass sighed. 'This is really important. It's how they catch you.'

'How?' Kurt demanded.

'You remember, a few years back, the American Government launched a whole bunch of spy-satellites?'

'I think so. Like, rockets.'

Shylee groaned. 'He's too young. He must have been five when that happened.'

'No, I was ten. I remember. There were three. We watched it on TV. They were cool. They said, it would help for there to be no more terror. Mum didn't like it. It was after that…'

Cass proceeded. 'There weren't just three satellites. There were ten spy satellites in every one of those launches. And they launched more after that, from out in the desert, out there…' Cass pointed out to where the freeway led. '…but didn't tell anyone.'

Shylee stepped back from the window and shivered. She found her thick grey coat and put it on. 'The Bureau uses those spy-satellites, kid. It's random, but it works. So never rush in the open outdoors. We rush to the trees, over there, and walk down here.'

Cass nodded. 'Then there are the security cameras. They use what used to be the internet. We can get around them, but you have to be fast. Like really, really fast. Okay?'

'How come?'

'After we've rushed, we don't show up on digital for a few minutes. It's different for everyone; might be ninety seconds, might be one-eighty. That's how you steal. You have a limited time to shoplift, then you start showing up.'

'We look like ghosts.' Shylee hugged her coat tighter. 'Like shadows. But you can make us out. After about two, three minutes, we're clear as anyone.'

'So,' Cass nodded, and looked him in the eye again. 'If a satellite camera catches someone appearing out of nowhere, or a security camera in a supermarket catches one of us starting to appear, the Bureau's piggy-back program registers an 'anomaly of interest', and it sends the information, and location, instantly to Bureau 88. And Bureau operatives can offer lethal response within four minutes, sometimes faster.'

'That's the fourth three, kid. Three hours in the extremes, three days without water, three weeks without food, *three minutes* before the Bureau.'

'And you don't know you've been caught until they shoot you – no time to rush.'

Shylee walked toward him again. 'The 'spontaneous appearance' scan is the only real trick they have. It's when we're stealing they catch us. You think you're okay. But maybe you're tired. Maybe you need medical supplies; pain killers, antibiotics… you can't find what you want. Maybe someone sees you, and you panic. You can't focus over the panic; then the fear is the killer.'

A cold wind blew through.

'Fear creates panic, panic kills focus, without focus we're fucked. Maybe you don't have line of sight out of the store; if you aren't familiar with the terrain, you need line of sight. Maybe you rush in on a whim, find what you want, but the store doesn't have windows like you thought. Maybe there are shelves in front, you didn't see from outside. You're rushing aisle to aisle. You can't think of where your safe place is to rush to. The cops respond before the Bureau gets there. We're not immune to being hungry, and not thinking things through, or panicking, and not thinking clearly, not thinking smart, and we're definitely, definitely, not immune to bullets.'

Shylee pulled her jumper, tee and thermal up to expose the skin of her right flank.

'Nobody ever outrushed a bullet, kid.'

She yanked the material up in a high arch, but used her other hand to hold the material down, preserving her modesty. Her skin was a light tan color, almost honey, but the bullet in the flesh of her right side, just inches below her armpit, showed up bright pink. Then she let the material go, and pulled her collar down.

'This is one of the reasons we don't pretend to be homeless. They spot us in a second, and two in five are schizoid. They think we've come to melt their brains, or kidnap them to another fucking planet. Like that hasn't happened already.'

Kurt turned to Cass. 'You've never seen that, have you? She's never shown you her scars, has she?'

Cass gasped. 'You tried to hide with the homeless?'

'We're sisters, kid. Not lovers.'

'Sisters…?'

'Non-biological; we didn't grow up together. But we're as close as if we did. Still, you get older, there are still stories we keep to ourselves, even from sisters. But we are sisters. We're bound by this *thing*…'

'The Wrath,' Kurt told them.

'See?' Shylee let go of her collar. 'Some things, we just know. Right?'

'When?' Cass snapped.

She couldn't *believe* Shy had never told her this.

Shylee shrugged. 'How else you think these things get figured out, Cass? Someone had to try, and live, to tell everyone else that it didn't work. How many people got caught long-rushing before they figured out to hold their breath steady? I told a few people; the homeless get wise to us. I guess it got around.'

Cass gulped. 'How did you survive?'

'I don't know. Someone patched me up. Never found out. Maybe another homeless. I woke up in a storm drain. Drugged out of my mind. But patched. Enough to be getting on, anyway.'

'Holy cow, Shy…'

'I probably would have told you, sometime. If you ever saw the scar…'

God, Cass gasped. Hector had stayed too long. Trying to get… she couldn't remember. Some dumb flavor of the thing he liked, for his dumb birthday. He'd remembered his birthday. He'd told her. That was why she'd kept track. That was why she'd remembered things. Dates, and what day it was. It was May now. May twenty third, two thousand and twenty one. Fuck.

'When you get out there Kurt…' Cass uttered, hearing her own voice low and level, like it was somebody else's. '…don't rush outdoors. You can in the suburbs, but only in emergencies. The satellites are all in stationary orbit, but there's one right over the city. They take time to move, but there's always a chance it might be trained on a suburban drug bust, following a car or something. So keep it indoors. Satellites can't see through the roof, and they don't all have heat recognition. Just a few. Find abandoned places the homeless can't get to, places you can only get into by rushing; places that are locked up, that people have forgotten, where there are no cameras. Never kill a camera. They'll send someone. And never stay too long. Anywhere.'

'Try to rush only at night. Satellites are less reliable then.'

Kurt was going pale now. He was starting to freak out.

'Kurt,' Cass spoke softly, but harshly. 'You need to hear this.'

'The golden rule…' Shylee paused for effect. 'You must remain hyper-aware. Basically… rushing in the city, at any time… is suicide.'

And that was the moment when Kurt started to cry.

NINE: PISS

I

Mike Lincoln was a chancer from the wrong side of the tracks.

That's what they'd say about him in the end.

An old East End London boy, made good.

Traveled the world, taking meetings, making loads of money. Imports, exports, that kind of thing. Whatever brought in the dosh. Nobody ever really asked what, exactly, because, let's face it, all that was boring as shit. Which was half the point really, because, most people with half a fucking brain worked out that he was some kind of intelligence agent, left it the fuck alone, and moved on to something else.

Good thing too, otherwise if they asked too many questions he had to scare the living shit out of them and he didn't really enjoy seeing grown men piss their pants. But you could never be sure, unless they did, that you'd gotten the message across and they wouldn't blab. For their own good really. Certainly nothing to do with him, he fucking hated the smell of piss.

'Of course I hate the smell of piss!' He'd complained once to a contemporary. 'It smells like piss! You're supposed to hate it! It's fucking piss!'

But that was all a bloody tedious business as well.

Cover stories and all that shit.

He just happened to be good at it. Winding people up. Finding weak spots in organizations. Finding ring leaders and potential trouble makers and sociopaths and getting them pointed in the right direction, to do what his organization wanted them to be doing. Money or threats or just persuasion.

Political agitation, economic assassination.

All that came with it.

He just knew people, knew how to make them do things.

But then it had all started to change. He'd done what he'd done, most of his life, undermining countries and regimes that one day might rise to threaten the west. And at

the same time, he'd created individual loose cannons, nut cases that one day might give the west something to be frightened about but whom, because of Mike's involvement, the west could always locate and fine tune.

The Perpetual Terror Machine, he called it.

And then, one day, he just woke up and realized that it was the west, or at least, this well-funded social-engineering cell within the west, that everyone needed to be protected against. That the people who wanted control wanted it too much. The deepest and darkest core of the military-addicted American government had started to fear everyone, even themselves.

The fear was taking them over, and by proxy, taking over everything.

You see, Mike told himself, the individual nut cases that would blow themselves up in shopping malls, or take people hostage in amusement parks, they were a necessary consequence of global control. This was despite the fact that, although their random acts could be swayed this way or the other, manipulated, exploited, propagandized, they could not, in the end, be truly controlled. They could be used to make people think this way or the other; that there were people out to get them, and that we, the people, needed to be protected from them. Hailing from wherever, really. Wherever was useful at the time. Wherever the people who put them down said they were from. It could be claimed that the people there were mad, bad people. Or that this bad land created an unusual amount of crazy homicidal maniacs, and that they were all joining forced, creating a terror network… that they were all out to get them, get us, get anyone and everyone who wasn't them. But the main this was that we were always, ultimately assured that the government could always deal with this unfortunate consequence – of being the most prosperous nation on Earth. And this was all true, at least from one perspective, because these people were real. Their acts were authentic, so they seemed completely authentic, top to bottom. Everyone was pretty much on board with that; they understood the risks, and essentially accepted the losses.

And it almost, always, played.

But then, one day, Mike Lincoln started to see... the individuals weren't necessarily coming from anywhere they were supposed to be coming from.

You see?

There were too many of them, and some of them weren't legit. Some of them had been wound up by people other than those who worked with, or alongside, Mike Lincoln, cheeky-chappy hard-man, Import-Exports of London, and they had been pointed, quite deliberately, in quite unexpected directions.

So it seemed that there were people, other people, trying to control things. Or at least, adding a new element of potential terror, from which they might seize control. Then, it seemed to Mike anyway, there suddenly seemed also to be a few too many of them, both the wound-up, and the winders.

There was only one answer. The western governments had gone spare. They'd gone way overboard with security. They'd gone way overboard, hiring paranoid people to protect them from psychopaths. Then they'd started hiring psychopaths, and sociopaths, and the homicidal variety of both; the openly, bloodthirstily Machiavellian, to protect them from... what, Mike had to wonder?

What was worse than that?

Did anybody know any more?

Certainly, Mike Lincoln didn't.

So he'd scarpered.

Wound himself up, and done a runner.

Changed everything, vanished into the night, and pissed off to some remote island not even he knew the proper name of, to drink and snorkel and pay a harem of all the best local whores to screw nobody but him.

The dream, in other words.

Until he'd heard the voice in his head.

II

Mike traveled by coach now because he knew they were okay. That was a kind of unspoken interdepartmental agreement that the coaches weren't properly monitored for ID, and that the security tapes were erased after twenty four hours, if not sooner.

And on top of that, it was thinking time.

Cameras were everywhere but until he did something, until he made a move that gave the game away, nobody would look for him, and his face was still off the register. He still had old mates who would have seen to that. He'd done enough work in Australia to know his way around, and maintain his brief accent. They liked the working class down here, still maintained the façade of an egalitarian national psyche, something that hadn't truly existed anywhere now for a generation at least.

Still, after the big crash, at least Australia was where it had come to die.

They still called them Greyhounds here, although they had some kind of generic name now. Central Coach, something piss poor like that.

Our motto: 'Don't Get Too Comfortable'.

He'd booked in person but used a fake ID and spoken with a French accent and a stutter. The woman would remember that. When, and if asked, she would tell them; no, that's not him, that man was disgusting. The man you're looking for in the photo you showed me is a handsome old dog, who I'd shag after a few… what did they drink here, again? Bourbon and Cokes, or something horrible like that. The man I spoke to was a freak. You could always depend on people to be cruelly judgmental, especially these days, when everybody was so bloody unhappy.

Mike Lincoln had kept in excellent shape, and at fifty five was in better shape than most young men. He got off the bus in a long tweed coat and beret, hunched his shoulders down and pretended, when it was handed to him from under the bus, that he could barely carry his own small carry bag. Then he went into the station's Men's and came out looking about as nondescript as was possible; slacks and shirt and zip-up polyester jacket, all different shades of blue-grey.

On the pavement outside the bus station, he and everyone else were greeted by the local cops. Not city privates but the so-called proper cops, who were all mean as hell now because they hated being paid less and treated like second class cops to the corporates or privates.

And quite frankly, who could fucking blame them?

They were handing out half hour tags, barking at people to get a move on.

'Excuse me, thank you officer…' He spoke in a proper English accent to the cops. They were the most likely to still respect a random authority. 'I wonder if you might direct me to the nearest bed and breakfast?'

There were two cops; a young man, maybe nineteen, and a decade-older woman.

'Bed and breakfast, mate?' the woman had a deep twang.

Mike made his best effort to smile at her, charmingly.

'Or, something akin? A youth hostel perhaps?'

The boy spoke. 'Keep going, down there on the right. It's an old pub. You won't miss it.'

'Don't take too long. Half an hour, or you're in a cell for the night.'

'Many thanks.'

'Oh, mate,' the women sniggered, 'they're not *youth hostels* any more. Just *hostels*.'

'Oh really? Well, cheers. Thank you officers…'

The woman nudged the boy. 'Lucky for you, eh?'

They both sniggered as he walked on, pretending he hadn't heard.

Mike smiled. He appreciated not their despicable joke, but his own.

'Lucky for you...' he uttered. '...I don't end your life in a second and vanish into the night.'

Cops. Talking like that. To elders. On duty.

The world had truly gone to shit.

He walked on.

'Kill me...'

The voice in his head asked again.

Begged.

'Please... *kill me...*'

TEN: WARM

Kurt was asleep now.

Having nightmares.

They'd worn him down, given him the rules until he'd started bawling and passed out. Now the rules would sink in. It was kind of the way it worked.

No sooner had he fallen asleep than Cass had felt the call. There was another hour, at least another hour, until sunrise. She had wanted to tell Shylee that it was okay. That she understood. They'd maintained their modesty, together, on the run. There had to be something. And that some of those stories… they were connected to their bodies.

Connected to how they were, and their scars.

'Shylee, that thing I do. I have to do it.'

'Now?'

Shylee had already retreated to her side of the room. She liked the hay bales. When it was dark, and she went to the far corner where she slept, Cass couldn't see her. Although she knew what that space looked like in the light, somehow in the night, the dark, it took on a different aspect. It was like a cave. Shylee's cave. And when her voice came from the darkness, there was something about the timbre that made it seem like it was coming from much further away. Somewhere dark and holy.

'Okay.' Her voice came out of her den. 'I know, but… promise me, like you said, you're not… you know… having *alone time*, in the kitchen…? That would be too icky. Go to the woods if you want to…'

Holy…

'I told you…'

Cass rolled her shoulders a bit. She knew that monsters were real; they came in all shapes and sizes. But she didn't believe in any of that spiritual crap. Monsters were real. As real as she was, as Shylee was. There was nothing... *holy* or *unholy* about them. *Nothing.*

'I am. I mean, it is alone time. But it's not... *that* kind of alone time. Not what you're thinking. I'm too tired for that. I can't remember the last time...' Cass sighed. 'It's more like... a personal ritual. I think it's more to do with...' They didn't usually use this word. But Kurt had said it. And they were saying it more as time went by. '...more to do with the Wrath.'

Using that word more frequently.

Since they'd started killing.

But they still didn't like it. It was in every hyperpsychic's head, yet none of them knew what to do with it. They couldn't gather in any one place, certainly no more than three or four, and not for more than a few days at most, so all they could do was acknowledge that it was there as they passed in the night, and weave a subtle conformation between them, spread throughout time and distance, that it was somehow real. Like people who had seen ghosts, she sometimes thought, or flying saucers.

She heard Shylee rustle in her cave, rolling over her hay bale nest.

'Are we good?'

She'd sat up to ask. Cass could hear it in her voice.

Cass let out a tension, in her gut and shoulders, just the one degree of it all that had ramped up on her when Shylee had shown her the scars.

'Of course.'

'Sure?'

'Promise.'

'Okay. Keep watch and wake me in a few hours.'

'Okay.'

'We both need men, Cass. At some point.'

'I know.'

'Just to… just to feel.'

'Go to sleep.'

Shylee fell silent and Cass went out to the kitchen. There was an old chair and table there, painted red. She sat for a while, for a few minutes, until she sensed that Shylee had fallen asleep.

Then she went outside.

Immediately, it was bitterly cold.

She tried to take her mind off it, take herself away.

She recollected her thoughts from before. So, because of Hector, she had been thinking, she remembered things. Things that others allowed themselves to forget. Hector had remembered his birthday. He'd remembered that stupid flavor of ice cream. He'd counted the days, until he could allow himself to have it; allow the risk of stealing it. He'd looked and looked, digging into the bottom of the freezer in the stupid little shop. The shop, he said, that always stocked that flavor.

Cass walked on toward the water tanks.

There was a shower attached to the middle one. It wasn't much, just a chain and some mesh really. You pulled the chain, and water came straight down an open pipe into a catchment, like a baseball hoop with the mesh inside it. The water just fell through and spread out, like a shower. You pulled the chain again and it stopped. Shylee had recognized it when they'd first arrived, and had somehow known how it worked. She'd climbed to the top of the tank on what had turned out to be the last warm day at the end of autumn, when neither of them had washed in days, and fixed it. Pulled some leaves out, reattached something. It had been glorious.

Still, it was effectively just a cold, outdoor shower. Fine for washing on a hot day, even a mild day, of which there had been a sparse few since, but not much else. The farmer must have used it a bit though, probably just to dose down after a long day in the field, because there was a patch of worn ground underneath the shower head-hoop, marked out by a circle in the dry earth where the surrounding, mangy couch grass had never grown back. And, if there ever had been a curtain to hide would-be naturist sight seers, it had long since been stolen, or deteriorated, or just… blown away. But such a thing would not have been strictly necessary; there was no line of sight behind, where there was the hillside, or ahead, past the edges of the house.

Still, it was odd though.

More than odd, coming out here, answering the call.

It always made her wonder.

About being guided. By something.

Walking out, into a cold shower at, what? Four o'clock on a freezing cold plains morning…?

Why else would you?

Shylee had once, after the one before Dancer, maintained that when she shot the pedophiles, or slavers, or serial killers, she felt as though she had been guided to do it.

She had stated something about… what was it?

'There's a spiritual concept, called…'

It was so cold out here, and she was still… *so fucking tired*… that she was having trouble thinking straight.

And yeah, like she'd always said, she didn't believe in any of that crap anyway.

So… every time she did this, out here, it seemed insane.

And yet, every time, and this was, what? The fifth, sixth time now? Even though it seemed like a dream, and afterwards she had to convince herself it had really happened, every time she did this, something changed. Her *scoping*, like she'd done with Dancer, to read his mind, became more acute, or her rushing more precise. Subtle things, yet important things, and useful.

But all that; that wasn't… spiritual. It wasn't holy. There would be an explanation. Some kind of dimensional thing, a frequency thing, that humanity just hadn't discovered and explained

– yet. Except, they had discovered it, and they didn't want an explanation. They just wanted to kill it.

The third time she'd done this had been the time her hair had changed color. It had gone from plain auburn to a kind of bright honey orange, with dark yellow streaks underneath.

Shylee hadn't asked and she hadn't, really, said anything.

Although they loved each other dearly, and depended upon each other sometimes by the very second, there were still things like that between them. Like Shylee's weird spiritual side. She was happy to kill the evil, corrupted old men with a single bullet through the forehead, but at the same time she believed all that crazy stuff. Like that shurshes still meant something to the world.

'I don't know…' Cass had shrugged, the morning she had woken with her new hair. It had been down way past her shoulders then, but now she had Shylee cut it a little more even, to the blades, just in a straight line. Slow, keeping still. Easy, a straight back, a straight line. And lately, she'd even been thinking about bangs. '…it just happened.'

Cass stared up at the shower. She was aware, again, that on a night like this it could kill her. The hotter the days, the colder the nights. This really could kill her.

Yeah; so, she remembered all that. The global warming, slash, climate change thing. It was happening, for sure, but it didn't seem so important now that Bureau 88 had frightened all the Asians out of the western counties, and rounded up all the African Americans into prison cities.

So she'd heard.

With all that going on, man, there was more to worry about than the freaking weather; managing climate just didn't seem to be on anyone's agenda anymore. But the predictors had warned people; Adelaide was going to become like a desert city. And almost no autumn or spring. She had always thought, back then, that she would just cope with that.

She took off her gloves and stuffed them into the pockets of her deep-crimson frock coat.

She'd just assumed that people would move, migrate, to accommodate themselves better. Perhaps another, smaller, more southern city somewhere on the South Australian coast would blow out, as people moved toward it, adjusting for the shifting equatorial regions, as they upped and went, down to a more moderate climate. Maybe even Tasmania. She had always thought; this is what they're missing. People adapt. They move.

But Cass had not expected to be homeless, or living like a homeless person, when all this went down.

She removed the coat and hung it on a long nail. It seemed to be there, just for that purpose. For the farmer's shirt and pants, she assumed.

There was a meme running through the hyperpsychics about that. Her clothes. Everyone they met seemed to have adopted it and realized it was true. Some American girl, a hyperpsychic, a beauty queen or fashion guru or something, who'd turner hyper and fled here after The Purge, after they'd taken her tiny, sparkling pink phone away, probably, had come up with it, apparently.

Fine.

It was; don't dress homeless. We're not homeless, the hyperpsychics. People will tell you're faking. The homeless will spot you a mile away, like we all spot fake beggars. She supposed now that Shylee had been something to do with working that one out.

Go figure.

And don't try and dress normal, to fit back in. People will spot you, feel uncomfortable. Even your friends. Everyone you knew, who had been comfortable around you, would now try to get rid of you. At the very least, they would unconsciously try to push you away. At worst… well, they'd almost all experienced that.

Once you're gone, expelled, hunted… dress like a hyperpsychic. Dress, look real, like you're *someone*, but do not dress like you *don't belong*, or *don't care*.

They all did it now. It had become a whole neo-Dickensian thing. Coats and scarves and mittens and even hats, sometimes.

The idea worked, Cass thought, as she unwrapped her brown wool scarf from her lily white neck, and unbuttoned her thick dark-gray waistcoat, because of vampires. Vampires had a look. If you ever saw a vampire, you would know. You would run, and you would maybe freak out and tell your friends, or maybe even tell no-one. Because it sounded crazy. If you saw someone who looked like a hyperpsychic… well, half the world didn't believe they existed anyway. Probably more than half.

The American girl had made hyperpsychics into *something*, and therefore, they had weight. The very idea of them could possess someone, and scare them if they had a sighting. They would maybe call the cops, or even Bureau 88. But their response, should you describe a Dickensian hyperpsychic, was more likely to be; well, she's mad. That's what hyperpsychics look like in the public imagination. Really, nobody dresses like that. Especially not the hypers. Alternately, the sighter might think; that was a real hyperpsychic, because it looked like what they were supposed to look like. They might think twice, because, if they called the cops, and the cops chased the hyperpsychic, and the hyperpsychic got away, then it might come back around after you… and it, the hyper-monster, might be *pissed* and want *revenge*.

Burn out your tiny fucking mind!

Raaah!

She smiled to herself as she hung the waistcoat over the coat.

It also gave weight to the 'pretend you didn't see it' response. You saw one, a hyperpsychic, but… let's just pretend you didn't. It's all a bit weird, and far out, and potentially dangerous. Let's just… let it be.

Fuck it was cold. Her shirt was faded, but still bright orange, and she unbuttoned it quickly and slipped it off. She still wore a bra, although she didn't know why. Shylee only squeezed her boobs into that business suit when she was going for a kill; she said it was something to do with wanting them to know part of the sacred, assertive feminine was responsible for her moment of Wrath.

Okay.

But the rest of the time she had that old wooly jumper, and that massive black overcoat, that made her look, with her serious face and beautiful dark eyes, like a European Morticia Addams in a penguin costume.

Now the hard part.

She unlaced her Docs quickly. There were two layers of wool socks underneath.

Was it faith, what she was doing? Using?

Faith?

Faith in something wasn't required if the something was real, was it? That is; there could be a person, who you loved. And that person was real, and said they loved you. But you had to have faith that the trust you placed in them wouldn't be betrayed. And would last.

Shylee might have been spiritual before all this, but Cass hadn't been. She'd never believed in most of the things she could do now. Not before she'd actually started doing them. But here she was, taking her clothes off at four in the morning, the coldest part of the night, outdoors, hoping it would… happen again.

So… that person you loved was real. And love itself was real. So the faith was… trusting. Was that it? Fuck. If she'd gone the church, or even fucking shersh, when she'd been asked to, like a good girl, maybe she wouldn't have been so frightened and confused about all this now. Maybe she would have been…

Nah.

She doubted that, quite strongly.

She put her shoes aside. The ground was so dry it crackled, even without her weight in them. Socks next; fuck, she could already feel the cold of the ground, through the two layers of wool, the Earth, under her feet. This was insane. *Insane.* She was already weak; she would catch influenza. But she fought the fear, and slipped off one double-layer of socks, then the other.

Fuh-uuuuhck.

She squeezed her jaw and clenched her teeth.

She could feel every toe, distinctly as the massive bundles of nerve endings on her soles responded with pain; a terrible warning. Higher and sharper with every second.

'Haaah. Haaah.'

Nothing *fucking* ventured.

The black jeans came down. It was a relief as she raised one foot, then the other, then repeat; harshly painful again as she returned each to the ground again, moving, walking just a few steps. Off with her thermal stockings, rolling them down, lily white legs, one then the other, gooseflesh like the surface of a golf ball, then her panties.

Nude; fuck!

Nude outdoors, in the cold!

A sports bra, when she wasn't killing. Shylee. When she wasn't squeezing all she could out of the girls. But not Cass. Still wore a normal bra, with a normal…

Unclasp.

She liked the feel, the normalcy. It was civilized, not just for warmth, like the sports bra, it was...

Oh, *for fuck's sake*, did she have to analyze every *fucking little thing*!?

She looked down. The starlight made her pale skin glow. The last time, her milky pink nipples had retreated like tortoise noses. This time, they were sticking up like demon's horns, and were about as hard. She was covered in gooseflesh. The end of her nose, and the tips of her ears *stung*.

She looked up and made a weird, primitive sound.

She could see the massive stretch of the Milky Way.

Familiar enough to her now, even if she had forgotten all the names.

She pulled the chain.

The cold metal was painful to the touch.

The water fell.

She thought she could see the cold.

And then, she remembered.

Oh yeah.

Righteous anger.

That was what Shylee called it.

Cass stepped under the shower.

ELEVEN: DARWIN

Ink was in Darwin.

He went there a lot.

It didn't take long, simply an elevator to the third sub-basement of the Central Security building.

Ink had requested the chamber and they had created it for him.

In the early days he had waged a security war with the Bureau that he had won, ultimately, and this had been part of it.

There was no surveillance here other than his own, and that was necessarily limited. The best way of seeing what was down here, apart from a small but efficient security system he had set up for emergencies, was to come down in person.

When Ink had started to realize what was happening, he had realized just as quickly that he needed to find a way of sedating the hypers. Even his allies in the Australian government would not sanction an order that would allow hyperpsychics to simply be tagged, or recruited, and then released to roam free. But if he could catch and contain them, then at least there was some oversight and deniability; even duty of care. All those things politicians were supposed to worry about.

Ink had managed to find one, weak and dying.

He'd fed her, but with high doses of all the things the rumors said diminished their powers. The rumors, it transposed, had been true; high doses of processed sugar, refined salt, trans fats and… well, all that good stuff. Fluoride worked, certain kinds of flavor enhancers and preservatives. MSG. Corn syrup.

The sugar and salt was probably where the old wives tales came from. Salt the ground, keep evil at bay. Meaning; other. Sugar treats to ward off the ghosts at Halloween.

So here they were. The others, the ghosts. Dosed and sedated.

He'd done his best. Turned Tamara's rumor of a northern Australian Shangri La against her, in favor of the hypers. Monitored and, when he was able, secretly supported the underground traffic system that helped get them all here, to Australia, then to Adelaide.

Then there were some, like Davy and Kelli Kennedy, who hadn't needed his help, who'd been fine on their own. They had made their way successfully to Detroit, then to Seattle, then commandeered a small yacht and sailed the Pacific down to Australia.

How the fuck they had done that was anyone's guess…

But they hadn't been the only ones.

People had been doing it, in fact, for many thousands of years.

And now, if they were desperate enough, and canny enough, they were still doing it.

They were smart kids, from good stock. Generations of wealth; well fed, well exercised, and well bred. Good bodies, good brains.

The office tower had been a genuine anomaly. There was no way Tamara would have found them. But he had requested their records from NUSA and received them, then studied for a weakness. Tamara and her men just hunted; she did not study profiles. Her theory, and to her credit it had been tested and found viable, was that eventually they would all try to come here, and eventually they would all slip up. How they got here, she didn't care. All the better if they were killed along the way by someone else; Tamara was not vindictive in that way. But once they were here, all she had to do was wait.

Until Ink had arrived, the Australian arm of Bureau 88 had been based in Canberra. Tamara's agents on the ground had called in any confirmed sightings, and Tamara had chosen whether or not to respond personally. Usually she had, with relish, in military choppers. And despite her protestations to the contrary, she had indeed taken them alive, several of them, if and when she'd been able.

And tortured them, in whatever secret lair she had created, in whatever city they had been apprehended.

She had to torture them, she'd reasoned, or they'd escape.

Ink had found another way to prevent them escaping.

He kept them safe, and didn't kill them.

He made a deal, and gave them sanctuary.

He made them a promise, and they had faith in him.

True, many of them had little choice.

But some did, and almost all of them had agreed.

Bureau 88 kept a record of all known hypers not to have been killed or apprehended. Davy and Kelli had been near the top of the list, being the children of a wealthy Texan media baron who was now big in the N'American government. He'd impressed his fellows by marshalling troops to track his son and daughter, who by all accounts had spontaneously and simultaneously emerged as hyperpsychics during their school prom. They had been attacked. There had been casualties, and they had fled. It had been nasty. But piecing it together afterwards it had looked to the cops as though Davy had been planning an escape for some time, perhaps preparing for his sister's emergence as The Most Wanted Woman in Texas. The route via which they had made their escape had seemed too good to be true; it had to have been chosen in advance for its bad reception, satellite and ground cover, and overall unlikeliness. Davy had led Kelli up the Colorado River, but had diverted in unexpected ways so that, by the time the cops had exhausted all the false leads Davy had planted, the fugitive kids had been long gone.

Vanished into the wastelands of Detroit, it seemed.

So Ink had studied the high school personality profiles of Davy and Kelli Worth, assuming that if Davy were that resourceful, he would get here, to Australia. Ink now controlled it so that all the railroads ended up here, in the one point three million plus capital city of the good state of South Australia, but somehow Davy and Kelli had travelled under their own steam, and ended up here anyway; perhaps guided by other hypers who told them it was safe and quiet.

More likely, guided by something altogether different.

And ancient, and scary.

II

There had been a lot of crazy decisions made after the crash of '07. A lot of papers burned, files deleted, people vanished. Business had abandoned secondary cities like this one, like Perth and Brisbane, and centralized in Melbourne and Sydney. Whole tower blocks had been gutted and abandoned, or odd sections of skyscrapers closed off between floors, with nobody knowing any longer the key codes to make the elevators stop there. Huge, unclaimed gaps, empty floors, tiny rooms where nobody went any more, randomly spaced, all over the city.

He thought, maybe, that was how Black Dog was getting around.

Or the kid who watched, but always moved on.

The Cat in the Hat.

They'd caught his image, just once or twice, but… it was almost impossible. They had no idea who he was, where he went, how he was hiding. Nothing other than Ink's theory, that Ink had kept resolutely to himself. Just that a lot of his Darwinians had mentioned seeing him.

The Darwinians were kept in cells, but they were comfortable. Like padded cells, but better equipped, with constant television and a constant supply of bad food.

It was a compromise he could live with, because it meant they could live.

Maybe television did rot your brain. But that was nothing compared to one of Tamara's bullets.

Tamara entered Darwin and stared at Ink.

She had tried again this afternoon to have them all killed, all these hypers in their secret little mental institution.

Tried again and failed again.

She didn't understand it.

Nobody would tell her. Ink had convinced them that the hypers should be caught and… was it tamed? Could they be…? Would they be able to turn them into hunters? She didn't know. What was he doing down here? Getting them hooked on something, so that they would be forced to obey him? Wake at some point, and do his bidding?

The notion had an appeal.

'The two Americans, the brother and sister.'

'Their names Kelli and Davy Worth.'

'Naming a psychic is like naming a killer shark as it jets toward you, smiling.'

He turned to her. She'd been home and slept, changed. He had too, but unlike him she had done a full makeover, as she seemed to every day. Today she was a black bra covered by a bright rose camisole, black pants and jacket. Her long hair was down, and sculpted messy, with thick black eyeliner.

Ink smiled at her, deliberately.

Like he wasn't hot for her any more. Like he hated her any the less.

'They're in the city. We have a kid who saw them, told them where to hide.'

'Bring him here.'

She touched her earpiece, making Ink think she was activating it, when it was always activated, always recording their every word. Sometimes, she liked to go back and listen to the sound of her own voice, working the boys.

'Bring him in.'

Chambers would be listening, would hear and obey.

'One of the abandoned office towers, apparently.'

'Leave them alone, Tamara.' He turned away again. 'I want to deal with them personally.'

Personally? Why? She was totally perplexed.

'Rutger, listen to me.'

He turned and looked at her once more. He was as surprised as she was. She was being earnest. It was completely spontaneous, but it seemed real. Seemed to her, maybe even to him, that she really meant it.

'If I take a team out and kill them, who would care? My people, my contacts would...' She shrugged, her voice light and soft. '...they would cheer me on, Rutger. Half of them would be happy to do it themselves.'

'We must mix in different circles, Tamara.'

Tamara gestured around, widely at the line of windows that surrounded them.

The cells.

'Rutger. This is an abomination. I would poison that food you're serving them in a second if you would just...'

Ink stepped toward her. She stared at him, looked into his eyes. Slightly taller; that always irritated her, but she couldn't function in higher heels. He would lick these five inch Casadei pumps before he died. Run his tongue down the spiked heels, and love it. But that look, now. She'd never seen it. Did he... love her now? Was that a look... of love in his eyes?

'I pity you, Tamara. I pity you, truly, because I know that right now you are being earnest. You think that because you are beautiful, and I know that you are beautiful, that it can change things between us. It can't. You think that because you hold power over men, with your sexuality, and cunning, you can get your own way all the time. I pray that this is not one of these times.'

'What if it were? Would that change things for you?'

'Change things?'

She could see that she had really surprised him now.

Yes, she thought.

You didn't think I really wanted you, did you?

Let me fuck you, Rutger. She was getting quite steamy now. *Let me fuck you to death…*

'Change what, Tamara? If you did that, if you killed all these kids in here, you would not be responsible for saving the entire human race, as you believe. On the contrary, you'd be responsible for our total extermination.'

Neither had moved an inch since the conversation had started, both were tense as dogs, waiting for the attack.

'I know you have to keep these monsters sedated, Rutger…' Tamara offered this quietly. She would not make the first move. '…so your people can't be too solid in their convictions.'

He was going to, she could see. She could see at the base of his throat, a growl was forming. An attack growl.

'I…' The growl came out as. 'I… do know the people you know, Tamara. And you're lucky our vigilante friend…'

'Friend? The Black Dog is our *friend* now?'

'…you and your people are lucky someone hasn't yet made the connection, made them a target. Don't threaten me again, Tamara. And if those American kids are so much as breathed on by your pack of animals, I'll personally poison someone in this room. Someone wide awake, and watch them as they drift away.'

'You're not man enough to take me.'

That was it. He moved at her, just a fraction.

This was it.

Fucking to the death.

It begins!

Then Chambers came in with the kid and fucked everything.

TWELVE: PAIN

The pain was always so intense, at first, that she never felt it.

It was a bit like what she'd heard about childbirth. The pain was such that the brain basically forgot it, erased the memory, as a biological imperative. Otherwise, no woman would ever even consider conceiving a second time.

Cass would have screamed, stepping under the ice cold tank water, and in fact she did. But no sound emerged; her scream was so high nobody heard it. Maybe a dog, if there was one within range.

Then…

It must have been something about the shock, the pure body shock, that triggered the magic.

Such as it was.

She felt the magic on her soles immediately; her agonized nerves tingling.

Then her toes were warm, then her feet. Then her calves, as her soles returned to normal, then… she still could not truly believe it… *warmth*.

Her calves had been about to cramp… then they were warm. As though she were standing in a tank that was slowly filling with warm water. Slowly heating. Then the lower curve of her buttocks, and between her legs. The underside of her breasts. The heat arose from the earth, under her arms, under her chin, under her numb pointy nose, her lips, and to her icicle earlobes. Then, it was surrounding her.

Then the water was hot. The water from the pipe, from the mesh, was hot. As hot as any hot shower she's ever had, and constant. There was steam, forming a kind of shroud. She reached out of the steam and grabbed the bar of soap from her coat pocket, fumbling, her arm quickly cold again, her fingers instantly chilled. She could feel, beneath her pale white toes; it was the ground, the ground was warm. Not quite hot. She could stand on it. But the heat was coming up, through the ground, through the barren patch of dark brown earth. The rising steam was surrounding her from there, like a solid curtain.

Cass just stood there, in it, as the hot water sprayed into her shoulders, her back, the curve of her lower back to the top of her bottom. The sensation forced her to realize how thin she was now, how little body fat there was between flesh and bone and muscle. She turned and leaned back, looked up and let it pound her face, her chest and breasts. She soaped herself up and down, and felt her ribs with the flat of her palms, especially pronounced as she leaned backwards.

It was impossible.

Later, she would forget that it was real.

She would question it.

But it was.

It was real.

When she'd soaped her fire-orange and canary-yellow hair, and washed her face, she let the water spray her again, then opened her eyes.

Shylee was at the door.

Watching.

At first, Cass couldn't tell.

What..?

She froze.

What was she feeling?

What were either of them feeling?

There was no connection; Shylee's face was impassive, cold even.

Then Shylee she took off her coat, and tossed it to the ground. Then her jumper was off, roughly over her head, then she ripped off the tee.

'Shy…'

Her heavy shoes were off, then her socks, then the jeans.

'Shut up…' Shylee snapped.

Cass thought she heard her say that; then the sports bra and the panties were off. Shylee shivered then, savagely, as though she'd just been electrocuted. Then, bringing her arms together, her fists clasped under her chin, she approached.

Then her giant lips moved.

'…before I lose my nerve…'

She stepped under the hot water.

They were face to face, staring at each other.

'Cass, I don't, I wish I did…'

'What?'

'I don't feel that way…'

Then Shylee gave Cass the strangest look.

'Shut up!'

'Shy…'

'Neither do I, you idiot… but we have to do it this way; *you're making it work.*'

She smiled. Cass felt relieved. So relieved. And then she started crying. She couldn't help it. Shylee held her arms out and she pressed herself into them. She wrapped her arms around Shylee, and felt her start to shake as well. She was crying too. With their bodies pressed tightly together, their arms wrapped so tight, they wept and wept beneath the hot water, bound together in the reality of the impossible.

THIRTEEN: CRISPIN

Crispin stood on the pedestrian bridge and waited for the sunrise over the hills.

It would be a while yet.

A half hour, maybe a bit less.

The bridge was over a train line and under a massive concrete overpass.

He could not be detected here.

He did this every morning, if the night hadn't been too taxing.

He'd found that if he smoked, nobody thought twice about him.

His mind was too powerful now, to be affected by the sedatives, and he didn't expect to live long enough to be made ill by the poisons.

It was pleasant enough, a few smokes a day.

Was it time?

He wondered.

The pixie, Cass, and the assassin, Shylee.

The American bro and sis.

The black dog thing.

Was it time?

FOURTEEN: SCARS

'If we live through this…' Shylee smiled. '…whatever this is, we'll come back, and build a spring. A hot spring, like in Bath. And around it, we'll build a shursh.'

Shylee could tell, Cass thought she was mad.

But why not? Who wouldn't? This was all mad, after all.

'What are they?' Shylee asked, soaping her black hair, feeling her scalp under the bizarre, mystical hot water.

Shylee figured that she might as well ask. You never knew how pale someone was until you saw them naked. And Shylee could see now; Cassandra Casperelle was white as a ghost. But there were tiny scars, up and down her left arm.

Cass shrugged. 'I stopped doing it when I met you…'

Shylee stopped massaging her scalp.

'Stopped doing it?' She looked harder at the tiny scars. 'You were… self-harming?'

Her hands came down and she grasped Cass by the arm, lifting it quickly but gently, with no resistance. Shylee stared intently in the moonlight. Yes. That's what it was. There were tiny white scars, cuts, all the way down and across the middle section of her arm.

'Why, Cass?' Shylee demanded softly.

Cass gulped. Shylee looked up. The hot water was running down her face, which was bright pink from the heat. But somehow, with her hair flat, exposing the sharpness of her ears, she looked more foxlike than ever. Shylee put her hand on her cheek as Cass started to cry again, as they both started to cry again.

Cass gasped. 'Hector. To punish myself. For surviving. For running. For living.'

Shylee saw the pain of it, in her friend's eyes, for the first time. The true pain, and the loss.

'Oh no, no Cass, no…'

Cass lifted her other arm to show her. Shylee's heart twisted. It was the same. Tiny white cuts, healed now but whiter than her pale pink skin, all the way up and across the middle section.

'…and these were to stop me, when I couldn't stop remembering, after I'd forced myself to remember…'

Shylee cupped Cass's face in both hands. She could feel her own hands shaking. Cass's lips were trembling. Shylee kissed Cass on forehead, and cheeks, one at a time, and on her lips, just a peck, but a good one. With feeling. Over and over in that order, like some weird benediction. She didn't know what it was really; she couldn't help herself.

'Oh, no, Cass…'

Cass was fully weeping. Shylee wondered if her cupped hands over her cheeks weren't all that was keeping Cass on her feet.

Forehead, cheek, cheek, lips.

'No, Cass… no, no…'

Her cupped hands, tight.

Forehead, cheek, cheek, lips.

Then they embraced again, tight under the water.

'I'll never let anyone hurt you again…' Shylee could feel a pain in her jaw as she clenched her teeth. 'I'll never leave you on your own, Cass. Never…'

Shylee pressed hard into her, her whole body, all the surface she could, her arms wrapped tight, one hand gripping her upper arm and bony shoulder, one under the other arm, against the top of her protruding ribs. Shylee felt Cass angle her head under her neck for a while, like a puppy. There was soap running out of her orange-yellow hair, and she watched it roll down Cass's pink back.

Slowly Shylee felt Cass relax, and release her muscles. Her crying stopped and she started breathing heavily, but normally. Then Cass looked up. There was gratitude in her puffy blue almond eyes. There was an urge there, to communicate the emotion, to unleash again what had underscored so terribly their last exchange of telepathy. But the physical proximity, the intimacy there, seemed enough. They ended the embrace and separated, still tenderly patting each other's upper arms, until Shylee found the soap again at the edge of the couch grass and bent down to get it.

When she stood again, they were normal. It was over. Shylee smiled and shrugged. It felt stupid, but she didn't want Cass to see. So she turned around as she soaped her loins, then turned back to rinse them, looking slightly over Cass's shoulder.

'You shave still?' Cass asked.

Shylee was surprised. She glanced down, very quickly.

'You too?'

Cass shrugged as Shylee returned the soap to her.

'It's the whole thing, the American girl thing. We have to stay normal, as normal as we can. Keep things up. We belong, Shy. We belong here, in this world. We're not supposed to be… killed. Like animals. If we live like animals, we'll die like animals.'

Shylee nodded. She'd been thinking the same.

'It's not just survival, is it? At least, it shouldn't be.'

'Can you feel the others?' Cass asked.

'Not feel. But I see them sometimes. There's a Robert Redford boy…'

Wow. Where the hell had she pulled that name from?

'…I saw him last night. It's as if we're both looking into a mirror at the same time. You?'

Cass shrugged.

'There are two of us in an office tower, hiding. There's are two more in a warehouse, near an abandoned train station. Maybe eight more, in the city, on their own. And… more than that, somewhere here, in the city. More, but… weak. Together maybe. But I don't know what that is.'

Shylee was surprised. 'You can tell that?'

'Here I can. Under the water, in the warm…' Cass squired. '… and Shy; something else. Something… heavy, and dark. There's…

those dark things everywhere, but here's another one of us, who is…'

Cass gulped.

Shylee nodded. 'That's okay. I thought there must be.' She was getting it now. 'And all this from… the heat? The energy?'

Cass shrugged again, nodded again, gulped again.

'There's stone under out feet. We're standing on something solid. And; glass. It's when I see people, in the reflection of glass, or a mirror. And here, the house, it's all, mostly, wood.'

Cass frowned. 'I don't see the connection…?'

'Natural substances?'

'Maybe.'

'Who are we Cass?' Shylee couldn't believe she was asking this. 'I mean; why do we even exist? The world, the world we used to know…'

Shylee shook her head. She'd had these thoughts a while. Kept them in. Too depressing, too much of a downer. But; she'd been that kind of person before all this. Studying history, and art, and pissed with the world, dissatisfied.

'Cass, before that this, I was angry that here was too much suffering the world. I had a good life, and I wasn't about to give it up, but I thought, maybe, from there, I could do something. Maybe that's why people with conscience are born into wealthy families; or, just, half decent western cultures. So they can help the rest of the world form there, but…'

'But you never thought things would be this bad?'

'We remember, Cass. But kids are being born into this. Thinking it's normal. I think we both know how these things run; the people in power write the histories. Re-write them. Cass; who are we? Who are we *really*? What if we're like this, like, empowered, because we are supposed to stop it?'

'Aren't we doing that?'

'No; I mean stop the Bureau. Maybe all these awful ghouls are just practice. Maybe we should start looking higher…'

'Higher?'

Shylee let out a long, shaky breath. The water seemed to become warmer.

'At those three towers, Cass. At Bureau 88.'

FIFTEEN: VODKA

The hostel was okay. He'd used an old code word to get an upgrade, nothing out of the ordinary, but one that would not get him flagged or draw undue attention. It would simply be written, by hand, on a roster, that would be assessed at the end of the month for anomalies. Or, not assessed, if things were still the same. Assessed only in it needed to be; not enough for anyone with half a brain to stop keeping it.

Useful.

It was almost like the cold war days, again.

There were secret signs, outside, that said that certain code words would pass here. That there were private rooms with their own showers that people traveling on private business could use. Central business that central did not monitor, for deep cover or private assignments and… all that jazz.

He showered and worked out and went downstairs.

The food was well prepared but filled with shit.

He ate it, because he could stomach it once in a while, and occasionally it tasted good. Like fast food had once tasted good, before everything tasted like fast food. There was a Ukrainian woman in good shape, in her thirties, who was up for a shag, so he gave her one and they both enjoyed it. She had a private room as well, and he could tell she was a roamer, out here with nothing to do, traveling, reporting anything she saw.

'Anything out of the ordinary?'

She remained unclothed as she offered him vodka.

'No. You?'

He shrugged. 'I don't know. Just got here. Everything's changed.'

'I've been here too long.'

'I might not stay. The Bureau seems strong here; they tend to get in the way.'

'In my country they are all junkies. My government hooks them and keeps them under control. We need no Bureau; they are the Bureau. All this hunting and killing; what use is that? A waste. Terrible waste.'

Mike nodded.

'I only ever work for Central Government. A lot of my generation bailed out.'

She nodded.

'I don't care why you're here. I like you.'

He smiled. 'Good.'

'Why are you here?'

'I've come to put down the Black Dog.'

She nodded.

'Good. I can't help. I know nothing about that. Maybe let him kill a few more old pedos before you dispatch him.'

'Maybe.'

'You want to go again, or sleep now?'

SIXTEEN: DEBRIEF

Sharon Coyer wanted them to be lovers, and Ink had not discouraged that. But he'd not yet given her a signal, or allowed her anything to indicate that it was time. He wondered if he ever would, given how things were playing out.

She entered the office, and stood by the door as he watched the sunrise over the gloomy city. She waited a few seconds, then she closed the door.

'The two girls who've been raiding the city supermarkets.'

'Yes.'

'They've slipped up. The cops have them; they must be too weak to mentally teleport themselves out. Tamara's people will be upon them shortly. As soon as she gets back from… wherever she's gone.'

Ink knew; Tamara had gone for the night. Most of her men had vanished as well.

'They would be caught already if Tamara hadn't taken the evening for herself. They've got until morning to escape the police, or we'll bring them in and set them up down below.'

'We have footage of them. Just two girls… one might be indigenous. I don't think they're the assassins.'

'No?'

Ink knew they weren't. The assassins were too good.

'No. The other is Chinese. With an accent. Our one witness to the assassins says both our girls, the suspected assassins, are Australian.'

Ink nodded. 'Do you know where Miss Chant went?'

'No. Her counter surveillance isn't as good as ours, but in this instance it was very effective. But, she let her men go, and most of them are out drinking. Three unaccounted for, but they're probably with her.'

Ink didn't like it, but he accepted it. Tamara was so rarely absent, even for a day, that it was practically ghostly not to have her and her men striding about the carpets, making their presence felt. But Tamara's ghost, he could live with.

As for the living?

This was the time, Sharon would have thought. They would do it here, in his office. Tamara would never know. It would be just like one of the boardroom dramas that had become so popular again, that played on TV, endlessly each night, to fill young women's heads with such nonsense. But Sharon wanted it to be real, and Ink was fighting off loneliness as he'd never felt before. Still, Sharon was nice. She would do. But she wasn't his equal.

It wasn't just that Sharon was younger; just that she clearly had no talent for office politics. Not beyond a clandestine, forbidden romance. She was a lifelong technical administrator, brilliant at surveillance but always remote, never in the field, or on the ground. She had an imagination, and an eye. Where and how to plant cameras, hide microphones. Secret office sex between herself and her older, more experienced, Daddy Issues Lover was some tiny scenario from within that seedy world she so often observed, and considered, that had gotten her mind inside, that she could translate to her world here; a little of the TV soaps she sometimes watched, too. Ink was pretty sure this was how things would be for Sharon Coyer, but it meant that she had, therefore, no idea how dangerous Tamara Chant actually was.

How could she?

Ink himself was only just starting to learn.

Ink waited a few seconds. He could have looked at her reflection in the office window, framed her with the night and the neon, but instead he turned from the window and smiled at her, hoping he would not see a look of longing, or expectation.

'I'm going to leave you in charge of the office for tonight.'

'You're... leaving, sir?'

She'd hidden the longing and expectation well; but this was too far in the opposite direction. After all, if he wasn't here, how could they begin their long-delayed romance?

'While I'm gone, I want you to pay special attention, in case Davy and Kelli turn up. They might be born survivors, but they are still running scared, lone survivors, and they will be wearing thin, in every sense.'

'Davy and Kelli?'

She squinted a little. He could tell; she thought that was too personal. He was too close to it all, clearly.

'The Worth siblings.' Ink nodded.

'They escaped the Dallas executions. I mean, if they'd been caught; in Dallas they executed seventeen hyperpsychics a month later...' Sharon smirked. 'Sorry, you know all that. We all know all that. Sometimes it helps to process how horrific things have become if you just keep talking about it. Over and over...'

'It's good you find things like that difficult to process. It's a sign you're retained your humanity. Although what you're doing with humanity, in the Bureau...'

Sharon smiled. 'God knows what they've been through to get here, but they'll probably try and head north sometime soon. If they break cover, we'll have to act first. If they do it while you're not here...'

'I'll be back before daybreak.'

'What about other girls? The ones the cops have?'

'I'll be back.'

'Will the Worths be sent back? I hear there's a backlash against the Bureau in the States. Does our hyperpsychic extradition treaty still hold, now that Atlanta has started executing as well?'

Ink smiled at her, as reassuring a paternal smile as her could muster. 'Nothing would persuade me to start sending people back. Parents in every N'American country are still turning their children in. To be killed... inevitably.'

Sharon nodded. What could you say?

'I can cope.'

Ink smiled; that was about as good a response as he could hope for.

'I believe you.'

Sharon stared at him as though he'd gone mad.

'I suppose you do. You brought me into this after all. I suppose you had to see something in me.' She flinched a little. 'Sorry. That sounded a lot less slutty in my head.'

Ink let out a short, polite laugh. 'It's been a long night. I've had… some intelligence. Otherwise I wouldn't risk leaving. I need to follow it up personally. If I leave, now, and I'm back before nightfall, Tamara won't know. But I need you to cover.'

Sharon nodded. 'There are no reports sir. It should be fine. The remaining hyperpsychics are the best; whether we like the way it happened or not, they're the smartest and most cunning. None of them are breaking cover any time soon.'

Ink nodded. 'Sharon, I brought you in, because…'

'I know.'

'I'm sorry?'

'Because I don't want to kill the hyperpsychics. I'd never say it while Tamara was in the building, but I don't think it's right.'

That hung in the air between them like an unanswered marriage proposal.

'I don't know if I should have said that or not, but I don't care anymore. They're people. They're humans. They're not animals. Sometimes I think they're quite the reverse. Critics say we should have done something about the corporations before this. About the fact that they attracted and supported organized communities of… narcissists, and sociopaths, without empathy. Exploiters and fiends. That we should have changed the business model, that we should have prevented them from rising, stopped them conspiring, made some kind of laws against Machiavellian business practices.'

Ink smiled. 'People do say that, yes.'

'But what were we supposed to do? Burn *The Prince*? Ban Sun Tzu? Back then, there was no clear psychological process for defining sociopathic behavior. Now they have so much power they seek out their own; know their own, and advance them.'

'They used to say that about the Jews, before Hitler's Germany.'

'Exactly!' Sharon huffed. 'And; that is the most shameful period in our long, long – '

'The current N'American government may be doing it again, to the people of color. Who knows what they've done to the Jewish population.'

Sharon shook her head. 'From all reports they've been left alone. As though; been there, done that. I'm sorry. That sounds horrible. But it's true. It's all so… calculated. To appeal to the ignorant and uneducated. The mean-spirited and the terminally bitter. The worst of us.'

'Formula.' Ink growled. 'Tried and true. Different veneer, different victims. You're right. It is horrible. And calculated. And it works. It always works.'

She squinted again. 'But if we declare war against the sociopaths; we're just as bad. Aren't we?' The squint was growing on him. He liked it; she did good angry, good frustrated. He liked her, it seemed. More than he'd thought. 'Where will that end? Surely that makes us just as bad?' She got angry about the right things. Even if they were… naïve? Or just, too late? He threw her a bone.

'But, Sharon, that's been the liberal, the peaceful, high-ground excuse for not waging war… forever. Look where it's gotten us. They have crushed us.'

'But...'

'We have the moral high-ground? We can still win?'

'I don't know...' Sharon shrugged. 'I thought… I thought you'd have the answers. I just… try. And hope. I don't have faith in anyone or anything anymore, I just hope, and try.' She gave him a nice smile, sympathetic. She knew that wasn't enough, but it was all she had. 'I wanted to be here. You brought me in, but I got myself to a point where you could bring me in. Where you, or someone like you, would see me. For what I was doing, for what I was *trying* to stand for...'

'And I did.'

'And I thought…' She shrugged again. 'I don't pretend to understand how you put up with her. I don't know why you have to. People say that you had to accept her as your deputy; that in exchange for the position, using whatever political favor you had, or have; you were forced to accept her.'

'That's true.'

Ink felt his fingers tapping at his desk.

The headline of the morning was: STUDY PROVES – AUSTERITY WORKS.

There was a small scrap of paper there, tucked under the headline, that wasn't his. He ignored it.

'But, sir…' Sharon sighed again. 'Rutger? There are ways of putting her in her place, surely? She wouldn't hesitate to do the same, if the positions were reversed?'

'I thought you didn't hold with power plays.'

'Power must be wielded, sir. Just, not unjustly. Not with cruelty. How much more…' She huffed. 'How many more…?'

'How many people need to die, need to vanish, before people realize that? That's where you were heading with this train of thought, weren't you? That eventually, people will see? Rise up? They've thought of that. This is it now, Sharon. People won't rise up any more. There have been so many governments, so many dictatorships, so many forms of fascism and organized cruelty now, that they've learned every way it can fail. We had a chance; then they managed to convince people that psychology was quackery. That spirit was a delusion. And now we're done. Humanity is being ruled by its least human members, it's least compassionate, and most ruthless. They're not even logical; Tamara is impossible to predict because undermining her ruthless, logical mind is a temperament of a child. She swings, to and fro, up and down. It's not true that psychopaths have no emotion; they lack empathy, but they are capable of great emotion. I think maybe it's to make up for that, it's where the emotion goes that would otherwise be used as empathy; enormous bursts of sheer, brute emotion.'

Sharon was staring at him. She looked almost hurt.

'You sound…'

Ink was surprised.

'…sound what?'

'You sound like you admire her.'

The little bit of paper was still sticking out from under the headline.

'I admire the sheer animal guile of Mother Nature, to create such a seamless intra-species predators. I admire her, like I admire a shark, as it jets toward you.'

'A shark? But…'

'Tamara would kill me if she could. If she could manage it, without her superiors knowing. I'm sure she's killed several of her opponents already, but I have no proof. She is most likely out there now, lobbying for permission to have me removed. That's why I must make my move, make my counter-arrangements immediately, while she's gone. My single advantage is that she underestimates me. She thinks I am some variety of 'holier-than-thou' crusader. But my past is drenched in blood. She doesn't know my true past. She does not know me, what I am capable of. She thinks she had all my records. She doesn't. But she is correct, in that I sought this position, traded every last favor, and made promises that will cripple me if I fail, to seek redemption.'

'The hyperpsychics?'

'I have information.'

'I assumed that you did. But…'

'She will kill me, Sharon. And she will kill you, and everyone else here who has openly sided with me. Even a few of those she suspects would side with me, if they had the courage, just to make a point, just for good measure. This is old school, old style rule Sharon, make no mistake. This is a fascist bureaucracy in all but name. Evil controls the western nations. And they are ushering in an age of even greater evil, that we cannot imagine.'

Sharon gulped. She was terrified. He had terrified her. But she walked toward him anyway, crossing to his desk, to stand almost right before him.

'There's a lot more to this, isn't there. The hyperpsychics?'

'I think so, yes.'

He turned to the desk and she examined the papers with him, the headlines.

'I understand this. This desk. You don't want to give her anything.'

He reached down and took the receipt from the morning paper.

He did not want to look.

Sharon nodded to herself.

'I don't pretend to understand everything you're hinting at. It's enough that we agree, she's evil. She represents unrestrained evil. But, I think, you are playing…'

'…a very dangerous game?' Ink smiled. 'You *have* been watching those dramas, haven't you?'

Sharon smiled. 'I used to like watching things. As a child, on Saturday mornings. Then they stopped them, and I missed them. The shows. I like escapism. We all need some of it. Some pretend. Even if its Central propaganda in the form of a cheap soap opera. The words get in. The stupid phrases that the lazy writers use. But that doesn't mean there isn't more behind them, when I let them slip through.'

She looked up at him.

'She won't kill you. She'll make a fool of you. She'll keep you on, humiliate you, make an example. I don't know how people can be like that. How they can maintain it; but people like her will do that. I think you should do everything within your power to prevent that. But in the meantime…'

She came forward. The tips of her fingers rested softly on the back of his hand. The hand that held the receipt.

'We've played this out too long. When you come back, will you take me out to dinner? I have waited, and I do deserve it. Maybe, things can be better? Maybe, that can be your version of escapism? Even for a little while?'

Good Christ, she was sincere. And, so sweet.

'With people like you still in the bureaucracy, maybe there is hope.'

Sharon smiled. 'I know some people too.'

Her fingers left his skin, and she turned to the door. She paused a second, then walked away. He watched her bottom, though the clean black fabric of her sensible business pants. As was her intent.

Ink let her leave, then looked at the receipt.

His blood ran hot, then ran cold, then hot again.

It was a receipt from and exclusive elite lingerie store. A black suspender belt and garters. She had paid a fortune.

She had known.

She had known, and now she had ruined something he that had, at the last second, come to think that he might enjoy. He would never know now, if and when he initiated something with Sharon, whether or not he was doing it out of sheer frustration, as a fuck you to Tamara, or to fake out Tamara that he was affected by this ploy, or to show Tamara that he wasn't. Or, god dammit, that he was affected by her ploy. Because he wanted to see those black…

Drama and cliché.

Worked.

Every damn time.

Sharon was one of the few remaining people in government, certainly in the Bureau, who had a heart. A good heart, still, after all this time. A morality, a belief. Faith that… something would prevail, in the end, that was worth it all.

But now, all he could see was Tamara Chant.

In black suspenders.

Waiting.

SEVENTEEN: RUDDER

Tamara liked to drive fast and didn't think twice about it.

There were no speed limits on the freeway anymore, but there were speed limiters built into cars now, controlled via satellite by Central, or whoever.

As one of the Central Elite however, Tamara could drive unrestrained, at any speed she desired, and liked to interweave through all the other cars, all pushed to satellite controlled maximum, all soaring along at exactly the same speed. She liked to weave through them, at speed, like a video game, with her heart pumping overtime and her adrenalin steaming, jetting from her nostrils.

She pulled over at Four-Two for massage oil, healthy snacks and fresh fruit. And some ice cream which, if she was prepared to risk the lives of everyone on the freeway, including herself, which she was, would not melt beyond refreezing by the time she reached the beach house.

Four-Two felt weird. Like someone had just done an enormous poo right outside the store, but had just cleaned it up in time. It felt colder there too, which she liked. She noticed that Ansel had hiked the prices again, but said nothing. Four-Two customers paid through the nose because they liked to, because they could afford it. It was a sign that they belonged, that they were as elite as they thought they were. There had never really been any question in her mind as to her elite status, right from the start she had assumed; no, know it. But it was still nice to have that feeling confirmed once in a while.

Still, Ansel was clearly taking liberties and sometime soon… Maybe.

That didn't interest her tonight though.

She parked under the balcony of the beach house and went directly inside, through the front door, and straight to the freezer. The ice cream went straight in, and she saw that there were two other tubs that she had forgotten, and remembered that she had done the same thing last time; raced here to maintain some over-priced ice cream at a reasonable temperature when she hadn't needed to. She felt pleased about that; it meant that somewhere deep she liked being here, liked what happened here. That she wasn't bored of this yet.

Tamara sighed, and dumped the bags of groceries, and the massage oil on the grey marble kitchen bench.

She was still in the red and black outfit. She liked red and black.

She removed her black jacket and hung it over the back of a kitchen stool.

There was a modern Old Wives Tale which stated that schizophrenics preferred red and black. It was a nonsense from an ignorant time when schizophrenics were still thought of as people with so-called split personalities, who could turn on a dime, pleasant to horrendous and back again. But that was exactly why she liked red and black; because that had been a powerful false meme. It was still stuck in people's minds. It made them ill at ease.

She removed the bright rose camisole as she went to the stairs, up to the first floor, and hung it over the lower bannister.

Along with that went the old idea, from various ancient schools of mysticism, that black and red represented 'The Devil'. Or even 'Satan'. Absurd of course; there had been red and black sports teams throughout the world who had called themselves 'The Demons', or 'The Bloods'. The bottom line was though, that it looked good. Red and black always looked good. It had been used in marketing for decades, and along with white or yellow had represented some of the previous world culture's most powerful brands. Some of them, Central had allowed to keep going. Central Security's logo was red and black, after all. Planning was black and blue, Government black and orange, and she had corresponding outfits for all occasions. But she had worn it today to turn Ink's head; to make him see. And she had slipped a gift into the papers on his desk, to let him to know she knew, and that she would be thinking of him.

She stood on the balcony now, in black business slacks, and her black bra. She pondered herself and eternity, as best she could, for a little while. The low waves crashed softly in. They calmed her as the salty breeze blew through the hair she'd kept deliberately teased all day, as she had teased Rutger Ink. She stared out at the ocean's horizon, at the stars above, as though awaiting a signal. She felt important.

Behind her was the first floor living room, but she crossed the balcony and entered the code to open the bedroom door. She liked to come in from here; it was the best view. The beach house was not huge. She had not desired the maintenance, but she had paid to have it designed exclusively, and even more to have the designer assure her that nobody would ever have anything like it.

Quite simply, her whole apartment was monochrome; black, white and shades of grey. The bedroom featured minimalist décor, as though it were a blank canvas; a set that had been cleared and was ready for some kind of art designer to arrive, to prepare it for a fashion shoot. The bedroom's central feature was a four-poster bed, which was raised on a low dais and elaborately swathed in sheer, flowing, translucent fabrics of clean white and gossamer grey. The bed sheets were black, Egyptian cotton.

Trey was still sleeping, but he woke as she entered, and stared as she sat on the edge of the bed. His body was spread, his arms out and his legs parted, like Da Vinci's Vitruvian Man. Except that Leonardo had not drawn his subject with a raging erection. She took hold of it in her right hand and placed her left on his forehead; he had a fever, still, and she felt like the captain of a little boat, one hand on the till, leaning forward, guiding her vessel through a storm.

Trey was very handsome, and quite muscular. She had to be careful; he was exciting to look at. Like many people of her personality type, once sexual arousal was initiated it was difficult to snuff out. Women like her, with psychopathic tendencies, were like men, it was thought. They were quickly turned on, and reached orgasm quite readily, in a matter of minutes if all went well. Efficient, and fast, like men.

But that was not entirely true. That was, again, a remnant of an age when, for some reason of which not she, nor anyone she knew, could entirely fathom, female sexuality had seemed entirely off-putting to several generations of Victorian and Edwardian biological scientists, and had therefore been represented to the world in weird, rigid and inaccurate forms. The false idea that women could not orgasm quickly, and were slow to arouse, had given rise to the idea that women who did were more masculine somehow; perhaps that was true as a broad generalization, but in practice, she had never found it so.

What was the point in the so-called 'office quickie', then? The kind Ink and Coyer would have engaged in, just now, just as the night shift was starting, if her plans had come right. Or the famous British 'knee-trembler'? What purpose, if the woman could not benefit? If Sharon did not want Ink inside her, right there and then, fast and hard, as the cliché went? She wondered. Would he be stabbing into her against the wall, against the window, or on the desk? The desk, she decided. The greatest cliché.

Beneath Trey's body, the sheets were damp with his sweat.

His body was covered in moisture.

He had been a swimmer, and played tennis when he had been able to find someone worth playing. His profile was a trail of sports clubs from one side of the world to the other. Nothing fancy, he had not wanted attention. He had wanted to kill with the impunity he had been promised, by holding up his end of the deal and remaining anonymous. He had been one of a handful that had been allowed this, and his discovery had represented the start of, and essentially been the reason for, the rise of Bureau 88.

She examined him, her prize. Not her prisoner exactly, although he certainly could not leave. She wasn't sure he even wanted to leave now. She was pretty, she knew. She had looks; not soft pretty but exaggerated pretty. Her jaw and smile were massive, her breasts were too small to exploit well, but she was, in all, an attractive, pretty young woman. In the world at large, she might have been able to attract a specimen such as this for a night or two, but she would never have been able to keep him. This was something else, and it excited her no end to have him contained, and touchable.

And nobody knew.

The flesh of his erection was warm on her hand, which she knew was cold from the night outside. The air that had come in with her, off the balcony, had gusted through the open bay windows and into the warmer air that had escaped. That had made the hair on the back of her neck rise, and the muscles in her pelvis contract. The warm air had been musty. It had been sweaty air, that smelled of his sweaty body.

His mother had been Jamaican, his father British. They were both dead, had both been killed in a terrorist attack on the London Underground. They had not seen each other for years, until a few weeks before, when he had brought them together, at first against their will. But something of the old fire between them had rekindled and they had started going out together, to the theatre in London, to nice restaurants, to decent hotels where they had again become lovers. They had been on their way to a popular musical when the bomber had detonated a backpack of nitroglycerin and taken out almost all of the passengers in their carriage, bringing London to a screeching standstill for the better part of a week.

Subsequently, Trey had hunted down all those who had been responsible, tortured and in the end killed them. Nothing had stopped him.

His erection did not diminish with the coldness of her closed palm, nor with the chill from the open balcony. Granted, it was there most of the time, and probably had nothing to do with her. But she liked to hold it as though it did, as though it were a sacred jewel, the glass cabinet for which only she held the key.

Trey had done two hundred laps every day, and worked out, every day, while he had been free. He had designed his own weights and fitness program. He had been dedicated. He had believed that a healthy body led to a healthy mind.

He had been the fittest and deadliest hyperpsychic on the planet.

Just, not the brightest.

'More bad dreams?' She asked him softly.

He nodded, very gently, against the black pillow.

He wasn't one of those muscle men who had an enormous neck. He had taken pride in his good looks, paid attention to himself, the gift of his genes and biological pattern, and had not wanted to spoil his natural form and symmetry with anything grotesque. When she looked at him nodding, she was informed of exactly which parts of his neck and shoulders had gone into that. She had seen it, felt it acutely in the palm of her hand, even from the tight, wet skin of his forehead, even with the slightest of little nods he had given.

She understood the practicality of it also. Fit men attracted attention, but body builders stood out. In those days, he had been okay, being noticed. Being admired. It had greased the wheels. People thought he was a swimmer, or a tennis player, or maybe an underwear model or a television actor, something along those lines. They would drift off from the real him and into their own fantasy of who he was, and what he would do to them if he was in their life, their world, their vagina or anus.

He was straight, she knew that, so he would not dislike the attention she gave him. He would not respond to her beyond this, as he had from time to time, if he did not want to. There were so many men, like that, left behind in the trail of wreckage of her sexual adventures. Men who hated her, who she had made hate her, who had fucked her all the same. Not even hate fucking, a lot of the time. Some kind of perverse enjoyment, usually. Passion was strange.

Tamara's hand rested on his chest now. The skin was tight over his muscles. Soft but stretched. He had last worked out a few days ago, last shaved a few days ago. She would let him, now, while she was here for the night. While she slept, he would cross train in the gym she had installed for him, and be back in the bed when she woke.

She didn't sleep beside him, he was too restless. And he was capable of projection. She had not enjoyed sharing his nightmares. She had not recalled them clearly, but she had been jittery all week after that, and initially not wanted to return to her own beach house. She had been unusually sadistic with her boys. Gotten one of them killed, in the end. Then it had all gone way, and she had returned here, to Trey, understanding.

Trey needed to kill.

When he had killed, he could sleep.

Trey had essentially classic Caucasian features; handsome British features for a handsome secret agent. Caucasian with the glorious exception for his lusciously thick Negroid lips, and his milk-coffee skin, amusingly almost the exact shade of the latte she ordered and drank every morning from the café bar in the lobby. Many white men had hair as dark and thick as his, but with the lips… he could probably no longer walk the streets in N'America safely, at least not in most of their ridiculous, new, so-called countries.

Corporate strongholds, was what they were.

He might pass in California, where apparently they still didn't care if you were only half black, but it would probably not be worth the risk. They were completely insane, of course. You thought California had been crazy? No. The true crazies ruled there now.

Tamara was prepared to admit that people with her mindset, those of the different subsets of sociopaths, were not like the majority of people, the motes. Not normal, if you will. But she could at least explain herself. She could tell you why and how she was making almost every move she made. Maybe not at the time, but at least in hindsight. Maybe it did not match the ethical and moral standards that had been established in the pre-crash world, the mote-ruled world, or even still, today, outside of the non-corporate, non-Central world. Outside of business. But at least she could explain herself.

The combination of racist, sexist mote-maniacs and dumb, dictator-model sociopaths who now controlled what had once been the United States of America could not, however. Frustratingly, their mote madness and murderous idiocy had filtered through, down here, to Australia somehow. Down here, to where they had treated the Asians the same as the N'Americans treated the blacks. Worse, actually, in some ways. Central here hadn't simply enslaved the Asians, they had banished them. Actively rounded them up, put them in camps, and commandeered cruise liners to sail them away, to randomly dump them on the islands of Indonesia.

'Go back ta where ya came from!'

Some had been rescued, some had perished, some had remained and were flourishing, still, to this day, apparently.

The world was bizarre; there were never a truism more true.

This was a beautiful man. The notion that he could be persecuted for just one of the simple ingredients that made him so…

She sighed aloud.

The motes.

The motes were so…

Ugh.

Tamara could understand killing. She could kill, would kill, if somebody was in her way. She would order it, or do it herself. If and when somebody tried to stop her getting what and where she wanted, there was no question. Without hesitation, she would act to have them removed from her path, if she could, as soon as she could. For ambition, for power, even for insult; insults could be toxic, like a wound, a cancer, could linger and last forever.

But for skin color?

That was about as perverse as things got.

Even so, she still, *kind-of* understood; there was, after all, a biological imperative that many people possessed. It was hardwired into their minds; the fear of other. The different. It was partially a tribal thing, that the other would infiltrate and take over. It was also a genetic thing; that mating with the other would make your children more different, and less likely to be accepted by the collective sameness of the tribe, and therefore it would become increasingly more difficult to for the genetic imperative to be passed on, and to proceed. But that was all so simple, so basic, so totally irrelevant in the modern age, that it was easily undone; the mind was, surely, so easily unconvinced of this most basic and primitive of notions, and the pathetic imperative circumvented, like any other basic loop of the primal brain.

She sighed.

The mocha sheen to his skin, and his chocolate nipples. So deliciously beautiful. His penis was darker, too, browner than most men's, that she'd seen anyway. The stalk was almost blue, it was so black, the head a striking purple and brown mélange. If he did pass in America, he would have to remain fully clothed at all times, and have sex in the dark.

In Australia though, nobody would blink; if they realized that he was half Jamaican, they would assume it was a wealthy half and that was what he was doing here. Any blacks in Australia were wealthy, integral parts of Central. There were even some Asians, still here, who had made themselves or their families indispensable. They had unconvinced those who insisted they leave.

And yet, it kept returning.

She could use it herself; others of her kind, higher in government, had used it. Deployed racism with the ease they would confidently deploy any weapon. It was so reliable; all you needed was an uneducated, frightened population. And they were always so ready, the populations; it was as though their collective ids couldn't wait to be transformed into the monster armies of a culture run on entrenched bigotry.

She looked back at Trey.

Coffee Trey.

Trey had the look of a dog, hopelessly loyal to a master that beats him.

She didn't want to beat him.

She didn't; but she did discipline him.

She leaned down and kissed him, gentle on the lips.

Thick and dry.

'Nasty bad dreams…'

Trey laughed. It sounded a little cynical. His erection shifted, raised and tightened in her hand as his body laughed, just a bit. She squeezed it, just once, lightly.

'We'll make it all better.'

She looked down at his body; the male form, when it was worked like this, was so seamless. His pectoral muscles were like plates, his sixpack abs like a layered series of heavy springs, his forearms and thighs, like weights. It all made sense in its glistening layout, hard and molded, like lava had been poured into the pure, ideal shell of a man.

She looked across at him and he saw her admiring him; he had virtually no body fat and his face was the same laying back as it was when he stood. A small nose and a long jaw, a wide mouth, and those lips. Deep check bones and sunken eyes over jet eyebrows and a high forehead. A mess of thick black hair, cut short but furious, everywhere. His emerald eyes glistened, staring back as she cast her gaze about his cheekbones, the kind that seemed to protrude like tiny horns at the edges of his face. She ran the tips of her fingers along the line, beneath his left eye, as though she genuinely might cut herself, draw blood. He did not cease staring back. The skin of his face was like soft leather;

she felt the stubble beneath his ears, small and flat against the side of his head, ran her fingertips along the stubble of his jaw, pronounced, where his mouth seemed to sit, set within it like a six-pointed jewel, smoky pink and brown.

He was lean, but not brutish. Clean, and efficient. A sleek killer, a homicidal vehicle.

She released the rudder of the man she controlled, but ran her open palm up, over the head, and made him shudder with it.

'A shower first, while I change the sheets. You can go and work out a while, if you like. I have some calls to make.'

He sat up on his elbows, his collar bones so pronounced, so sleek and purposeful, that she brushed them with her fingertips as he went, to make sure they were real. That they were flesh and he was not some kind of android machine that she had forgotten she had made. She watched him as he walked out of the room, his cock still hard in front of him, no nonsense, directly up at fifty five degrees, his buttocks, the backs of his legs, the beautiful machine, so simple, just walking.

She took her phone out of her pocket and put in her headphones. She gulped and cleared her throat, trying not to sound worked up. Nobody could know she wasn't alone.

'Ma'am.'

'Report.'

It was Ackerman.

'Coyer doesn't know I'm here.'

'Where are you?'

'In your office. Where you told me to stay.'

'And?'

'Ink is going somewhere.'

'Where?'

'I don't know. He's going to be gone a while.'

'A while?'

'That's all I heard them say.'

She didn't care. Ink wasn't capable of resisting her. He could do what he liked.

'Have you moved?'

'No ma'am.'

'Have you touched anything?'

'No ma'am.'

'Don't touch anything. There's one item in my office. I kept it in my panties all yesterday. If you can't tell me what it is next time, you'll get the love beads back. Until I am back in charge of the Bureau. Don't touch anything. Don't leave my office. Do you understand?'

'Yes ma'am.'

'What, Ackerman? Are you crying?'

She knew he wasn't.

'No, ma'am…!'

'Find it. Be a fucking man.'

She hung up.

She called Chambers.

'Ma'am?'

'Report.'

'Coyer has made a discovery. Random inspection of supermarket security showed that two girls were entering the store on a regular basis, but neither were seen to leave.'

'Where?'

'Central Mall.'

'They kept this from me?'

'Apparently ma'am. I heard her tell one of her nerds that they were clearly attempting to hide in plain sight by teleporting themselves into the crowded supermarket, but it's a trick they've used once too often.'

'In the middle of the city?'

'Elite food ma'am. The hypers don't function well without –'

'I know that. I wrote the bloody book on how fucking hypers fucking function. Do nothing. If Ink is moving, I can't move until…' Damn. But she needed this. She need this tonight. Or she would be vulnerable. The more attracted she was to Ink, the more generally horny she was around him, the more likely she would slip. Maybe she did care where he was going, and for how long. The urge to control him was getting stronger. To hold his cock as she held Trey's. This was getting exciting.

'I'm leaving. Meet me at the usual place.'

She ended the call.

So Ink had hypers up his sleeve. Knew about hypers he wasn't telling her about. And now he was off somewhere. Where would he be going?

Gone for a while.

No, this was no good.

'Trey! Shower! Now!'

No fucking good at all.

EIGHTEEN: KISS

Ink slept on the helicopter as best he could, and woke likewise when it was coming in to land. It was a regular country flight, a regular drop to a regular town, and the pilot was an acquaintance who didn't care one way or the other about hyperpsychics but did hold to favors for old war buddies. Half an hour before the regular drop, the pilot made a quick pit stop and Ink disembarked.

Ink had friends still, friends he trusted, and that was what got him through sometimes. But those friends still had to tell him sometimes who else to trust, especially out here in the country, and that was all just part of the general risk.

Every step removed was another degree of risk.

Trying to change things for the better was the whole of it.

'Bud Kerr?'

'Yep. You Ink?'

'I am.'

'Then…?'

Ink handed him a chunk of cash.

Bud Kerr looked at it. 'That's okay.'

'That's the agreed amount.'

'No worries mate, I'm sure it is. You wanna go to the old church ruin near Forbes?'

'Yes…'

'Not a lot to see out there…what there is to see out there…'

'I know. Is mainly church ruins. Old homesteads.'

'You got water?'

'Yep.'

'You know which way to Queensland?'

Ink pointed, very casually. 'It's just called North Australia now.'

Bud Kerr smiled. 'Guess you know yer way about then?'

Ink smiled. 'Suppose I don't?'

Kerr nodded. Ink's pilot buddy had told him that Kerr had been out here a long while. Never went to the city any more.

'My first kiss, in high school. Turned out years later she was one of these mental telepathy kids. A hyper? Is that what ye call 'em now?'

'Some do.'

'They shot her in the supermarket, in West Wyalong. In front of her kids.'

'I'm sorry.'

Ink was silent a few seconds.

'Here's a map. Burn it when you're done. It'll take you to the right church. There are signs to the one they say, but it wasn't that one. That will take you to where it happened. Really happened.'

'Thank you Bud.'

There are some things we never forget, Ink supposed.

NINETEEN: FORCE

'The club was quiet.'

Kelli was still in her chair, still reading.

'Have you got another one somewhere?'

'Another what?'

Davy rolled his eyes. 'Another book.'

'There's a couple I took off the boat; over there in the corner.'

There were three, lined up against the corner of the room, like the world's most pathetic collection of anything.

Fuck.

The club hadn't been quiet.

It had been on fire.

He'd walked to his alcove and there had been a couple having sex there.

They'd had their backs to the street, and her face, her cheek, had been pressed up against the glass where last night he had stared at himself, where he had seen the brunette, with those lips. If he could find her, they could bang it out, like he had with Zara. He'd exploded with Zara, within a minute, then waited, then hammered her a second time, for almost an hour. Then they'd met again, two days later, when Kelli had thought they'd gone, and then two days again after that.

Davy had felt so good after that, he'd gotten them a boat and sailed them across the Pacific God Damn Ocean.

It had been like having an affair, with the secrecy and sneaking about, the adrenalin, but with no consequences. It had just been make believe. Even if Kelli had found out, and he knew she'd suspected, she probably would have been happy for him.

But he had wanted to keep it for himself; he had needed the risk, the cheat.

He could have stayed with Zara, if it hadn't been for Kelli. They might have had kids by now, colored kids they took with them on the road, stealing baby formula. She would have given birth in a barn somewhere, during a thunderstorm. Maybe the kid would have been the savior of their kind, the Christ Child of the Wrathful Ones…

Fucking Hell.

'What?'

Had he said that out loud?

'Sorry.'

Kelli laughed. 'It's okay, Davy. It's just, you don't usually swear like that, out of the blue.'

'I didn't realize I had.'

'Did… something happen?'

'Nothing I can't…' Davy sighed. 'Sis, I'm going a bit crazy.'

'I know Davy. I…' She seemed so sad, all of a sudden. '…I'm sorry you're so lonely.'

His head was aching. 'I don't know what I can do…'

'We need to find someone again…' Kelli stared at him, sympathetically. 'Like Zara.'

The tension in his jaw made him feel like his back teeth were going to just squeeze right out.

'You… you do know about Zara?'

'I thought…' Kelli shrugged under her cloak. '…well, I do now.'

I practically asked her to do it for you, bro.

Davy knew, that was what she was really saying.

Asked her, so he wouldn't…

Despite his feelings of tension, of pressure, all over his body, he could still feel normally. He wasn't angry. Not entirely, not in an all-consuming way.

'My mind…' Davy heard himself utter. '…is wandering to strange places.'

He felt sad. He'd been feeling sadder every day.

His anger was just that, turned inward. Frustration at their situation; Kelli, his beautiful sister, in rags, in his face, bearing up, every day.

'The path ahead feels…darker.'

She deserved so much more.

'You're not going to…' He heard Kelli gulp. '…*do anything,* are you?'

'Like what?'

'At the club?'

Now Davy gulped. Now he heard himself, his swallow catching in his thorax.

'The club?'

What had she seen? What had there been to see? Nothing; just his sadness. The sad loner, the outcast, watching, night after night.

'Kelli, can you… read my mind?'

'No.' Kelli shook her head, resolute. 'Even if I could, I wouldn't. One night I followed you. That's all.'

He nodded to himself. He wasn't even angry. It was a relief that she knew.

'I just watch…' It was the truth. '…it reminds me of…' Now what? Suddenly, he was confessing? Being honest with himself? '…the old days. What our lives used to be.'

God, she was so sweet. The look in her eyes. The open pity. The empathy.

'I know, Davy. But we need to get some food, before we do anything. Davy, I tried to rush. While you were sleeping. I could only get down a few floors. I walked back up. It took a while. Then, I slept. I… couldn't help but sleep.'

Davy stared at her. 'That's bad, sis.'

'I told you we needed to eat. Yesterday.'

God. Had she? Yeah. She had. She had.

'I'm sorry. When I get there… I just get stuck. Mesmerized. The people coming and going. So… like us. How we used to be.'

He saw Kelli smile to herself, an edge of wry. She knew; he'd meant the guys. The us was his boys, his buddies. How his gang had been.

'And then I think, what if someone else takes the papers? So I stay. The truck never comes at exactly the same time.'

'What about tonight? Will you go back for the papers?'

'Later.'

'Davy...?' Kelli's voice was a little more nervous now. '...you didn't get seen, did you?'

Davy sighed. 'No.' Although, he almost wished he had. 'The opposite. I saw something. It made me...' He felt awful. But he couldn't get the image of that girl out of his mind. The girl, tonight, who was being hammered, had blended with the face of the dark haired girl. The girl he'd seen tonight; her eyes had been closed, squeezed shut, her cheek sideways to the glass, but her face... that tense face, almost a snarl, on the border of ecstasy. It had been so long since he'd seen it. More than a year. That earnest grimace of a building...

'I saw something that made me realize. I need to stop going there.'

His feet felt hot under his sneakers.

'You're right. We need food. I need shoes. We need some warmer clothes.' She smiled. 'Cloaks that don't have rips and holes. It's time we took the risk, Davy.'

Davy nodded. 'I have a few short rushes left. I'm sure I do. I can get us some blankets, some food, and get back here, at least a floor or two. Nobody knows we're here. They can't know. Then we can eat, and... I don't know. Head north.'

'We can stay...' Kelli offered it softly. '...if we're careful. Do you really believe the north thing? Darwin?'

Davy walked to the window. He stared out. There were two other skyscrapers this side of town; the abandoned, post-crash side of town, that they could see. Probably six or seven more behind them. But from the view here, there were really just two buildings close by, dominating, one each, diagonally, out to each side. And they, in turn, framed their view of the new city, right before them but blocks away, and the three imposing new towers that Central had erected. That part of town was so bright, so present, that

sometimes, the other two older towers, with no power, always unlit, always dark… well, you forgot they were even there.

But… just then.

Just for a second…

'What?' Kelli demanded.

Davy turned. 'You felt that?'

'I can't read your mind but I always feel a burst like that, when it's that intense. Did you see something?'

What was happening?

'Davy, do we need to go?' Kelli tightened her cloak around her and sat up. 'Do we need to go now?'

The concrete floor had changed. It was hot, like exposed concrete in high summer. He'd noticed it before, but he'd thought it was just something weird, to do with the tension… the rapidly diminishing soles of his old sneakers… but he was walking around, trying to not to feel the heat through his sneakers.

'The floor is hot.'

God, she did. She knew him so well, and they had such a connection.

She untucked her knee from beneath her, from under her cloak, and slipped her leg out, stretching her calf. She only had socks and leggings on; her little shoes were under the boss chair. She'd been sleeping. Her leg was so thin, so slender, and her foot so tiny. Her little toes were so adorable when they stretched out and touched the floor.

God, she really deserved… so much…

'It's not hot…' Kelli assessed. 'It's… *prickly*…'

He wasn't listening.

He was thinking. He just needed somewhere to put it, to hammer it and have contact. Just flesh. It didn't matter. It wasn't like they would be declaring sexual love. Or, like, starting a family. She could just turn around.

Now, in his mind's eye, she was there too, along with the thick lips, and the cheek pressed and eyes squeezed closed.

They weren't even... in the world any more. That world. Where those rules applied.

It was coming up, through his feet, this feeling; his nerve endings on his soles, right up to his brain. It was making him hard. And, what did it matter? Her tiny lips, so pink and soft. What did it matter? It wasn't good for her, either. Not healthy. She might never get to do it again, with anyone. Not with anyone. Could he deny her that? She was tiny, and he was big. She would feel it, it would be good for her.

She's not like that, she's not made like that, this isn't you, what are you thinking? Why are you thinking...? ...there's something... there's something else here...

'Davy...' Kelli was shaking. He realized that he had been staring at her the whole time. The whole time he had been contemplating...

'Kelli...' Davy was stunned. Hot, weak, horrified. He had not been going out of his mind. He had gone out of his mind. Just for a second, something underneath them had exploited his weakness. Found his most brutal, callous, primitive self. '...Kelli. There's something under...'

'I know...' Kelli uttered. 'Davy, I was going to *let you...*'

He fell to his knees and dry retched.

He started coughing, then weeping.

'It's found us, Davy.' The terror in Kelli's voice was terrifying in itself. 'It's found us...'

His palms were on the concrete floor.

Aching, sizzling heat, right up through his wrists and the tendons of his...

He stood and staggered toward Kelli. He grabbed her, up from her tiny, slim hips, right off the chair, and threw her onto the desk, down on her back. Then he was climbing onto the desk, over her. She was winded, prone, he'd lifted her too fast, brought her down too hard. She moaned, helplessly, terrified, as he straddled her; there was just room enough for them both, his arms on either side of her shoulders, his knees either side of her thighs, and she was quivering beneath him.

Davy froze and listened.

Scuttling. Some kind of…

Kelli was breathing nervously. Her eyes were closed, her expression confused but clearing.

'I had a nightmare last night…' Kelli uttered. '…that someone broke in.'

She was talking up, into his throat. He could feel her hot breath. He was looking out, his neck to the side, to the corridor that led to the open elevator doors.

'Last night?'

'After you'd gone…' She was breathing hard, still terrified. 'I went down and checked.'

'It's all locked up. Nobody could get in.'

'I was tired, too quick. I went down, then back up. I don't know how you do it every night…'

Every night. That reminded him of the club. The thing, the presence here, was telling him; it would be so easy. Just flesh. Just mechanical. Make everything better. Make everything easier. Keep her here. Feed her the bad food, keep her docile. Stay here forever. But now he knew.

'It's here, Kelli. Below us, under the floor. It comes up through concrete.'

'These things. They're everywhere, Davy…'

'I know. We know. We just forgot.'

'Killing people slowly. Driving us all out of our minds, keeping us apart…'

'I know.'

'It likes concrete, Davy. It likes to travel through concrete, and asphalt, to the dark places, abandoned places. It lives where we hide…'

'I don't know why we didn't know that it was here, before now...'

'It couldn't have just found us now... could it?'

Davy was perplexed. 'Wait.'

He rushed; down to the tenth, where he knew it was okay. Still on his hands and knees, still hard. He sat up slowly, to kneel. Then he pushed, one leg, then the other, forcing himself to a stand. Weary. Aching all over with tension.

The thing, wherever it was, had made him objectify her.

Cave men, he thought. It's been around since then. Whatever it is, it can still tap into the caveman mind. Fuck everything. Spread the gene. Kill the mutants. Raise the beautiful.

Why had it come here? Why tonight, when they were at their weakest?

Just lucky?

He supposed these things hunted...

Coming through from wherever they...

...wherever they came from, whatever they were.

He didn't like being scared. But he was angry.

And, over the edge now.

His temper.

Ready.

And he was willing.

Willing to use –

A sound. A sad sound. Crying.

Coming up from the elevator shaft.

Darkness in his mind that he needed to walk toward...

He rushed before he knew what he was doing. He knew the spot, in the lobby; where he could appear without chance of being seen from the street through the glass frontage. Then he was there, down in the dark comer. The lobby was colder than normal. Almost freezing. The night outside seemed more dense somehow, darker and blacker than it should have been. The street was empty but the lights outside were dimmer than usual, way dimmer. His rushing down here hadn't done that to the street lights; they weren't close enough. Something else had done that.

He stepped out into the lobby. One, then two strides into the wide open space.

The backwards signs were there, in the window.

This was home.

PRIME OFFICE SPACE

COMPETITIVE RATES!

Pasted over with:

SITE CONDEMNED

DO NOT ENTER.

He shivered. The chains that had bound the old fashioned handles were hanging down, limp. The sliding doors on this side of the entrance alcove were open. Not broken; opened with a key, and pushed aside. No power, just unlock and push. The front doors to their condemned home were wide open to the street, and the deep darkness outside. The lobby had been exposed to the evil of the world. Anyone could have walked in. Anything.

…someone, something, had.

His head was reeling.

What was happening?

He looked down a long corridor to the side of the open elevator shaft. To the immediate left, the stairwell.

Was there… light?

Flashing down there? In the basement, down to where the… *crying* was coming from?

His brain felt like something at the base of his neck was… fizzing.

It was natural; an alarm. An alarm, in his mind, for something humanity had not seen for many ages. Some part of the human mind that had laid dormant for centuries, millennia… was going off, now. It was creepy, genuinely; a part of his brain completely unfamiliar to him, warning him a thing that *crept*… was coming. Had come. Was here; was there, down there, down the stairs to the basement, where the flickers of flashlights were coming from.

He moved toward it, knew he had to, knew that he could do something… that he was supposed to do something. He found that his feet were moving down, one step at a time, then he paused at the blind corner where the concrete stairwell turned one-eighty and descended into… what? He didn't hesitate, just briefly poked his head around, like they did in the movies. Nothing. Blackness. He held his breath involuntarily as he descended the remaining stairs. When his feet touched the linoleum of the corridor floor he smelled stale alcohol. Maybe urine. Could have been homeless people. Might have been kids down here, drinking. But underneath it all there was something worse. Fetid. He didn't want to be down here, but he wanted what was here like crazy. More than a woman. More than anything. He wanted to kill it.

His eyes began to adjust.

He'd been down here before in daytime, when the thin, street level windows had allowed a modicum of light through, into the doorless rooms and the long corridor beyond. The floor had an H-shaped layout, with just three long corridors, he remembered. To his right, the corridor ended where the street began above, with a sealed emergency exit. To his left, the corridor ran directly and uninterrupted to the other end of the basement. Halfway down, the centrally dissecting third corridor started off to the right. But there was nothing here. The crying had stopped. There were no sounds. If he moved an inch, his rustling clothes sounded like an avalanche. He looked for the shaking flashlights, to give him perspective, but realized somehow that his eyes were adjusting to the darkness better than they ever had, better than they ever should. His vision flicked about. There were no other light sources. In a matter of seconds, then, he began to acknowledge… he could see in the dark. In a kind of greyscale, sure, maybe a tint of blue, but… he could see. He shifted his eyes about, up and down the wall, across the floor.

The blue seemed centrally focused. It seemed to travel along, wherever his eyes moved. Was the blue *coming from* his eyes? His eyes, or something on his face…?

No. His eyes. They were *glowing*.

This drive he was feeling… it was fear, and anxiety, his heart pounding in his ears, even approaching terror… but it was also adrenalin. The hunt, the need to find this thing, his loathing for it… all of that was activating parts of his mind… his body.

Through his greyscale vision he saw the wavering shadows from a powerful flashlight, then another, coming from his left, from way down the other end, making the corridor that extended before him seem like a haunted mine shaft. Definitely two. These people had come in, looking for something. Gone right to the end of the basement, and now they were on their way back toward him. He backed into the stairs again, edging the side of his face out to see.

He could clearly see the dissecting corridor now. And something else. Something on the square patch of floor there, where the two corridors intersected. Right in the middle of this corridor, just meters down from where he was standing. Was it this weird vision thing? Or… no. There really was something there. The floor had shifted. The two people were walking toward it with their torches, they hadn't seen it. Then the thing raised itself, like a camouflaged manta ray rippling up from the sand of an ocean floor. It seemed to oscillate, then flowed backwards down the middle corridor and was gone. There was a scream, a girl's scream. Like she'd had a shock. Then she screamed again; this time prolonged, three or four, in terror. Then… silence.

Davy saw now as the two approaching people broke into a run, with their flashlight beams darting jaggedly everywhere, that they were cops. They hadn't seen the manta ray thing, even as they ran up over the spot where it had been lurking and veered sharply off in the same direction. Davy didn't hesitate. He ran down toward them, but stopped about half way, as he realized his old sneakers were squeaking on the bare linoleum floor. But he halted too abruptly and they squealed louder than ever. Damn. He ducked into a room, but it was a sure bet now that anyone else down here with him knew they were not alone.

Here was the old staff kitchen, the basement tea room. Abandoned with a punctured metal urn heater in the corner, like someone who couldn't steal it had stabbed its base with a knife. It looked chrome, shining with the increasingly 'bluescale' light from his eyes. He heard a rustling sound, and felt the urge to pull himself away, out of the room, to go back, to up to the lobby, to rush up and… the eerie feeling washed over him again. He felt sick. The acrid scent of decay became suddenly more acute. There was something malevolent in here, in this room with him. The sound came again, louder. Rustling, clicking mandibles. In his mind's eye he saw slime and slithering blackness. The urn. There was something in…

His blue light vision swung back again and fully focused there.

The thing inside scuttled up, flinging the lid off. The sound of the aluminum disc hitting the floor was like an explosion. His mind said it was a cockroach the size of a cat, then it vanished into the wall, as though it were slipping under a liquid surface from a muddy bank.

Davy was totally shocked.

He closed his eyes, squeezed them shut with the reverberations of the tin explosion still ringing. He'd seen them before, but not for a long time. He'd tried to forget them; the feeling they brought…

What…? What *were they?*

The creature had been disgusting, and yet… he opened his eyes again. The blue was gone, but the greysight remained. Feeling a twisted nausea in the pit of his gut, somehow pulling him to find the thing again, to find all of these things, he moved quickly to the door, less careful now with a sudden identification of his target.

Down the corridor there were voices, a man and a woman, and a third person, maybe the girl who had been crying, all in a panic. The cops were shouting, real cop shouting, like; *down on the floor, hands behind your heads*, but Davy was so suddenly exhilarated, so angrily sickened, that he found that he no longer cared about being discovered. The relief, the liberation, was immense. Somewhere deep but strong in his mind he knew that all that other stuff was done. The cops were here. Something bad had happened. But they couldn't help. Only he could help. He had been born to deal with this. He needed to do that now, then get Kelli, then flee.

Find this thing and…

And kill it.

He went directly to the T and headed down the central corridor.

And there it was. He couldn't fully make it out, he just knew that in front of the door, the door to the room where the two cops and the girl were, the floor was quivering.

It was there. Sitting flat and waiting. The manta thing.

Inside the room, the cops were pointing their flashlights inward, at something low.

One of the flashlights swung about and pointed, out of the room, at the floor.

It brightened and a cop emerged, staring at the floor where the flashlight was striking it.

'What's… *happening?*'

The cop was young, her flashlight hand was shaking.

Davy remained totally still.

'Get back in here!'

The other cop sounded older. Davy could tell from his heightened tone that he was totally freaked out.

'The floor's moving! There's something under the linoleum!'

'There's a gas leak! It's making us hallucinate!'

Davy watched as the manta thing raised the front of itself a few inches and slowly reared its head, which seemed to be in the shape of a snail; tense eyestalks zeroing right in on him as though pointing him out with two fingers. Then its mouth opened and it hissed at him, exposing two even rows of terrible little fangs.

The cop pulled her gun and crossed her hands, one over the other, targeting the manta-snail's head with the torch. Then she realized; the thing was directing her to look down the corridor.

She saw Davy right away. She kept the torch on it, then pointed the gun at him. He raised his hands in surrender, but didn't take his eyes off the thing.

'I heard screaming…' Davy offered calmly.

Inside the room, the girl burst out in wailing, horrified tears.

'Officer…' Davy began. '…can you see that thing? It's…'

'Shut up!'

'It's not just me, is it?'

It hissed again.

The stench was obscene.

She swung the gun back at its head, then swung the torchlight at Davy.

'I heard screaming…' Davy repeated, blinking in the brightness. 'I was on the street… I saw the doors were open… this place is condemned, nobody should be in here… I thought someone was in trouble…'

The girl inside was wailing still.

'Dierks!' The cop with the light in Davy's face was shouting in a high pitch. 'Keep her bloody quiet!'

'I fucken…' Dierks did not sound okay. 'Stoll, I fucken don't know…'

Dierks clearly didn't know what was happening. Then it sounded to Davy as though he might be vomiting. Davy couldn't help what he was going to say next. The manta-snail-head-thing… it was part of The Fear. It was part of everything that had been going wrong. Not just with him, not just with him and Kelli, and everything before that, but…

'I can kill it.'

…God Damn Everything.

Stoll flinched. 'What?'

'I'm here… that's what I'm here for.' Davy couldn't help it. He had to say it aloud. He could feel the bile at the back of his throat, the hate for it. Hate for evil. 'I'm here to kill it.'

The Fear thing spat out at Stoll, a thin tendril from its open, hissing mouth. It wrapped around her wrist like a grappling hook and she immediately began to shift her stance. She didn't scream, but she opened her mouth and hissed as well, as through the burning she was feeling was too much to express. The gun, still held tightly in her captured hand, slowly began turning, to point back at Davy.

'Officer Stoll…' Davy spoke, level.

'I don't…' Stoll gasped. 'I can't…'

Davy took one step forward. 'Stoll, don't shoot me.'

The thing hissed up at him again.

'I can't…'

She would, Davy knew. As soon as the gun was aimed at his head. Aimed anywhere that would hit. She was trying not to, but she wouldn't win. It had her, and she couldn't process, couldn't believe any of this was happening. For her, there was no resistance to that. But Davy could; he could feel it. If he could bring it forward, out of the pit of his stomach. He could kill this thing.

He stepped forward again.

One more step and she would fire.

She would fire in a second anyway.

The thing shivered as Davy raised his hand.

'Kill it…' Stoll uttered. '*Please, kill it!*'

The thing's head raised. Its eye stalks extended toward him. Davy stepped back. Then back again. Stoll's hand was shaking. He was further out of range now. The thing had to twist her hand, push her arm further. How much strength did it have?

Davy took the risk.

He strode several times, quickly, reached and grasped Stoll's forearm. The thing retracted its tendril instantly, then vanished beneath the linoleum, into the concrete beneath, before either of them could truly comprehend what had happened. They just stood there, Davy holding Stoll's still-raised arm, staring at the space where it had been. Then, gently, Davy released Stoll and stepped past her, into the room.

He could feel part of himself being amazed at his lack of caring, the other part totally possessed by the urge to kill these things. His primary attention, his forward consciousness, was directed totally at finding…

Dierks, still vomiting.

Davy stepped around his bent, lurching form and went further in. It had been some kind of small conference room. Maybe an AV room, for screenings. There was a scraggly homeless woman and a body at the end of the room. It was impossible to tell if she was young or old or sane or not. The flesh of her arm was withered. Not from needles, she was nothing like a junkie. She was a victim of some other kind of total evil.

Davy moved to the corpse at the end of the room, spread out on the floor of a horribly unsanitary makeshift home. Dirty blankets had been propped up with old wood like a child's fort. He saw the skeletal corpse of what had to have been a homeless man, but was now a mere outline. The bones were dried and twisted, like dead vines, and covered in gel, slime and some kind of slug-trail excreta. That was all that was left of him now, just mess, congealed inside his clothes, as though he had simply lain there, accepted his fate, and been consumed.

The rustling thing, the other creature…

The Fear.

The Fear had eaten him.

With his clothes on.

Fed on his despair, then his flesh.

One of the vine-like bones crumbled and turned to dust, even though nothing had touched it. Everything he had been, even the bones, were still wasting away before his eyes, rapidly decaying and decomposing within the shabby wet clothes.

Then he heard it again. The Fear. Not the manta thing. This was the first creature, the giant roach.

Further in, further down.

But… how could it be?

Davy was at the back wall.

It was draped, propped with horribly stained sheets…

But it was there.

He could feel it with his mind. Smell it like an open sewer. And there was cold, real bone-chilling cold, coming from there, radiating like a glacial wall.

He had to kill the fucking thing –

He still had to –

'Hey!'

He turned back.

Dierks had cornered him in a shooting gallery.

He understood immediately.

The *fucking thing*… The God Damn Fear… was *intelligent*.

Maybe, The Fear had been here all along, dormant in the abandoned tower basement, watching him, watching Kelli, until these two poor homeless bastards had just come along, and conveniently provided them with a meal. The Fear must have taken the man easily, maybe he'd already been ill, and then it started to feed on the girl, through her grief and helplessness. How long? How long did these things take to eat someone? To consume, and vanish them? He didn't know. It didn't matter. Maybe the sustenance that The Fear had gained from them had allowed the creatures to possess the courage to move up, to the room at the top, and try for him and Kelli.

Maybe they really were just weird-animal, weird-insect predators, and it really was all just that simple.

But Davy was starting to sense something else.

Aware of its enemy, it could plan, and use other people, other victims, to adapt, lure and trap. The two cops had seen that somehow the homeless couple had broken into the building. Recently. Maybe last night, maybe the night before… maybe even before that. Davy had been neglectful there, he had to confess. He'd allowed himself to become distracted. He'd been too focused upon the club, on his pathologically insistent libido. While all that sinfulness had been going on, these bums had broken into his home, maybe days, maybe weeks ago now, and set themselves up down here. And somehow, the girl had started crying, wailing in grief, a final desperate siren call for attention, just as he and Kelli had been at their weakest. When they had been about to do something terrible and irreversible. When, maybe just after, maybe even during, if the cops turned up, they could simply not fight back.

Davy's head was reeling with options, scenarios, swirling like ghouls in a maelstrom of fury and shame.

Maybe it went further back. Maybe The Fear had chased him and Kelli here, led them here and let them grow weak. Maybe it had found them here, maybe it had sniffed them out, maybe it had led the cops to find the homeless victims, to then find him and Kelli, to weaken them further, and would attack again, later tonight in a concrete cell…

But he knew for sure, for definite:

These things had tried to get him to rape his sister, then hate himself and want them, ask them, beg The Fear, to come and kill him. Then it would simply take her, his physically exhausted little sister, who he would have all-but plumped, slaughtered, oiled, roasted and left out on the table for them.

The world would never know what had happened to them.

Just the tattered old clothes they'd abandoned, and fine dust.

He saw it, playing out in his mind within a millisecond, and understood.

But he knew also now that The Fear needed to feed, before it attacked the Wrath, no matter how weak the Wrath had become. It needed strength to attack; and that meant, the Wrath was a viable threat. *He* was a viable threat.

All in seconds, he put it together as his world fell apart.

This was it.

Dierks had thrown up down the front of his uniform. The mess that The Fear had left of this poor homeless bastard was so awful that Davy hadn't smelled the puke pile over it, but he did now. Dierks was right there in front of him, his vomit right there, right down his cop shirt like a baby's dribble. Davy almost threw up himself, but forced it back down, acid down his gullet. The awful taste of it. In all his years; the body of the fed-upon homeless man had made this veteran cop sick. Stoll was tougher, she'd seen it before maybe, seen worse things sooner, younger, adjusted faster to how the city had descended so quickly, while she was still a rookie. The older cop would never get used to it, not shit like this; never. Whatever we were born into was normal. The Fear was more prevalent now. It had grown with this awful government. This world government of neo-fascism that stood only for corporate enslavement.

Getting bolder.

Ready to make a move on the weaker Wrath.

Where was this coming from?

How could he know this?

But he did.

He did know it.

Davy had the Wrath.

Bad.

Kelli.

The cop demanded something of him.

'Who the hell are you?'

He didn't know.

'I...' Davy's voice rasped. 'I'm – no-one.'

'A Yank.'

Stoll had re-entered the room behind Dierks and was holding the homeless woman up, cradling her withered arm.

'Stay where you are!' Dierks demanded.

Davy was frozen to the spot. 'I heard a scream...' He was surprised at his brain, still working to lie. '...I came in from the street. I know that this place has been sealed for years...'

Dierks was pulling himself together. 'Dirty freak...' That was all he had ever been exposed to; everyone was that to him, everyone but the other cops. 'What do you know about this?'

Stoll still had her gun out, but it was limp at her side.

'What?' Davy protested. 'Nothing; I heard...'

'*Who are you?*'

The homeless woman raised her good arm and pointed.

'It's him!'

Davy raised his hands in surrender again, and backed away. 'No!'

The roach rattled behind him, behind the curtains, behind the wall, in the wall, in space that wasn't there...

'Don't let him go...' Stoll demanded. 'He knows something...'

Davy looked up and rushed.

TWENTY: PRESUME

Bud Kerr had given him a car that he said, if he followed the map, would not be recognized, but also was not registered. Ink said that would not be a problem; Kerr said he could keep it.

He had told him something else too, at great risk, that had surprised him.

But that didn't matter right now.

What did was; the map was true.

Along the road there had been signs to another church ruin, clearly claiming to be the one he was looking for. There were a few other church ruins as well, all in plain sight along the way. The roads had been long, and Ink had moved fast, exceeding the speed limit. Everyone else he passed had been doing the same, out in the country.

He drove for more than two hours, at first through cultivated farm plains, where here and there an enormous, single gum tree extended high into the grey winter sky, alone in the middle of a grazing field, then noticed as the gums became less sparse. Appearing first in clutches as the terrain became harsher, then eventually thickening out, the gums now formed a forest, and the forest was closing in on the edges of the road. Then, more bridges, and more streams, and jagged rocks everywhere. Instead of being carved through the hillsides, the roads began to rise and fall, sometimes undulating in quick succession to accommodate the steeper hillsides, and there were patches where he had to steer back and forth, up and down, between them. Ink was in the ranges now, the Weddin Ranges, where lawless bushrangers had hidden out one hundred and fifty years before.

After more than almost an hour through the ranges, Ink found a dirt road, which was indeed invisible to anyone who had not been directed there, and plunged the car along it, into the dense forest. A mere few meters in, he could no longer see the main road, back in his rear view. He grimaced. He might have been in the middle of a mountain range anywhere, a much deeper gum forest, thousands of miles from civilization, rather than an hour's drive from a country hub.

Either way, if anything happened, nobody would find him here for days.

He followed the dirt road past the ruins of several colonial houses, and realized that at some point, maybe more than a century ago, a town had been born, failed, and died right here. Prospecting, he supposed. There had been gold, for a time. Thousands of people and many small townships like this. Now only the farming centers remained, and even then, only just. Ink was driving through a ghost town now, overgrown with a gum forest; a dirt street that had once been the old town's main road, probably. Nobody even remembered the dead town's name any more. Gold rushes were like that; some towns didn't exist long enough to let a proper name stick, some came and went so quickly they never even had the chance to be named.

The clearing Bud had mentioned was almost indistinguishable from the rest of the mass of bush foliage, but he had been told where the second turn off was, and about fifty meters up, there it was.

The church ruins.

He'd been told not to bring a gun, but he was not crazy. It was in his pocket and padded, so it could not be seen.

She would know he had it.

But in turn, she would know that he wasn't stupid, or naive.

Besides, people still came through here, once in a while.

And who knew what kind of people came to a place like this?

A shrine, a memorial.

The road stopped well before the church. The clearing was pretty big. He looked out as he stopped the car. This distance seemed respectful; it would have been wrong just to drive right up.

Ink had swapped his decent shoes for hiking boots back at Bud Kerr's property. They made no sound on the ground as he got out, the ground here was wet. It looked like it was going to rain any minute, but it always did out there, this time of year.

Just a little one-room church. A wooden entrance alcove and a side vestry, all burned away.

Nothing inside; he could see from here, through where the blackened stone wall had partially collapsed. Someone had tidied it though, someone had made sure it was not a vacuum for the famously abhorring nature that totally surrounded it. Although… there seemed to be a ring of stools inside. Maybe… slices of a large gum trunk? Ink looked up at the treetops surrounding him. They were enormous, right through in every direction. For many kilometers, if the long drive had been any indication. But then again, who knew? You couldn't really see that far through any long section of gums; this area had been, and still was, well-farmed. Ten strides past the back of the church, past those huge gums, there might be farmland, yellow-gold with an endless flat horizon. There might even he a house, and a patio, a verandah and a swimming pool. Australia was like that, to a point. Where there were people, and farmers.

But he was pretty sure that was not the case.

He was pretty sure there was nothing, for miles.

And now, all he had to do was wait.

Maybe he would see; stride over and check? But through this undergrowth, ten strides wasn't that easy. You could get lost in a kilometer of forest. Lose your sense of direction, which way you'd come, turn sharply, twist your ankle on the rocky ground and one freezing cold night later be dead of exposure.

Why the hell would anyone build a church here?

This was, essentially, a church already…

Although… perhaps that was why?

Or, was it the other thing? The old, classic church, planting a flag, making a stand, against paganism and nature worship? He hadn't researched. Might never know, might never care to know again. The white gravel crunched underfoot as he approached.

It had probably been something, ten years ago, when it had burned.

Closer now, you could indeed look right through and beyond the charred and ruined frontage, although the main altar wall had survived. You could see parts of the forest behind, up high, where a stained glass window once might have been. And someone had imported gravel, into a gum forest, to have a path leading up; a nice English white gravel path…

Recently.

Who the hell had maintained such a bizarre thing?

Who did now?

A cold breeze passed over him. Behind him, he heard two light crunches out of nowhere. He turned around and found a gun leveled between his eyes, an inch from the bridge of his nose.

'Amy May?'

She smirked.

'…you presume.'

TWENTY-ONE: HUNGRY

I

Kurt held his head in his hands.

Cass felt so sorry for him, but they had to keep going.

'Just remember; the Wrath disrupts local energy fields. Whenever powers are used to blast something, it can affect anything from a PC to a power line, and if it's a slow day and they're looking… the Bureau is given a point of reference. So, we're actually very comfortable living out here, without electricity.'

'How? How will I?'

'You can't go back,' Shylee insisted. 'You know that, right? You gotta break all formal ties with society, establish no forms of ID. You're family's dead to you.'

'I know, I know…'

'You're just a kid, so it shouldn't be too hard. You're not entrenched in the system yet.'

Cass rolled her eyes. 'He barely knows what the system is, Shy.' She squatted down in front of him. 'We've taken steps to ensure that neither of us are registered on any computer. It was hard but we did it. You're a lot younger, you shouldn't have to try too hard.'

Shylee kept going. 'So now, given all that, all we've told you, within that framework, you've still got to learn to steal, okay?'

Kurt shook his head. 'I don't think I can do it.'

'Yes, you can. People like us, we're here for a reason. We're meant to survive.'

They looked at each other. Cass knew; something seemed to have been acknowledged between them since last night. They had both slept deeply all day, since just before sunrise. Perhaps more deeply than either of them had done since the start of all this. Then they had each awoken, ravenously hungry, just before sunset.

'Even if it's just a few of us,' Shylee growled. 'We're meant to survive.'

Cass could feel it. It was true. 'Kurt, it…' Even so, she couldn't believe she was going to say it, out loud, with something close to confidence. 'It won't always be this way…'

Cass sighed, but when she looked to Shylee, she could tell she felt the same; that she knew, as well. Still, even though Cass was determined for it to be true, she didn't quite trust it yet. She could only just say it.

'It's going to change…' Shylee uttered darkly. '…soon. But until it does…'

Suddenly Cass was the bad cop. 'Until then, the sad truth is that you need to get used to being alone. Most victims of Bureau 88 have first been victims of their own desperation, or stupidity, or just –'

'Jesus!' Kurt stood suddenly. They weren't eye to eye, but it felt like they were. 'I know, I know! I get it! Fuck! You told me all this!'

Cass looked to Shylee. Shylee smiled, relieved.

'Good, Kurt. You're ready.'

'So we can go get food?' Kurt demanded.

Shylee smiled wryly back at Cass.

'We're going to help you…' Cass offered. 'But you wait here, and we'll bring back dinner.'

'Breakfast.'

'Whatever. It's food.'

Kurt's narrowed his eyes. 'Really?'

'Sure,' Shylee shrugged. 'Why the hell not?'

Cass leaned in again. 'You have to remember though; it's the food that keeps the power going. That's something you can never forget. Good food. Unprocessed. Stuff the elites eat.' She leaned back. 'To be honest, I'm starving too… I could eat a whole bloody cow right now.'

Shylee smirked. 'Rushing and blasting always leaves you starving. Add that to the list.'

And the first time he does it, Kurt will need painkillers.

Shylee gasped. Cass suddenly realized; she had psyched her. And… it hadn't been there. The desperation, the pain, the pure emotion.

The telempathy was gone. Cass looked at Shylee. Shylee stared back. It wasn't often these days something took them equally by surprise. Maybe it would be okay?

'Are you… like Robin Hood?' Kurt asked hopefully.

'Like, steal from the rich?' Cass smiled. 'If we're desperate, sometimes we steal a carton of milk from a corner store, but we try not to let things get that desperate. Because of the recession, we only steal from the big chains in the safe suburbs; we don't want anyone who's already struggling to suffer more, especially not because of us. We're trying to stop all that.'

'Really? How?'

Cass ignored him. 'You know about the gated communities? The getaway communities?'

'Where the rich people go on weekends?'

'We wouldn't go inside any of them, but on the way, there are stores that stock elite food. It's less tampered with; enough so it doesn't fuck with the Wrath.'

Kurt perked up. 'Well… maybe I could come with you? To watch? Learn some more?'

'I don't think so. Shylee thinks… we both think… we don't think you're quite ready for that yet.'

'But…'

'You should eat something first, before you do anything on your own. We should too, before we go, but we can't. We're going to have to take the chance, and steal hungry.'

Shylee threw on her big coat. 'And you should never shop hungry, kid. Even the normal know that.' Kurt smiled at her, tired but grateful. 'Will you be okay here on your own, kid?'

'Where are your boobs?' Kurt suddenly asked with a cheeky smile.

Cass chortled. 'Kurt!'

'That's only when she kills, isn't it?'

They both froze.

'It's okay. I know you need to.' Kurt's stomach rumbled. Hard.

Cass shook herself out of it.

It was actually painful to hear, and only made her hungrier.

'When will you go?' Kurt asked.

'As soon as it's fully dark, we'll walk to the woods.'

They waited another ten, until Kurt had fallen asleep again, then as they watched him sleep for another minute, Shylee stretched up and collected her gun from the top of an old wooden cupboard. She'd never hidden it before, Cass thought as she looked down at Kurt, sleeping the same way she did, curled over the grain sacks.

'The hunger might wake him again…'

'He'll fall back again.' They knew this; it was how it worked. 'And we won't be long.'

'I feel clean…' Shylee told her on the way to the forest.

'Me too. Inside and out.'

She'd surprised herself, saying something like that.

II

In the city the Bureau mostly piggybacked off of speed cameras, but there were hardly any out here, on the outskirts. Too much trouble to maintain, too expensive, no dividends. Some on the freeways, to monitor accidents, and the occasional one underneath to monitor an underpass, but generally, none.

They could often profit here, Cass had realized, where Central could not.

In the time they'd been together, Cass and Shylee had spent more than their fair share of summer days under the shade of a concrete freeway, somewhere in the middle of nowhere, where two important roads to two more important somewheres crisscrossed in a blind spot. Satellites couldn't see through overpasses and underpasses. Cameras couldn't see around pillars. Even so, most of their confirmed blind spots were the result of human flaws; the inevitable reality that many office-based security staff were just bored. There was only so far most workers would go for their cubicle job.

In the back of her mind, Cass feared that one day Central, or the Bureau, would find some way to install the cameras everywhere, and surveillance would be invisible, forgotten and ever-present, like it was in the new skyscrapers, on the new city streets. That it would be everywhere, like oxygen. But not today. For now, their time would more likely run out when some minion of Central, who'd already figured it out, needed an idea to save their job, or to get a promotion.

The hypers might be moving out to the country, they might be hiding between the city and the second towns. Why don't we monitor under the freeways and bridges?

That would happen, one day. But until then… it was virtually unspoken between them, but it was why they had remained all this time, since the start. They were both twenty two, almost twenty three by now. Cass knew that, although they sometimes got so hungry they forgot. They had both been born here, and had grown to young adults here. They both had a second sense, here, in this city. They knew their way around. For as long as they were careful, they would not get caught.

III

There were several long stretches of freeway between the city and the ring of second towns that surrounded it. The second towns were named because so many of the elites had their second homes there; a string of beach hamlets, former fishing villages and surf communities along the northern or southern coastline of Adelaide's west-facing beachline; farm and country service towns, and wealthy hilltop vistas in the eastern arc of hills and ranges.

The Four-Two General Store ostensibly serviced one of the smaller, almost abandoned towns along the northern beach route, lodged conveniently in the middle of the long freeway. It had once, surely, Cass considered, been an actual general store, probably going back to the first colonies. But now it was a well-stocked last resort in the gap between week and weekend. It could be accessed easily from the freeway both back and forth, and never closed. The food was good; hugely expensive elite food containing almost no preservatives, additives, stimulants or sedatives, and the store was always well-stocked, cunningly positioned for the elites to grab whatever they needed as they rushed toward their holiday shacks for a micro-break, or rushed back home to an empty larder, summoned by Central. Whatever had been forgotten on the way, whatever someone called ahead to tell them to bring back, everything was there; from milk and bread to solar batteries and lady shavers.

Beneath the overpass, Cass and Shylee looked down at Four-Two over a grassy, weedy slope to a small, three-way traffic island. One road came straight in, off the freeway and went straight back, the second veered out, into the trees and darkness to who knows where, and the third came in from the opposite side of the freeway. So far as they were aware, only they knew; Four-Two was not only a money fountain for the owner, but a golden blind spot for thieves, with just one external camera, across the street, facing the entrance.

In the beginning they had scouted for days, even risked going in and buying a few things with paper money to eyeball the monitors behind the service counter. They had been seen, but not registered. They couldn't rely on that, Cass sighed to herself, but you had to love the elite's tendency simply not to see the poor. Genuinely, not to see them, when they were right there.

But now they knew; it was clear, it was safe, it was fish in a barrel.

It was theirs.

IV

All through the early part of the evening they watched as the elites came and went. They would speed up in their oversized, military-style cars and park wherever they liked. They would dash in, sometimes leaving the engine running and the door open, the keys in the ignition, then run out, clutching something expensive, vital and precious.

They watched the lights within Four-Two become brighter as the night drew on.

'You got him?' Shylee asked.

'Nearly...' The waves that were coming at her were jagged; dark crimson and dark blue. 'He's really worried about something. I just need to get past that... make sure it's not us he's worried about.'

'It's been weeks, now. Months. He's never twigged before.'

The human mind was amazing, Cass had to concede. Even if the vessels, the people who contained that mind, were not. Her own mind was particularly amazing, even though what she could do with it, her abilities, had never felt particularly special. At least, not since the initial discovery and integration of those abilities into her consciousness.

If that's even what had actually happened.

After all, how could she be truly sure about any of this? There'd been no-one there to tell her, not at first anyway. Regardless, her abilities, while objectively amazing, had never felt more special to her than when she'd learned any other new mental skill. Or, in the end, even having the ability to understand a language, or perceive distance.

Right at the start, when she'd found out that she could use telepathy and read people's minds, and sometimes raise heat from the ground, she'd realized that it was meant to be. That it was all part of who she was. Then, she had found out something else. After a long while of running, stopping and starting again, then realizing that maybe, just maybe, she might survive, she had also realized that in the spaces in between the panic and anxiety, where she could rest, that she also had the ability to extend her awareness, and to leave her body.

Okay. That had been a bit more shocking, and amazing, but, probably…

'Not…' She had tried to explain it to Shylee once. 'Not *shocking* shocking… you know? More like… I remember back before all this, that there were sometimes people who had never played an instrument in their lives, then they pick one up, like a violin or something, and just take to it. And they're pleasantly shocked that they have this skill, already, inside them. Is there a word for that?'

It wasn't as though she hadn't thought about her abilities as they had developed.

Not just the floating away part, but all of it.

Cass was doing it now, reaching out, into Four-Two.

To do this, she was employing a part of her mind, an extension of her awareness. It was as though she could expand a giant sphere of energy around herself. Maybe she was even extending *herself*. It was hard to tell, still, after all this time. It was as though this field of herself, her mind or her consciousness, an invisible part of herself, floated away on the surface of the expanding sphere. At first she had likened it to standing on the bow of a ship, but then she had realized that the ship would be moving through, at her best guess, another part of the atmosphere; so it was more like being strapped to the bow of a submarine. But then again, if she generated some willpower, she could stop and start, forwards and reverse, and eventually, all around. This will to move, to expand and contract the sphere, or move in any direction across its surface, was different again; it was more like flying. Flying underwater, she supposed. But, no; still different. Like red and blue made purple. And always tethered to herself, her body, at the center of the sphere.

As she traveled like this, she could feel the pressures and tides. Of… something else, another force, around her, around everyone and everything. There was an invisible sky-ocean of it, everywhere, and if she closed her eyes and half-concentrated, but half-let-go and allowed herself to feel it, in a more abstract way, then the part of herself that was extended, out there and sailing around, became her primary awareness.

She quickly began to decode the streams she saw, and the wave forms she sensed; the ripples and tides, and the colors, the same colors everyone saw… but different. These colors weren't attached to anything. They were like streaks of light, or cloud, or glares or auras, but they weren't necessarily bound.

Soon Cass found that she had been able to read these color signals within the field, and decode them somehow. Her ability to perceive and decipher them seemed to have simply just emerged out of the field itself, out of wanting, and trying, out of studying and making connections. It had just taken form in her mind and then, one day, it had become… normal.

She had wondered sometimes if this was how babies discovered color, or language, or numbers, or even depth; hand-eye and all that. It was just the same as, she supposed, as a baby would first make sense of the sounds, of color and movement, and eventually figure out it was a face, or a finger, or a nipple.

Meaning: love, play, sustenance.

She could feel the mental vibrations too. She could feel the energy pulses and the waves they generated, the colors they formed, the echoes and ripples that people and things sent out through the invisible sky-ocean; their sounds and movements and emotions, through growth or contraction, expression or tension. She could still see everything as it was, in ordinary perception, but it was as though she were seeing it through, or along with, a much denser, more complex atmosphere. It had taken her a long time, a year maybe, to understand that, and understand the feedback, once the decoding had been done. Roughly the same time, she thought she remembered, as it had taken her to learn to talk as a toddler.

V

It was cold beneath the underpass. Behind her, Shylee shivered and shifted impatiently. She had tried a few times to extend her awareness like Cass did, but she just couldn't do it. Like Cass had tried to melt things, but couldn't do that either.

'Does it get any quicker?'

'Huh?'

Shylee huffed. 'The more you do it. The reaching. Does it get quicker the more you do it?'

Cass wasn't rising to her cranky bait.

'Reaching?'

'It feels like that's what you're doing. Doesn't it?'

Cass kept her eyes closed. 'I suppose. It's like reaching into the dark. But I've done it so many times, the dark doesn't seem dangerous anymore. It's quicker in that regard, in that I don't hesitate anymore, or get confused at what I'm sensing.'

'Tell me…' Shylee demanded softly. 'Take my mind off things.'

Cass sighed. It *would* actually take longer this way. But it would take longer *anyway*, if Shylee kept pulling her focus.

'He's the only other stationary person around for miles.'

'What about the people on the freeway?'

'They're like… sharks in the distance.'

'Sharks?'

'Cars are like sharks.'

'Okay.'

Cass sensed him from his head and heart.

'He's dark blue and murky crimson.'

Cass had learned over time what this represented.

'That's almost dread, isn't it?' Shylee asked.

Cass smiled, pleased that she remembered.

'It is when it turns brown.'

Shylee grumbled. 'What's he thinking? Up front?'

Shylee *had* listened over the past few months, since Cass had started telling her more.

Cass had told Shylee that she could also adjust her awareness, like an iris, just by thinking about it, just as she could her general sense of vision. She could broaden for a landscape, or tighten it like a microscope. Concentrate for a telescope. She could adjust this also to hear the different levels of *voice* in a person's head.

'This is just an example…' Cass had told Shylee. 'But, we're going to steal, right? Now, we were raised in a culture where that's bad. So, you to have a focus of intent that bypasses that; the guilt and moral judgment. You have to make that new voice the front voice. But then you have to fight the paranoia as well. So, there's one voice that's saying, he's not looking. It's saying, get closer. It's saying, be calm, walk past, hand up, grab and stash. It's calculating. The smooth criminal. That voice would feel like someone is blowing hard through a straw on my forehead, and seem very clear blue. Very focused. I would probably, actually hear that voice, in his voice, almost like he's talking to himself out loud. Because, it's the thief actually telling himself what to do. Verbalizing his thoughts inside his head. Then there's all the stuff you need to repress; like I said, what we were all raised with. All the bright crimson energy behind it; fear, panic, don't do this, it's wrong, it's bad, you're taking something that doesn't belong to you, stealing, thief, criminal; you'll get caught; there will be shame and pain…that's like a halo you're standing in, but it's also like the lighting in a room. It's just there, and after a while, if you focus on the deed, you forget about the light coming out of the ceiling.'

'I know that guilt…' Shylee had nodded. 'It doesn't matter who we steal from, or why, I still feel it every time.'

'But now…' Cass uttered. 'I am sensing that not from myself, the person about to steal. I am sensing it from the person we are about to steal *from*.'

'Oh. That's…'

'Not great, huh? I mean, his background? His aura, I suppose it's called? Tonight… it's like that too. It's dark blue and deep red, and I get a kind of tightness in the scalp, where you're trying to repress all the fear of all the other voices, telling you no, don't, you'll get caught, you're not good at this, you'll stuff up, not yet, not now, someone will see you… all of that.'

'So… he's stealing too?'

'I think so.'

'What? Stock? Cash from the till?'

'I don't know yet. But; you know, when you go in, there's tension in your neck, where you tell yourself not to turn around, not to look guilty, not to be paranoid, to stay calm? And you know that tension in your jaw, holding back the scream of anxiety, and fear and rage that you've even come to this place, taking such a risk, risking such a transgression?'

'Jesus, Cass, we're just about to go in!'

'And in the throat; the suppressed squeal of fear, of adrenalin, even excitement? I can get all that, decode it from him. Here, tonight, now.'

Shylee took pause. 'Really?'

'You remember what I said about feedback?'

'You said it's the most important thing. It's their motivation. Right?'

'It's like a series of symbols that allows you to follow someone's thinking. If you've got it right, if you understood the symbols from the decoded feedback, you can really decode someone's thoughts. Not just surface, not just background, not just under the surface; the real stuff. All the stuff it's connected to, down deep.'

Shylee nodded. 'It made me realize… I keep seeing the face of my grade three teacher. She caught me taking a red crayon that didn't belong to me. Because I'd used mine all up.'

Cass shrugged. 'I keep remembering the first time I saw a saw a baddie get arrested on TV. He tried to get away and his car crashed and burst into flames.'

Cass knew; all this and more. Your local cop. Your Mum and Dad and their look of disappointment when they realized you had taken the cookie from the jar. The shock of that first punishment smack on the bottom. Worse, for some people. Or better, in a way, she supposed; some people were still chasing the excitement of that first smack, and that's how they rolled. All that, and all the other myriad variations of that, all the bedrock stuff that went together and, generally, created your own specific set of criminal tendencies…

'And I always see the end of *Bonnie and Clyde*…' Cass confessed. 'Every time.'

Sometimes, Cass knew, if she was really lucky, it came to life, like she *actually* was the person she was reading and decoding. Just briefly. Within this massive packet of information, the information that was someone's mental activity and attention right then, and there, and in the moments afterwards, she could almost think like her target; she could sift through and remember things that she had never experienced, but her target had. Even things beyond those forefront elements that were connected to his general focus at the time.

'You have to be careful with the emotions…' Cass remembered telling Shylee, years ago. It didn't seemed like such a big deal now. 'It's like turning the volume down on a movie. You could be watching something sad happening, but without the sad violins, or melancholy piano cues, there's distance. It doesn't suck you in as bad.'

Just the facts.

If you could manage that…

And bingo.

There he was.

She had him.

She had the packet.

She opened her eyes.

It was pitch dark beneath the overpass.

Four-Two was like a beacon in the night.

'Took you long enough.'

She blinked at the brightness of it.

The off-ramp oasis of neon.

'Well?' Shylee was always eager.

Hunger never helped.

Cass huffed. 'You are hungry.'

They were disembodied voices in the darkness now.

'So are you. You're dizzy, I can hear it in your voice. Can you rush?'

'Yes. Once in and out.'

'Sure?'

'Yes.'

'We can't lie any more about how thin we've become.'

Cass remembered. Holding her. Their arms wrapped around each other, hands coming to rest on each other's ribs.

'Ansel's worried someone's going to complain about the prices. He's skimming. He knows these… rich dickheads… will pay anything for something they need in a hurry.'

'You never said this before.'

'He's realized, lately, how long he's been doing it. He's been fiddling the books all this time. The stuff we're stealing is getting mixed up with his shonky high prices and crooked stock-takes…'

'If he gets nervous, he's going to ruin it for us.'

'It's inevitable that one day we'll have to find somewhere else. But from what I can tell, it's just the pressure. Just that it's built up. The longer you take a risk, the longer the risk seems risky. You know?'

'He's had too long to think about it.'

'He's had too long watching rich dickheads come and go and not give a shit. He wants a place of his own. If he was thinking straighter, and in less of a panic, he'd know that the owner doesn't care about the balance sheet. Didn't when he started, won't when he quits. This is just a pocket money for someone.'

'So what do we do?'

'We do… what we do. Until he gets caught.'

VI

There could be no on-camera evidence of Ansel talking to ghosts, of him saying a short hello to someone entering, someone who wasn't actually there on the surveillance recording. But Ansel's internal organs knew, instinctively, the dead spots in traffic. It was late on a Wednesday night. People had come, and people would come again, but right now they were there, or eating, or eating and thinking about going there, or sitting about and digesting. Ansel could take a break now. And now Ansel had answered the call of nature, they had ninety seconds. Ninety had always worked.

'Okay. Pants down…'

Cass opened her eyes again.

'Phew. I really did not want to go with him there.'

'Go?'

'Same as last time.'

'Exactly the same.'

'Okay.'

'Go.'

Shylee was gone.

Cass followed.

VII

What does it look like, when we take things?

What? I don't know Shy. I don't care.

The cameras don't see us. Like, when I take this big 'ol bread stick…

Shy, from the back…

Raise it up like this and put it in my coat pocket…

Rye, please.

It is. It is rye.

Okay, okay.

But, does the camera see, like, objects floating up, and… what?

Vanishing like the invisible man puts them under his invisible coat? And why don't our clothes come up?

I don't know the answer to any of those things, Shy.

Cass hated that stuff. She didn't care. Even though she knew that logically, if they actually did have the answers, they stood a better chance of using their abilities better, she still hated it.

Perhaps we bring in a kind of field with us?

Cass sighed. 'What?'

She could hear herself getting angry, even in the whisper she could feel it, but didn't know why. Shy was taking handmade toffees from a box, two each from the back. She wanted to tell her to take three, one for Kurt, then she did, she reached back and took one more of each from each box. Fuck. He was their son now. How were they supposed to dump him?

*Why do you get so cross about all this? We *should* know.*

'Because it's impossible,' Cass snapped aloud. Shy frowned back at her. *It's all impossible!*

But it isn't, Cass, obviously.

I'm standing here, psychically spying on the base idiot thoughts of a – thankfully constipated – fortysomething grocery store clerk, who can only think about how he wants more and more money, while I hope he doesn't poo for at least another thirty…

Shylee went to the back of the store.

Shy, get milk and juice last – it's heaviest.

I'm nearly done! Stick to your half! Look, all I'm saying is, if the security cams do pick up floating loaves of bread, and jars of apricot jam, then maybe there's an algorithm for that; or soon will be? Maybe there's a way we can stop people seeing that? If the guy really is covering his own arse with the skimming and the stocktaking, we've got it made so long as we don't fuck up. Why not try and figure this out?

Cass sighed.

Okay Shy. So, you think we bring some kind of 'energy field' in with us?

She started moving more swiftly now, keeping specific goods in mind. A bag of cookies, made by a local trader. All natural. In this store, that meant what it meant.

Sure! Why not an energy field of some kind? Look, Cass, how did that shower just heat up like that? We create an aura. There is some kind of heat, energy, we can attract. So maybe, when we rush, that energy comes out and for some reason, it obscures light. We're both still carrying it around now. Or, radiating it. And it hides the kind of light a digital camera lens registers.

They'd both worn their coats, chosen for pockets as much as warmth. They'd brought bags. One of each thing, but as many things as they could. Nothing there wasn't a lot of. Nothing he would notice. Take from the side of the pile, the back of the shelf. Reach deep.

Do you know anything about digital camera lenses?

No. I don't. I don't even know if they're any different from… what's the other thing?

The other thing?

The other… analog. I don't even know if they're any different from analog lenses, just that; obviously, we have something in us, or between us, that prevents us being seen by these lenses, these ones here, in this store. So, our light, just for a minute after we come through…

Are you keeping track?

So the energy that comes through the rush tunnel, acts as a filter, right?

Shy are you keeping track?

Twenty seconds.

Cass pulled out her second bag. She had actually registered Shylee's musings. *A filter… I suppose. Get the milk now. Cass considered a second. I was taught this. By someone I met, later… after. The cameras and everything. It was never really explained to me what the cameras do and don't record.*

Or how many of us does it take, to get killed, to find this out. Shylee gasped, then sighed. *I'm sorry… that was…*

Cass heard Shylee open the fridge doors, slowly and carefully, the light vacuum whoosh, but making as little sound as possible. She moved to the front of the store.

It's okay Shy. It'll be his birthday next week. I found you three months later. I thought it was closer to two, but that's nearly three years we've been doing this.

And we've never found anything this easy. We should be taking more. Hoarding for winter.

Shy, the security monitor.

What? What about it?

At the front. I'm watching you at the fridges back there. On the monitor. It's like… some fuzzy pixels. Maybe the door opened, but… if you're quick it's more just like, a… what did they call them? It's like an artefact or something. And the screen, the image is so small, you wouldn't see anything was gone. Not even if you were looking… I think we were right; we bring some kind of field in with us, and whatever we take into it, while it's there, just doesn't reflect light or something.

Really? You're really watching me?

Well, no. I mean, that's just it. I'm not! I can't see you! Shy, when I was a kid, they used to play clips like this on TV, from video, and try and convince you they were ghosts…

So we've been around a while, then? Our kind?

Shy, we need to go. Or we'll get caught.

We'll never get caught.

Cass stood there now, her pockets full, her coat heavy, with two fully-stacked carry-bags in each hand. She reached out to Ansel. He was still sitting, still blocked.

We've never taken this much before.

But there was something maternal. She understood that. Something about providing for Kurt.

Kill me…

What?

Please, kill me…

Cass spoke aloud in a harsh whisper. 'Shylee, *what?*'

What? Nothing! Shut up!

Shy, there's something… we need to get out of here.

No shit – did you remember th-

Now, Shy! Look – outside… it's so dark. I can't see anything…

She acknowledged the fear in her own mental voice as Shylee shuffled up to the counter and stood quickly behind her. The path from the front entrance went straight up to the counter, then on, past several shelves, to the back of the store and the back-room door.

'It happened, all of a sudden…' Cass glanced back at Shylee. Shylee grimaced.

Cass, you're freaking. You should rush. Now. I'll be five seconds a behind you…

Cass didn't. *The lights outside… the off-ramp lights…* Cass tried to swallow but her mouth was drying up. *The lights… they're different…*

Kill me…

Cass felt as though she had been stabbed with a blade between her shoulders.

Kill – me…

Cass – what just happened? – you just flinched –

Shy, that's really not you is it?

Shy uttered aloud, softly into her ear. 'What's not me?' Cass didn't answer. 'Cass…?' She hissed lightly into her ear again. '… what's not me?'

Cass couldn't swallow. Her voice was hoarse.

'The voice asking me to…'

…please… kill – me – …

'To what? Cass? Asking you to do what? Look, grab one more thing each. If we don't rush in two, we'll never be able to risk coming back here…'

'Shy, if we rush out there, back up to the bridge… what are we rushing into?'

Shylee stepped forward, staring out. Cass glanced up at the monitor. It was broken into four tiny quarters. In front of the main counter, where they were standing, there was nothing.

'It's okay, we're still nonexistent...'

Shylee kept staring at the entrance.

'Can you see?' Cass demanded. She was hoping that Shy could see, but also hoping she couldn't. Hoping it wasn't just her, but also hoping it wasn't real.

Oh. Oh, right...

You see it? It's not just me?

Cass, there's no...

Cass let out a breath. '...no reflection. From inside. No lights from the freeway outside...'

'There should be...'

'...something! *Some* light! But there's *nothing*.'

She could feel Shy tense even more, hear her breathing become irregular as she tried a few times to formulate a question.

'What could...? ...what do you think...? ...what's...? ...out there?'

Cass didn't answer as they stood, laden with stolen goods, staring at the lightless glass door and long black windows. It was as though the glass had been painted black from outside.

'Cass... what do we do?'

I was just going to ask you...

'I can hear a car...'

They both heard it approaching at speed down the middle road, from the other side of the freeway. Someone heading back to the city in a hurry, making a pit stop.

'Maybe we can go out the back...?' Shy suggested. 'Ansel might hear us go through, but by the time he gets his shit together...'

'Shy...' Cass felt completely restrained. 'There's something out the back, too... there's something closing in around the store...'

Shylee moved back, closer toward her, and pushed her arm, and the side of her body against her. Their bags rustled. Cass could feel Shylee summon the rush, to take them both, just back up to the rise, under the…

Cass, I can't get past it… Shylee gasped. *I can't… my mind's eye… I can't see past the door…!*

Cass could feel the telempathy creeping back. Shylee was starting to panic. Starting to fear for them both. Starting to blame herself. Then she turned, instinctively. Behind them, way behind them, outside the back of the store, there was something in the dark.

'It's behind us…' Shylee stated, low. '…isn't it? It's out there…'

'I can't look. I can't even try. If I put my mind out there, it will know we're here…'

'Wait…' Shylee looked quickly back to her with a deep frown. '…you mean it doesn't know we're here?'

It came as a revelation to Cass as well. Weak and panic-shrouded, she had been unable to decipher the very thing her instinct was trying so desperately to get through to her.

'The thing…' Shylee growled. '…and the car, it's not coming for us, is it? Why not?'

Cass frowned. 'We're so weak… it hasn't sensed us yet…'

'So our weakness… it's…*it's working for us…*?' Shylee took a step toward the back. The store was old, stone walled. The door was wood, and hard. 'Is it those things? It's those things… isn't it?'

Cass knew what she was thinking, why she was stepping closer. She was wondering if she could block it, or lock it from this side. Cass was becoming even more scared now, because… she'd never ever heard Shylee scared before. But the fear, the fear was in her voice. The Fear was out the back, out the front…

'The Fear…' Cass uttered.

'The Fear is here…' Shylee muttered, almost so Cass couldn't hear it, almost litany, almost as though she had said it before, long ago; a child's rhyme of protection.

Unable to turn, Cass passed her eyes over the ceiling directly above her. Could they get up, hide up there…? She couldn't see any access hatches at all.

'Cass, where is Captain Constipation? Has he closed the deal?'

Cass probed back, just for a second. Not outside, into the dark, just…

She grimaced. 'He's going to give himself a hernia…'

Shylee went quickly behind the counter. Cass saw her look down. 'Here!'

Cass came around. The room seemed to spin as she carried herself and her bags around the counter edge and looked down. There was a hatch. Shylee was already squatting, feeling the edges.

Here!

She lifted it. There was not much dust; people used it. But it was pitch black underneath, and a gush of frigid air plumed up.

Is it a meat locker?

Then something moved, at the edges. Something scuttled…

'No!' Cass hissed.

Shylee slammed the hatch down again.

It was as though that action had decided something; not just for them, but for whoever had arrived, for the Fear, and quite simply for the whole universal knot in which they were now caught. Harsh, cracking footsteps approached from outside; high heels on the concrete. They heard the back door of the store slam open, as though it had been kicked in. Something scraped on the underside of the closed hatch as Shylee rolled hard onto it, ducking with Cass beneath the counter so that Cass fell right beside her, almost into her lap. Out the back, they heard Ansel scream, then heard bustling as he collected himself and ran into, or was thrown into, the other side of the back-office door. Cass felt Shylee fumble and somehow recognized the gestures she was making. She was putting the silencer on her gun. Cass looked back to see, but her eye was caught by the security monitors. The front door opened and a woman entered, just as the back door opened and Ansel stumbled in, still pulling and zipping up his trousers as another man followed him and shoved him again, then caught him by the shoulder as though to jar and confuse him.

Ansel looked out in horror as he saw who'd arrived.

'Miss Chant! How nice to see you again so soon!'

Cass felt her stomach contract. It was as though her spirit had fallen through the hatch into the infested darkness below.

Tamara Chant. Black leather shirt, black heels, and a bright red business blouse and leather jacket. Red extensions in her explosion of blonde.

And she'd brought a psycho with her.

Ansel was stammering. 'I can… I can explain!'

'Explain, Ansel?'

'I was…'

'Ansel, I just came to restock the larder, what could possibly need explaining?'

'Then…' Cass could hear the pitch of confusion. '…why did you get your man to drag me off the…?'

'Really?' Tamara's voice was light with amusement. 'Did he do that? I just asked him to make sure you were ready to help me.'

Ansel immediately started babbling. 'Why, of course; as you can see the locals have again produced a… a *real bounty* of wonderful, *authentic stock…*' he stammered. 'I appreciate that there was no time to show you before; perhaps I can show you now? I hope you approve, Miss Chant…?'

Ansel proceeded to rattle off a list of most of the things they had just stolen a fraction of, and still had in their possession. As Ansel babbled on, giving his employer an impromptu tour of her own store, beside Cass, tight in the corner, something was happening to Shylee. But Cass couldn't move, to turn, to fully see her face.

Both of them, however, knew it was over.

Cass couldn't see a way out. There wasn't one now. Once Tamara Chant and her goons had you, once they were close, knew who you were, it was pretty much done. A few she'd met, she'd heard about, had escaped to tell the tale, for the name and reputation to spread, but nobody this weak would escape.

But Cass had started thinking; if they were going to die, then maybe they could take her out with them. Maybe they could kill Chant. She knew Shylee would be thinking the same. They would probably die in the act, they might die horribly; certainly they would, if they didn't take out the Bureau mercenaries as well. But they could take out Chant, and that would make their own deaths worthwhile.

Cass looked. She turned her head hard, just an inch or two.

Shylee's face, the dark severity of striking features, was fully in her vision. Her eyes expressed a terrible sadness as her lips parted and she mouthed.

'We – got – caught.'

Cass smiled back at her friend. She glanced down. Sure enough, the gun was there, the silencer attached. They both looked down at it now, nested in Shylee's coat, acknowledged what it meant, then looked up, meeting each other's eyes again. Cass mouthed back.

'We'll – never – get – caught…'

Shylee smiled. Her eyes glistened at the corners as she nodded, slowly.

Cass turned back.

Tamara Chant.

Everyone with the Wrath knew that name. It had gotten around. She was the one. Their worst enemy. She had killed the most, was hated the most. And then there was that feeling she'd had before, as though the universe had aligned for this, knotted them into it. What were the odds? The Fear and The Wrath? Here, now?

Shylee moved. Slowly, ever so slowly, she moved her hand. Up, over her side, just a few inches, so that when Cass glanced down, she saw the gun more clearly now.

Silver metal, black handle.

Cass suddenly wondered; now it was over, how many executions had they delivered? How many people had they tracked down and killed for their evils? It suddenly occurred to her, to wonder… how many men were there, in the store, outside, total? How many would Shylee have to take out, if they had even the slightest chance…?

Then she began to worry; how many bullets were there left? How many had there been in the clip to begin with? She'd never seen Shylee check. She'd never seen her reload. She'd never really ever thought about it.

The front door to the store opened again and Ansel abruptly shut up. On the monitor, they saw Tamara turn.

'What kept you?'

'I thought I smelled something.'

The Bureau psycho stood at the store room door, a few paces behind and to the right of where Ansel had ended up as he'd danced about, desperately trying to impress Tamara. And now there was, apparently, another man behind Tamara. He'd come in, spoken… but they couldn't see him. He didn't show up on the monitor. Now Cass felt her heart start to pound, very fast. So fast it was almost disorienting. She wanted it over now, it was too much. She wanted Shylee to start shooting, to shoot Tamara Chant and then… and then, their names, at least, would survive, if only in Wrath legend.

'Something?'

'Maybe. Gone now.'

They could hear the voice, the new arrival, clearly, only a few meters away. He sounded English.

'I see.'

On the monitor, Tamara kept staring at the empty space.

'Is this him?' The new man asked.

Tamara looked back to Ansel. 'Yes. This is the man I believe is stealing from me.'

'What? No!'

Cass had almost been Ansel for a few seconds, a few times, but she had never in all those times properly see him. As she turned to look at him now, on the monitor, she realized that she never would; not alive, anyway. Tamara was going to kill him. She had a feeling, an awful feeling, of an impending death. It felt as though his death was an active volcano, and she was flying up the top of the mountainside, approaching the crater. She would go over it, the death crater as it blew, be caught in the explosion of the death, and then…

There was some strange pixilation on the monitor and the form of a human, a tall man, began to appear like a shadow. It reached out a hand toward Ansel and he squealed, then snorted, as though he were choking.

'Yes!' Ansel cried out, spluttering. 'Yes! I took it! I skimmed! A little; then more! Then more and more!'

'How much?'

'One percent at first…' Ansel's voice was constrained, as though the words were being forced out of him. '…then five… I was going to stop at ten…'

'And?'

'The people who come through here will pay anything! Anything! They don't care! They just don't care! I could double the price of everything and they wouldn't care!'

'Double?'

Tamara laughed. She looked behind Ansel at the Bureau operative.

'Chambers, you're in change here now. Double the price. All stock.'

'Ma'am…'

Tamara pointed at Ansel. 'Take one percent of him.'

There was a flash, and Ansel screamed, crouching and grasping the side of his head. There was blood, but not a lot, and Cass assumed that Chambers had sliced off at least part of Ansel's right ear. It had happened so fast… Jesus. He was a stupid, greedy man, but he didn't deserve that! She jerked her neck back again and looked into Shylee's eyes once more, saw her sheer rage, saw her tense the gun, but still, Shylee shook her head, tightly.

Cass intuited; something else was going to happen, and they would move in the next moment of shock.

Shylee mouthed: 'On – three…'

'Three…' The rapidly appearing man said.

Tension shot through them both like an electric current.

'Five…' Tamara corrected. 'He said five next, did he not?'

'Oh yes… not three.'

Cass and Shylee kept their eyes locked.

Had he just… warned them?

'No!' Ansel screamed.

Chambers yanked up Ansel's wrist and without hesitation slashed the same Bowie knife again, cleanly severing all four of Ansel's fingers and the top part of his palm. Ansel

wailed in a high pitch, as Chambers grabbed his shoulder and kicked him on the back of his leg, so he fell hard on his knees, to a kneel.

'You can't do this!' Ansel protested, almost one long word. 'I'm an employee! I have rights!'

Then he sagged, and grasped at the disembodied row of fingers before him, reaching out with his good hand for them, but fumbling.

'Ten…' Tamara ordered curtly.

The knife came down again. Cass thought the move Chambers made was like some kind of Bushido; one foot forward, incredibly swift and forceful. Ansel's arm was severed above the elbow.

Ansel screamed in total shock. There was blood spurting everywhere, all over the floor in front of him. He screamed, loud and long for a few seconds, then stopped and made slow, panting, grunting sounds.

Fury burned in Shylee's eyes. She flinched, as though she might make a move.

'Stay where you are…' The new arrival was fully visible on the monitor now. He was a tall young man with light brown skin, almost beautifully handsome. Despite the cold he wore only a tight fitting black tee, with black slacks and business shoes.

Chambers flinched. Clearly, the next debt was one hundred percent.

'What?' Chambers demanded.

'Stay where you are. There is enough blood for you to clean. There will be people through here soon.' He turned back to Tamara. 'One hundred percent?'

Tamara stared thoughtfully down at Ansel, one arm folded across her breasts, her other elbow resting upon it, the fingers of that hand strumming her lips, as though Ansel was nothing but a piece of furniture she was asking him to shift.

'Yes…' Tamara opined, softly but definitely. 'The transaction is over.'

The man nodded and turned back to Ansel.

Cass watched on the monitor as he seemed to vanish again; but they could both feel his power, his… was it Wrath? Cass wasn't sure. It felt closer to the Fear.

But it wasn't that either…

There came a terrible stench as Ansel evacuated his bowels. Tamara laughed shortly, mockingly.

'Of course!'

Then they saw on the monitor as Ansel quivered, then seemed to explode. His clothes fell, limp, and the air around them looked to be filled with the liquefied remains of his body, then that turned to fire in the air, and in the proverbial puff of smoke, Ansel vanished. Only a few black flakes of soot floated down to their side of the counter as silence descended.

'When did you learn to do that…?' Tamara asked softly.

'Seagulls…' The man responded. 'They land on the balcony rail.'

Tamara kept staring at him, then she gave him an order.

'Go. You have your target for tonight.'

There was again a slight pixilation, and some brief blurring on the monitor.

He had rushed, Cass realized.

Then there was a finger held before her.

She looked back into Shylee's eyes.

The man had saved them, so they could kill Tamara.

So Shylee had thought.

But Cass knew; maybe, but there was another, more burning reason he had done it.

Owe me…

And there it was; and there was the second finger.

'Jump – her…' Shylee mouthed.

No stopping Shylee.

'Bang –' She pointed the gun out, then down. ' – bang.'

Cass got it.

Kill me…

No stopping anything now…

Owe me…

Cass leaned slowly back, enough to give her room.

Kill me, Cass, kill me…

Then Cass nodded once, sharply.

Shylee looked deep into her eyes. They smiled at each other.

Three.

Shylee was up, the gun out, extended over the counter and she fired. Cass scrambled behind her, was up and on the counter. She was there like a cat, like a predator feline, her hands down, back arched, feet tense, then as Shylee let off two more rounds, she launched at Tamara.

Tamara was stunned, Cass could see, but she was alert; energetic and fit. She leaped back as Cass launched at her, so instead of impacting the top of her body, Cass collided with her hips as she briefly sailed and descended, grasping Tamara's slender frame and crashing to the wood floor with her. Tamara came down cleanly on her back, the hair on the back of her head just brushing a heavy wood shelf behind her. Then Cass had her face on her belly, and was grasping at her as she squirmed.

The last thing she heard was;

'Out of the way Cass!'

…before a sideways black stiletto came at her face, stung her cheek, and then she was gone.

TWENTY-TWO: WATCHING

Blackness for a second, then total vision.

But; where was she?

She was looking down on the store.

Chambers lay flat on his back, arms and legs akimbo, dead eyes staring up at her. There were three bullets pancaked on his vest, with two more in the wall behind him, one each having passed through his cheek and forehead, sealing the deal. Shylee was on one knee, aiming down from the counter at Tamara, but Cass could see that her body had actually fallen hard, and oddly in her scramble to keep Tamara down, and appeared to have turned over when Tamara had… what had Tamara done to her? Her body was limp, and Tamara was using it… *herself*, as a shield, while her hand was writhing around the pocket of her black jacket, looking for a weapon.

Take it!

Shylee was hesitating; she was thinking, messing it up.

Take the shot Shylee!

But Shylee couldn't hear, wouldn't risk killing…

But – it suddenly struck Cass – was she alive, anyway?

Then Cass saw her own head.

Holy shit; there was a black stiletto stuck to the side of her fucking face….!

Tamara got off two shots from a tiny red pistol. They went nowhere near Shylee, but destroyed the security monitor in a shower of glass as the shells flew sideways on the floor. Shylee was startled though, and jumped back, off the counter. In the second she did that, Tamara slithered from under Cass's body and was on her feet. Cass could see her intent; to plant a shot right in her head, but Shylee was a millisecond too fast and Tamara saw. Tamara took the shot but was unbalanced as she simultaneously kicked off her other stiletto, and missed completely as she spun around a corner and into the store. Shylee blazed after her, like crazy, shot after shot through the tightly shelved store, blowing tins and jars and trays away in savage puffs of destruction. From above, Cass could see that Shylee was as reckless a shot as Tamara was a poor one, but Shylee was still missing Tamara. Then she changed her aim suddenly and almost hit her, spun the bitch around, the bullet passing so close to her right temple. Tamara dropped quickly and slithered further toward the back of the store, around and down another corner, deeper in. Shylee heard or sensed that she had dropped and stopped firing. Rising quickly, Tamara accidentally shouldered a tray of biscuits to the floor. It wasn't much noise but it was clear. Shylee glanced at Cass, almost bent down to touch the shoe on her face, seemed to sense there was nothing she could do and moved over her, defensively, in as protective direction as she could, and then with her back to the front window suddenly started blasting into the shelves again. Three more shots zinged back in response; the third sliced through the top shoulder top of Shylee's coat and she stumbled back, then a fourth went right over the top of her upturned face. A primal scream shrieked forth as Tamara rounded the nearest aisle and practically sprinted out at Shylee, then jumped onto her as she fell back hard.

Tamara brought her down heavily, but Cass heard them both cry out, then Tamara had her thumbs in Shylee's eyes. It was just a second; Shylee shot up a rocket-speed fist, drawn back over her gut and pumped up between them into the bottom of Tamara's jaw. There was a harsh click as Tamara's teeth slammed together, then blood poured suddenly from her mouth. Shylee's other hand clasped tightly on Tamara's throat, and squeezed as she slammed a second fist into Tamara's stomach. Tamara seemed to spasm, and scream, and threw herself backwards, out of Shylee's strangle and hard into a shelf, then crashed onto her bottom. From above, Cass saw something fly from her coat pocket as she hit the ground, spinning and flashing, and then clatter, but then she forgot, because Tamara was raising Shylee's gun. She'd gotten it, somehow, in the melee.

'Hyper fucking whore!'

Shylee stared back.

This was it, Cass knew. They were both dead. And Tamara would live.

No!

Tamara pulled the trigger.

Nothing happened. Just a dead click. She pulled it again and again. Click and click and click. She kept shooting, and clicking.

Shylee laughed.

'No!' Tamara screamed. 'No! You don't get to be that lucky!'

Shylee grinned. 'No luck…' She started to rise, leaning forward, toward Tamara. '…no bullets – *just brains!*'

Tamara's eyes flashed to the floorboards on her right. Shylee saw it too, amongst all the fallen foodstuffs; the tiny red pistol. But too late. Tamara had ducked and grasped and snatched it up before Shylee could get close. Then she spun about, still essentially sitting, and without getting too close, pointed the deadly little weapon right between Shylee's eyes.

'…so, you don't get to be that lucky. But maybe, I do…'

With all her focus, whatever she was now, however she existed, Cass quickly descended herself and, although she seemed somehow stuck to the ceiling, punched out.

'…eight rounds…' Tamara boasted. '…one left…'

She punched out and down at Tamara, with sheer mental force, at the top of her head. Tamara screamed and fired accidentally. Shylee spasmed and her hands went up in a hopeless defense, as she stupidly, pathetically, tried to dodge a bullet at close range, half jumping, half dropping backwards. Tamara's gun hand flinched as Cass's psychic bolt banged her skull. Cass was weak; she had only managed a force that was as though a baseball had dropped a few feet onto Tamara's head, but it was startling, and painful enough. Although the gun was still aimed, the event created a half second delay and made Tamara jolt, just an inch off.

Shylee's own blood splattered her face as the bullet passed through the palm of her left hand, sliced up the skin of her upper left arm, then shattered the window behind her.

'No!' Tamara screamed.

She threw the red gun away but snatched up Shylee's again, this time grasping it between the barrel and silencer. Shylee had fallen flat on her back once more, and was trying in panic and confusion to wipe the blood from her face with the very extremity that was pouring more blood into it, at the same time as she was attempting to fumble her way, with her other hand as support, to her feet.

Tamara came at her on hands and knees like a cave woman with a thigh bone. Shylee saw her through her bloodied vision at the last second, not quite on her feet, and rolled away. Tamara had been aiming for the back of her skull, but still delivered a savage cold-cock between her shoulder blades. Shylee cried out and dropped down a little, but pushed forward and was on her feet again, scrambling back toward the front of the store. Tamara staggered after her, grasping at her legs as she stumbled away, then standing, shaking.

As soon as she was stable on her feet, Shylee turned and went straight back at Tamara. The women collided as Shylee prevented the second cold-cock, her uninjured right hand slapping into Tamara's high gun-wielding hand, then clamping tightly under it, near the handle as the two women snarled, face to face. Tamara was only slightly taller, so the balance was essentially matched, with their other hands locked in a weird arm wrestle that seemed to be occurring in a completely different mental subset than the wrestle for the gun, drenched with the blood that was still flowing from the gaping bullet hole in Shylee's palm.

'How are you doing that?' Tamara snarled. 'How are you doing that you fucking hyper freak! I put a hole through you! You can't be doing that!'

Shylee clenched her jaw, her blazing eyes returning the heat of sheer loathing.

'Unholy freak!' Tamara shrieked, exasperated.

Shylee growled. 'Psycho scrag!'

Tamara spat a huge gob of blood, trying to get Shylee's eyes, but instead covered her right cheek, then her forehead, as Shylee flinched twice, trying to ready herself for a head butt. Then Tamara opened her wide mouth, her own cheeks and jaw still covered in the blood from where she had bitten her tongue, then chomped forward with her massive, glistening white teeth. She made one savage snatch for Shylee's face, at first trying to connect anywhere, then went again, precisely for her nose. Shylee lurched her neck and face back, then to the side, again and again, five or six times, becoming something close to disorientated. Tamara sneered into her then, eyes insane with hatred, believing she was getting there, was wearing her opponent down, was about to take a chunk of cheek, or nostril, even chin. Then Shylee grinned. She grinned as though she had woken from a dream.

'There were no bullets...' Shylee sniggered. '...never have been any fucking bullets... never will be any fucking bullets...'

Shylee twisted her grip where the two women were tightly grasping the gun barrel, lurched one foot forward and head-butted Tamara as she snapped forward for another go at her nose. Shylee's forehead connected savagely, as Tamara's jaw slashed out. There was a thud and a crunch. There was more blood, everywhere, all over their faces and down their necks, but Shylee was holding the inverted gun tight in her palm, with her finger on the trigger. Tamara twisted it away as Shylee fired. The shot went off, away from them, into the shop. She fired again, and again, each time with Tamara flinching in shock and confusion.

'No! No! It's empty! No!'

Still looking down, Cass could see now; there was no recoil, no smoke, *no shell expulsion*. But there were fumes, rising now, like a barbeque, from where their *other* hands were clasped. Tamara suddenly kicked up and kneed Shylee between her legs, connecting squarely with flat of her genitals. Shylee cried out in pain, flinched back and dropped the gun, and it clattered on the floor behind her. Both of them stumbled backwards. Tamara went toward the shattered window, staring back with horror at Shylee, who was reversing toward the door.

Tamara looked at her right hand. The palm and the back of her hand, where Shylee's fingers had left an imprint, were red-raw. Burned. Surprised, Shylee looked down at her own hand. The ruined pink and red flesh had sealed over with some kind of new, clear skin. Beneath her new skin, within her palm, there was now some kind of solid, fleshy energy; in the centre of what had been the bullet hole was a glowing inner core of silver-blue, like a light shining on an ocean surface, seen from underwater. Her muscles and tendons now seemed to be made of some kind of plasma, that was allowing her control of her fingers, each of which, along with what she could see of her wrist under the coat sleeve, were glowing shades of steel and shining metallic blue beneath her normal skin.

The wound was sealed. All the blood that had covered the ruined hand was caking and steaming away, and the flow from the wound had stopped. Everything had stopped now. Tamara just stood and stared, panting, and wide eyed.

'You have to be *stopped*!'

Bloody spittle sprayed out before her.

'No...' Shylee uttered.

'Killed!'

Shylee could feel a sting on her forehead; a bite. But it looked to her, through the wild, blood-stained face, that there was something askew with Tamara's huge front teeth.

'No...'

'Yes!'

'No, Tamara...'

Tamara seemed stunned at the use of her name.

'We have to be *started*. Brought to life!'

Still floating above, Cass saw the silver-blue glow in Shylee's palm brighten, becoming almost luminescent. She thought of her own ability to draw warmth... but this was something else. This was not subtle; this was the very strength, finally made manifest, that could melt an office safe at five paces. That could spit the idea of bullets, and make them real, through a real gun. One could not craft with this; this was the Wrath as sheer force.

Shylee raised the silver-blue fire of her palm to Tamara.

Then, like a jolt, they both turned to look at the window.

Disembodied, maybe even dead, Cass took an extra second to comprehend; she couldn't feel it, didn't understand what had stopped Shylee blasting this disgraceful excuse for a human being out of existence right then and there.

Then she understood.

The bullet had shattered the window. It had alerted something, drawn something to them. Shylee swung the silver-blue glow away from Tamara, toward the window, toward what was coming.

'You must be killed! They know! They know you must be killed!'

Something brown-black and sharply barbed, a long mandible of some kind, shot into the store through the window. It reared up at Shylee first, as though to strike, but was startled by her, the presence of the silver-blue light, and started to quiver. Clearly, it was not afraid, but it was angry, almost offended.

Cass could see it now, feel it; Shylee was toxic to it.

'Yes!' Tamara cried out. 'Kill her! Kill the freak!'

The mandible turned to Tamara and flexed, reared up, then slashed down and coiled tightly, quickly, around her waist.

'No! Not me!'

Shylee staggered backwards again, her palm flaring light; a brighter, chrome blue now, right throughout the front of the store, bursting from whatever source was deep within her.

The mandible held Tamara up, then lifted and swung her at Shylee as though she were a weapon, like an enormous dagger. Tamara cackled and clawed at Shylee in midair, slashed at her with her long red nails, grasping to get her. But Shylee just grinned and extended her glowing left hand.

'Take me Tamara!'

The tendril lurched Tamara forward again, almost as though it expected her to do something, to act on its behalf. But all Tamara could do was claw, and screech, and almost greedily snatch at Shylee. Tamara's right hand and upper arm slammed into, and connected tightly with Shylee's upper left arm, almost ripping the tough material of Shylee's coat, and the two grasped each other like a double clamp. Then Shylee twisted, so that the grip on Tamara's black jacket tightened, and the arm of the jacket started to smolder. The barbed mandible retracted something about itself to make it appear more like a tentacle, and gripped Tamara tighter. She opened her mouth and screamed as the tentacle flowed further into the store and around her, curling and coiling in through the window, rapidly wrapping around her six, seven, eight times. Other mandibles appeared and clasped around the edge of the shattered window, shaking the stone wall as though the whole store front would come away. Dust fell from the ceiling and the floorboards groaned. This monster, this Fear monster *thing*, was trying to pull Shylee back, using Tamara's grip. But Shylee's palm, hard down on Tamara's forearm, just seemed to flare brighter, somehow rooting her to the spot, giving her tremendous purchase. Cass heard a sharp, but low horn blow in the distance, and realized it was no distant call but a kind of warbling groan of unpleasantness from The Fear, now fully concerned at the proximity of this new and, apparently, surprisingly powerful Wrath agent. Was Shylee doing this on purpose? Was she commanding the blue-chome energy? The monster growled again; then Cass realized something else.

Although The Fear didn't like this, its expression remained that of mere discomfort, like getting too close to a snake, and pulling back. Then Cass realized something that was the most frightening of all; The Fear… it was not afraid of them. Not at all. They were just a thing to it, a potentially toxic annoyance, just as much as it was a deadly *thing* to them.

The Fear – did not fear.

Tamara's whole body shook, and she screamed as her jacket ripped under Shylee's heat, and the two lurched simultaneously backwards. But neither wanted to let go and they grasped each other's hands as they lost balance, their hands snatching and re-locking into each other's wrists. A blast of Arctic wind shot through the window behind Tamara, and blew over the closest shelves behind them, shattering another window and revealing more sheer black outside, spraying the back of Shylee's coat and hair with glass fragments.

'Faaark!' Shylee screamed. 'Fucking – ee – nuff!'

Tamara's hand, still gripping Shylee's wrist, was fuming now. Her flesh was burning.

'It wants me!' Tamara screamed triumphantly. 'It wants me!'

Shylee kept her grip.

'It wants me – to take you with me!'

'Burn in Hell, Tamara!'

'I wants me to kill you all!'

'Burn – alone!'

There were maybe a dozen mandibles around the window, but as the back of Shylee's translucent palm started to shine even more, with the blue-chrome taking on a stark, classically silver-chrome brightness, the mandibles started to shake, and tremble with effort in some bizarre, final, massive tug to pull Shylee back out. The front of the store would not hold; not with the force they were exerting, but Shylee remained rooted, welded, to the spot.

Cass saw the vulnerability emerging clearly, and tried again to communicate:

Shy it can't touch you! It can't touch you directly! Use that! Use – that!

But Shylee didn't hear; couldn't, she was too focused.

The massive tentacle changed its form again and flattened now, spreading allover Tamara like a sheath, right up under her outstretched arms, then down to her thighs, leaving her legs free. Her shoeless, black-stockinged feet wriggled and kicked behind her, as though she were somehow swimming, but without rhythm, flailing mindlessly in the air. Then the oily, dark sheath vibrated, and rippled forward. It flowed over Tamara's jacket shoulder and right up her left arm to her skin, to the back of her hand, then burst forth in multiple pointed barbs as it touched her flesh. The barbs sprung up, down her fingers, making a weird porcupine hub from her hand and long brown, spiked talons of her nails.

Shylee could see it coming. She raised her free fist, but with their right and left hands gripped in what was increasingly becoming a death lock, they were too far from each other now to trade blows.

The Fear stopped pulling, and pushed. Shylee seemed to panic; the silver-chrome flared brightly as they released each other simultaneously. Tamara screamed and slashed as the Fear thrust her forward again, as Shylee wrenched her head back, lurching away, staggering backwards.

Above, Cass saw blood spray from Shylee's neck, then the whole room flared bright silver-white, and her vision was gone.

This time the noise from the Fear monster was, absolutely, an expression of pain.

The thing dropped Tamara and she fell with a thud, face down on the floorboards as the sheath retreated, and the mandibles around the window retracted. The whole front of the store groaned, right across, as Shylee slammed against the wall between the two broken windows, then collapsed to a sit, propped helplessly in the spread of broken glass. Tamara lay face down, just two meters away, groaning.

Get up! Kill her! Make my death mean something!

Cass watched as Tamara looked up at Shylee. She tried to roll over, to get up. But she could hardly move. Then Cass realized: Shylee was hurt. They were both hurt. Neither could move.

It had worked; they were all going to die!

Here, now!

All three on the wooden floor boards of the most expensive store in the world!

Shylee raised her hand to her neck. Tamara's swiping talons had made contact. There were three long cuts where Shylee's flesh had been sliced open horizontally along the side. More blood. A lot of blood. Shylee pressed her hand against it, then removed it and stared at it. The slices were to her left side, the same as her silver palm. She stared at the glow, lesser now, but dull, light blue, beneath her wet, crimson hand.

Tamara arced her left arm up, over the floor boards, through the shattered glass and the ruins of her elite quality stock, and hooked it under herself so she could prop herself up to properly meet Shylee's gaze.

'You are… a very… lucky…'

Shylee spat at her, almost all blood, but it landed in a gob on the floor between them.

'…*creature*!' Tamara spat back. 'But…' She gasped. '…I know my anatomy.'

'Sick – *torturer*!'

'If I had hit anything major, you would have bled out by now…' Tamara suddenly stopped and ran what looked like a freakishly long tongue over her front teeth.

'What!?' She asked herself.

She did it again.

'No!'

Shylee chuckled as she saw through the blood.

Tamara's right front tooth was missing.

'No!'

Shylee's hand was fumbling for something on the ground beside her.

'No!' Tamara shrieked. 'No! No! No!'

Tamara was starting to move again. She brought her right hand up now, to feel properly. But that was even more horrific. Her whole right arm was a shriveled appendage, like burned bark; a weird, horrific skeleton of what had once been something slender, and graceful. She cried out, a pure, guttural expression of shock and revulsion, and as she did, the talons returned, slashing out of her left fingers along with the fist of porcupine quills. She kept screaming, again and again, as though the bursts of continued revulsion had become her very panicked breath, until finally she stopped and stared at Shylee, sneering.

'Give me back my tooth!'

Shylee laughed, once, low and wry.

'How?'

Tamara sneered even wider.

'Reach up…' Tamara grunted angrily. '…and pluck it out!'

'Whuh…?' Then, Shylee figured it out, even as Tamara told her.

'It's in your *fucking forehead*!'

Shylee closed her eyes and laughed.

'Pluck it! The fuck! Out!'

'…nah…' Shylee opened her eyes again. Cass saw then what she'd been fumbling for, on the ground beside her, as Shylee swung her silver gun over her lap and rested it there, easily aiming it between Tamara's eyes. '…that cute little gap gives me something to aim for…'

Then the front wall of the store collapsed.

It went backwards, into the asphalt of the car park out front, into the blackness. The old stones had been well-crafted, and the wall would have stood forever; but for a prime supernatural force, pulling at it for leverage. The mortar had cracked just above the base, so the whole wall went almost as one, effectively leaving a small jagged fence, the first layer of stonework, along the store front. Shylee barely moved as it came down behind her, apart from reflexively raising her hands. Tamara sprang to her knees, also reflex, putting weight on both her hands. Then she lurched backward, on her knees, and held both hands up before her, in a millisecond processing, realizing, amazed; that they both still functioned.

Part of the gutter had fallen with the top of the wall, but now the center of the roof and celling were badly supported, and made cracking, sliding noises as though they were about to give way. Tamara was faster and jumped out, into the black behind the window, and vanished as though she'd fallen into a vat of motor oil. Shylee wrenched herself into action and crawled quickly, further into the store, then rolled to her side as a plank of old wood from the gutter fell right where she's been. Then, glancing up, she threw herself sideways again as another plank, this one jutting with old nails and wood shards, swung down and fell, crashing onto the floorboards, again, right where she'd been.

Shylee waited on the floor a second, then pushed herself up, turned and collapsed forward again, landing on her chest and right shoulder, right onto the jagged stone wall, arms out, gun protruding. Blood was still dribbling from her neck wounds, onto her coat shoulder now, as she used the wrecked stone to steady her aim. The streetlights were all out; there was only a dim light from behind her, from within the store, along with the moonlight, and the distant glow of the freeway. But Tamara was still there, in plain sight, the ridiculously long curls of her fake blonde hair glowing in the night. She was only half way across the car park, limping hard as she staggered through the dark, trying to get to a huge black four-wheel drive, parked out by the road. Shylee blinked hard to keep focus. She'd never tried this hard to make a shot, not at this distance, not ever. Tamara was still three or four paces away from the car when she turned and something flashed in her eyes. Something stark, and evil; the murderer, casting a backward glance, looking to see if they had escaped their pursuer.

Shylee fired. Tamara's head whipped back and she fell, flat on her back. Shylee paused; Tamara rolled over, squirming, in pain. Then she started to rise again. Shylee fired again, and again, two shots in her flank. Tamara's whole body flinched with each shot, but then her torso twisted, and she kept rolling, kept moving, a wounded prey that would not go down. She was on her hands and knees again now, crawling for the car. Shylee shot again, and again. She saw Tamara flinch, again and again, but still she kept going. Then she was on her feet, moving, limping.

Cass was still watching. She was confounded; it was as though each time Shylee hit Tamara, it … somehow gave her more strength? Then Cass realized, as Shylee realized; Shylee didn't possess the strength any more. Each shot was weaker. She was basically shooting with the power of a paint gun.

Shylee humped herself higher against the jagged stone, pushed hard with her legs, against her feet, weak enough so that she had to order her body to do this, think it through, each physical move a successive, separate demand of her body. She used the wall to force herself to rise, up to her knees, then her feet. She heard a thump, and looked up. Tamara was leaning heavily against the car door. Shylee took aim and fired again. Two shots hit the car beside her, thunk, thunk. They made Tamara jump, and she looked over and saw that Shylee was standing, but she was panicking about something else now, slapping her black shirt, rifling through the side and inside pockets of her one-armed black jacket. She couldn't find her keys.

The idea of this sparked Shylee and she half-fell, half-rolled over the wall. Her Docs scraped down on the other side, onto the concrete path between the broken stone wall and the asphalt. Her ankles were wobbly; but she found purchase, and pushed forward, and was, remarkably, standing again on the other side, surrounded by massive white-brown stones. There seemed to be no stopping her momentum however, and as she staggered forward, through the wreckage, she came to realize that if she stopped, if she tripped and fell, she would fall and die. But she moved with the hapless good fortune of a cheerful drunk as she extended the gun again, as Tamara turned and saw, with total horror, that she was still coming. Shylee fired.

She was closer now, but no stronger. The shot hit Tamara in the shoulder, with a force no more than a push. She kept shooting as she closed the gap, as Tamara realized she would not escape her; not by car. She moved sideways, sliding along the side of the car, taking shot after shot that were more like hard punches now, as Shylee kept firing as she walked, gaining momentum. She could hear the shots hitting Tamara, hitting the side of the car, but her aim, her eyesight, was terrible. Tamara almost fell as she reached the back of the car, as Shylee, half way to her now, but still stumble-walking, found her aim and shot Tamara three times in the back, a tight pattern between her shoulder blades, in quick succession.

Tamara cried out at the last one, and Shylee increased her pace, but stumbled as she did. Tamara turned at the back of the car and saw Shylee almost fall, then correct herself, but stop. Then she was up again, aiming directly at her.

Tamara snarled.

Her spiked fist reappeared, the quills slashed out.

Shylee paused, aiming her shaking gun.

She fired.

It was a lousy shot, but it hit Tamara somewhere above her right breast. Blood puffed out from the bright rose blouse. Tamara stumbled backwards and screamed with rage as she realized that any closer, and Shylee's bullets would be as real as it got. She turned and ran toward the freeway.

Shylee closed the gap, keeping the gun before her. But she stopped when she reached the edge of the car. She could see Tamara. She was still running. In her disembodied afterlife form, Cass could see it too; she had seen it all, seemingly tethered to Shylee somehow. Tamara was running back, not under the freeway, but back onto it. She was still limping, but the limp seemed not to slow her now. In her odd, jerking run she was making decent speed.

Shylee wouldn't catch her.

She turned and made best speed back to the store.

Four-Two was a startling sight when she turned to see it; all the lights were out at the front, but the store was still lit from the back, perhaps a different power source. Somebody would come soon; there would be signals, security alerts, even out here, halfway between here and there, there would be basic services.

The front door and frame were, almost amusingly, still standing, alone, like a monument. Rather than strain herself again over the rock wall, she opened the door and went through, then the whole thing collapsed backwards behind her.

Cass followed, hovering above. She saw Shylee stare down at her body for one second, with the stiletto shoe sticking out from the side of her head, the killer heel buried somewhere in her skull.

'Cass!'

Shylee barked her name, as though she were angry with her, then she was on her knees, at her side. Gingerly, with trembling fingers, she touched the shoe. Hovering above, Cass felt a sudden and intense pain in her cheek, and lost her disembodied vision just for a second. Then Shylee grabbed the shoe and pulled, and Cass was immediately pulled back to her body by an intense sting, and searing pain all down the right side of her face as Shylee pulled the long, thin heel of the shoe out of her cheek. Cass opened her eyes and cried out.

'Ahhh-hahhh!'

But it was done. The taste of blood and, she supposed, stiletto heel, was already all through her mouth.

Shylee stared down with a look of highly emotional relief, and some telempathy crept through. In response, Cass belted out one, then a second weep, then Shylee allowed herself a burst of laugh-crying. Then a sudden sound outside, like a crowbar dropping on the road, shut them down again, and made them remember where they were.

'Black Casadei pumps…' Shylee held it up to her, the heel still bloodied. 'Kicked you in the face so hard the stiletto punctured your cheek.'

Cass propped herself up to her elbows. She guffawed, taking it from Shylee and examining it. The end of the stupidly thin heel was hardly a needle; it was maybe a centimeter diameter. Shylee could read her process like a book.

'It'll scar.'

Cass sighed. 'Well, they were named after daggers, after all…'

'Really?'

'Sure I read that somewhere…'

Shylee stared at her. Cass stared back. Shylee's face was covered in blood, her hair drenched with it. Both her eyes were bloodshot and she looked awfully, horribly gaunt.

'Let it scar, Shy. I saw everything…'

'What?'

'I was on the ceiling; out of body… I couldn't get back… I'm sorry…'

Shylee looked around at the destruction.

'Couldn't or didn't want to, huh?'

Cass touched her punctured cheek and immediately snatched it back, her fingertips covered in blood. 'Didn't really…' She winced. '…think about it, to be honest. I was just up there… watching…'

'Can you stand?'

'Can you?'

After a few seconds experimentation, they both realized they could, and helped each other to their feet.

'Okay…' Shylee grunted, one arm leaning on a shelf, the arm of her silver-blue hand wrapped around her chest. 'We need to get the bags…'

'The bags? Shy, we need to…' Cass winced. '… I don't know…'

'Get everything. We need everything. She came in a car…'

'We still can't go out there!'

'I thought you were watching? I just did go out there.'

Cass stared at her.

'Shy, why aren't we dead?'

Shylee stared back.

Cass growled. 'I was okay! I was okay with going out like that! Killing Tamara Chant!'

Shylee stared at her through narrow crimson eyes. 'We don't always get what we want!' She snapped. 'Pull yourself the fuck together! Wake up! There's some kind of fuck-off earth power shit helping us along. The Wrath…' Shylee sneered, fed up. '…whatever the fuck it's called. We need to get out of here. This is big, Cass, it's fucking global, it's fucking cosmic… I mean, *did you see that fucking thing?*'

'Only…'

'That fucking thing is real, Cass! And it's big, and it *fucking hates us*, like we *fucking hate sickness and disease.* It grabbed Tamara, it helped her, and it saved her – from me!'

Cass didn't know what to say.

'We need to kill it, Cass, we need to go out there, and *fucking kill it*! Now collect your shit and move!' Shylee shuffled swiftly past her, around to the back of the service counter, and quickly dumped all four bags on the counter. 'Come on! Get more! Get everything you can carry! Take it to the car!'

Cass could have argued. She could feel her tired inner voice start to formulate reasons against it, why it was never going to work. Instead she found another carry bag, larger than the one she already had, and started stuffing it with random foodstuffs from the closest shelves, and all the painkillers and bandages she could find. She lost track of what she was doing, then heard Shylee moving around the back of the store, doing the same, clinking bottles. Cass felt herself wondering what she was doing. What bottles…? Then she stopped, and didn't think some more. She kept going.

'All we can carry!' Shylee demanded from somewhere.

Cass was dizzy now. She couldn't pick up more stuff. She cast a weary, wary glance over her shoulder. It was still black outside. Jet, flat, black. So she kept stuffing the bag she had with… jars, boxes… cotton balls; she didn't know what else.

'Okay…' Shylee had several of the larger bags tied together near the front door. Cass brought hers and placed them there too, then her original bags from the counter. When she'd done that, she looked at the bags she'd filled and couldn't remember doing it. But her hands had left blood trails everywhere, as had Shylee's… so; she must have done it.

They could hear sirens in the distance, on the freeway.

'Shit…'

There were at least eight bags now; their original four, and four of the larger ones. But Cass was most surprised to see that Shylee had made several Molotov Cocktails from vodka bottles, and that they were now lining the counter top where the bags had been.

'I've flooded this place with grog…' Shylee spat as she looked around the counter. 'Where are the fucking cigarettes?'

'Shy…? Are you sure you want – ?'

'I'm not relapsing! I want the lighters!'

Despite her weakness, Cass could easily spy the tiny pillars of bright primary colors behind them, behind the counter. 'There, right behind you…'

Shylee saw the Bics, hiding in plain sight, and went behind the counter. She began stuffing handfuls of three or four at a time into her jean pockets from the box, snatched twelve, fifteen lighters, then hatch flew open. Shylee fell backwards, crashing into the shelves at the side of the counter, smashing back into a freezer cabinet, cracking and shattering the glass top.

Giant black scuttling bugs flew out of the hatch, over the counter and up the walls in all directions, as though they couldn't get away from Shylee fast enough. Cass rushed up to her as two of the horrendous things came across the floor and immediately parted, almost faster than her mind could process, like giant roaches. Shylee righted herself as the glass cracked further beneath her. Cass grabbed her hand as she reached out, and pulled her up. She saw stars at the effort and was amazed that Shylee was still even conscious.

'Are you okay?' Shylee asked.

'Me?' Cass scoffed. 'Are you?' Suddenly she spied something. 'That's…'

'What?' Shylee looked behind her to the freezer. 'What is it?'

Cass walked up slowly and removed some of the larger glass shards.

'That's the brand, he was looking for…' Cass leaned in and lifted a tub gently. She stared at it like a priceless trophy. 'That's his stupid brand…' She turned and walked

dreamily past Shylee, went to one of the bags on the counter and made the ice cream fit. When she turned back to Shylee, she saw a face of grave concern.

'Cass, turn around again…'

'What?'

'Do it!'

Cass obeyed. Since she'd leaned into the broken freezer, she was feeling quite light headed. She heard Shylee suppress a gasp. She wished she could turn around and see the back of her own head. If she were dead again, that would be easy…

'What, Shy?'

'When you fell, Cass. When she kicked you and you fell back. You must have hit the floor really hard. You split your head open. There's blood all down your back.'

'Split?'

The sirens were getting louder.

'How bad is it?'

'I can see… white.'

'What? Brain?'

'No! Bone, Cass. I can see your skull; just a bit through the… it doesn't look cracked, but you need stitches. We both… we both need… wait.'

Shylee went to the Molotovs and pulled out the drenched cloth she'd stuffed into one of the vodka bottles. Cass could see the concern in her eyes, but now everything seemed even more distant.

'Turn around again…'

'Shy, are you *sure*?'

Shylee took her by the shoulders and forced her to turn about; Cass didn't put up any resistance. She felt incapable. She heard a splash and felt cold on her neck, and then an immediate, shockingly terrible sting, like her whole head and shoulders had been drenched with hydrochloric acid. She thought she screamed, but she might have blacked out for a second. Suddenly she was aware, she could feel, the shape of the awful slit, its location and size. She cried out, tried to touch it, but Shylee snatched her hands from behind her, and in the process dumped another gush of vodka on it. Cass screamed again and threw her hands up to her ears, trembling. Shylee splashed her a third time, then threw the vodka bottle hard, way into the store, where it smashed somewhere out of sight.

'You got bandages, right? I saw you…'

'I…'

'You got the whole first aid aisle. You don't remember?'

'Jesus!' Cass turned back, her eyes stinging, the pain leveling. 'Am I..?'

Shylee turned from her and grabbed four bags from the counter, two in each hand, then went for the gap where the front door and frame had been. The collapsed rocks weren't as bad; there was still an open path.

'Come on, the car's right there; we need to get some distance, then triage…'

She was as grim she'd ever sounded, then she was gone, out across the car park.

'Shy!' Cass screamed.

She'd gone mad. She'd gone fucking well stark raving mad. Cass could barely comprehend this now; what was Shylee doing? What had happened? What the hell had occurred? Stabbed in the cheek, floating on the ceiling, back here, and a lethal gash…?

The pain… it seemed to have focused her. Brought the rest of her back off the ceiling. But she still didn't feel at all… herself. She saw Shylee drop the gear by the front car tire, roughly examine the lock on the door, then turn back.

'She dropped her keys!' Shylee cried out. 'Are they there!? Where the shattered window was!'

Cass had to force herself to think back, to remember. There was stuff all over the floor. It all looked fuzzy, all the same, all blended in. How could she be expected…?

Then Shylee was back, stumbling over the remains of the wall.

'Cass, the car's right there, but so is that fucking thing. It's back, across the street, under the freeway, where we came in. Like it thinks we'll go back that way. It must be watching to see what we do. Get the rest of the bags. Now it's seen we're leaving, it will try something.'

Shylee stomped over and grabbed one of the Molotovs from the counter.

'I…' Cass muttered. 'The sirens are getting closer…'

'Still minutes, Cass! We still have – quick Cass! I mean it! Get the rest of the bags, get to the car! Don't look under the freeway; the fucking thing is right there! I'll find the keys!'

Cass could suddenly visualize the creature. 'I can't! I can't go out there!'

'Cass…' Shylee stalked up to her, Molotov in hand. 'There's no way either of us can rush right now, right?'

'Rush…?"

'Cass, for fuck's sake, you're concussed! You're in and out! We need to get you…' Shylee's face twisted. Cass didn't understand. She was getting even more upset. 'Cass…I will stand between you, and it. It doesn't know what we are, it doesn't know what I can do. I don't know what I am, or what I can do, or if I can even…' She sighed. '…if I can even do that again.'

'Do… what?'

'Cass! Look, maybe it kills us, but maybe not. Maybe this isn't the end, but maybe, *maybe* this is just the start!'

'The *start?*'

Cass was appalled. Somewhere inside, she knew, and was angry about it; that she'd been ready to die; she'd *made peace.*

'We have to, Cass. We *have to* take the risk. Tamara knows us now. That's a Bureau car, it's not tracked, there's no speed limit; if we can get out fast enough the satellites won't know where we are! Eat on the way, dump it fast, and *rush*. But we have to find those fucking keys!'

Cass was coming back again now. She thought she might understand.

'She ran…' Cass nodded. 'I remember seeing…'

'Cass, we don't have time…'

'She'll call, won't she? She's elite; she will call and they will come. She'll get a satellite…'

'Her phone…' Shylee uttered. 'Fuck… her *fucking Bureau phone*…'

'No…' Cass could feel something. A memory.

'Hyper… fucking…' Cass uttered. '…whore?'

'What?'

'She said…'

'She said that; when she had my gun, and she fell on her arse, and thought she could use my gun to shoot me…' Shylee turned. '…over there…'

Cass didn't think. But she spoke. 'Look down the aisle.'

Then she grabbed the rest of the bags and went outside.

It was cold, and it was dark. So dark, weirdly, scarily, artificially yet organically dark, supernaturally yet unnaturally dark… that it almost wasn't real, despite being… she didn't want to try, but it looked… almost tangible, like… oily, bilious smog. Like black, gaseous sewage. Through this terrible blackness she could see the car, where it had always been, but now it was shrouded by the black fog. It was so dense, on the ground between it and her. She could see the street back there too, though. And the three-way intersection… but there was a translucent, vaporous liquid, inches deep, everywhere, right in front of her, around the white stones, past the car and all the way up to the grass, and the…

Again, she didn't think, she moved.

The black liquid rippled out with her footsteps, like walking through a giant puddle of water. And she could see, even though she tried not to look, the thing. Under the freeway; way back there, in the abyss. It was like a massive tree. But it was breathing, like a sick animal, like it had emphysema. The tendrils, the mandibles, the tentacles, extended all over it, seemingly resting, like exposed roots, like dead branches, but in reality tense and ready. Eager and hungry.

It was no tree, she thought as she put the bags on the bonnet, and lifted the others out of the horrid liquid.

But it was pretending to be one.

Old, diseased; nobody would ever go near it.

If they did, it would consume them, and spit out their fillings.

Cass looked back, away from the ugly monster tree.

Shylee was standing outside the store again, where the doorway had been, another two bags of stuff at her feet, a halo around her from the light at the back of the store. She was holding the Molotov, clicking the lighter, but she couldn't get it to spark.

'Come down…!' Cass called. 'You can walk through it!'

'Through what?!' Shylee demanded.

'The oil! On the ground…! It's just –'

'The what?!' Shylee snapped. 'Cass, there's nothing there!' She looked at the Molotov, frustrated, unable to get it to light. Then she grabbed it with her strange hand, and the cloth exploded into flame.

'Shit!'

Shylee panicked and threw it in.

There was an enormous *whoomph*, and the entire inside of the store caught fire.

'Jesus!'

Shylee staggered back through the giant stones, across the carpark. Cass watched Shylee as she arrived backwards, unable to take her eyes from the fire, then heard a weird tweeting from the car.

'They were there, right where you said they'd be…' She held up the car keys. 'And this…' She dug around in her coat pocket. 'This too!'

Shylee pulled out Tamara's phone.

Cass didn't like it. 'If we have that… can't they …*find us?*'

'Yeah, but, that means if anyone's watching, they think she's here. And it also means, she can't call for help. It'll take her ten minutes easy to run back to the freeway, and then she's got to hail down some elite speeding to the beach…'

Shylee opened the driver's door of Tamara's car and looked inside.

'My boyfriend had one of these, back in the day…' Cass watched from the passenger window as Shylee manipulated the dashboard computer. '…can't have changed too much in…' The engine started. 'Good…' Shylee grunted, then added in a strange mutter. 'Slight change of plan…' She closed the door, leaving the window open.

'Home!'

As the car began to move slowly away, she threw the phone in, then the car accelerated and drove out of the car park and away, down the road, back to the freeway.

'But…' Cass gaped, watching their escape plan drive independently out of sight. '…how do we…?'

'That psycho had a phone and keys too. And knives and guns and weapons.' Shylee kicked one of the extra bags. All Cass saw was vodka. But there was something else, underneath. 'I left his phone on him. Can you carry…?' Shylee looked at her. She froze. 'Cass, you're…'

'Huh?'

'Nothing…' Shylee winced. 'Your pupils… they're…'

'They're dilated, aren't they?'

'They're huge…'

'I can see something else. Some other layer; of darkness. Cass, it's not going to let us go.'

'I know…' Shylee glanced over, under the freeway. 'One *thing* at a time…'

The sirens were very close now, and they'd been joined by fire trucks.

'Hope this works…' Shylee uttered, pulling out another set of keys. She clicked them. They heard the identification signal from somewhere nearby, but didn't see the regular flashing lights. Shylee clicked again and they turned the other way. The *blonk-blonk* sound this time was accompanied by a muted flash of headlights, through some trees maybe. It was hard to tell now, with the darkness and the firelight playing tricks. It looked as though the psycho had parked around the corner, somewhere up the other road; the road that led to whatever town had originally spawned Four-Two.

'Up there...' Shylee uttered. 'Sure... he came through the back. Came through the forest between that road and the store...'

There was another *whoomph* from the store. Something exploded, briefly, upward in a plume, then something crashed and exploded out. It didn't reach them, but they flinched and drew back. Bits of debris fell a meter of so in front of them, and the lights of Four-Two went out for good.

Cass could barely see now. Everything was darkness. Black all around. But it was also glistening with the fire, and now everything was a fight between the black, and the fire, its vicious light spreading a copper chrome over the black, oily layer of drenched darkness that seemed to cover everything around them now. She liked the copper. The copper was hers, like the silver was Shylee's.

The cold was coming in strong, down from the freeway, across the grass, from under the pillars. Strangely though, her feet felt hot; almost fizzy, nearly burning, like asphalt and bare feet on a high summer day, like she would have to move them or...

Cass jolted as more shots were fired. Shylee's hand was stretched out; three, four shots, then something smashed in the distance.

'Fucking camera... by the time anyone checks we'll be gone anyway. Come on, we need to get to that car.' Cass saw Shylee look into her eyes. She was silver. Copper all around her. 'Cass, I don't want to leave you here, but if I can be quick, bring it around...?'

Cass could feel something behind her coming down the bank, under, through and above the oily surface. Down from the thing, from the sick and demented old mockery of a tree, the thing's tendrils were running like stream of salmon.

'Shy…'

'I see it… don't turn around Cass…'

'I…'

'We need to run, Cass…'

'We can't!'

'Cass, we *have to*…!'

Cass couldn't look, but couldn't stop feeling it. She just kept staring at the fire. She heard Shylee shuffle; her coat, the bags.

'Cass, I… need to remember where we were going. I can't remember. I can't remember where we were… I can't remember…'

'We can't outrun it…'

The evil fish swarm was at the road now, coming over it…

'If… if we give it something…' Cass heard herself suggest.

'No! No, Cass, don't let go of the food… don't let go of the food!'

Cass was shaking all over. She was terrified, but she was…

'It's what it wants, Shy. Without the food, we die. It's what it wants.' It got colder, suddenly. Much colder, and there was more wind. 'Shy, *don't put the bags down*. Shy, can you feel it?'

'Yes. It hates us. It wants to kill us.'

'No, Shy, it's different. It doesn't want to kill us. Can you feel it, Shy? It wants us to *kill ourselves*. To put the food down, and run from it, and to have nothing, nothing to eat, and to die. It knows; this is the start. But it doesn't want the start, it wants the end. Can you feel it? It's telling us; it's saying it will leave us alone, and go away, if we just leave the food…'

The swarm was over the road and into the car park now.

'I'm…' Shylee's voice was high suddenly, frightened like a child, trying to tell herself that the shadows, the ones moving at the end of the bed, weren't real. But they were; they were totally real. Realer than real. More real that her memories of childhood, before the darkness, when nothing had turned out to be real other than people, just mean or horrible people. Not like this; this was a monster, a real monster, lurking, lumbering slowly toward them, sending a tide forward as it moved and shifted and began to approach, always coming, right there, right out of the darkness.

'…trying to remember. Where we go… Cass, I got us here but… but I'm out, I'm out now… I can't, I just can't…'

'I need to give it something, Shy. I need to give it something of yours… is that okay?'

Cass was terribly dizzy now.

'Something of mine…?'

'It is the darkness, Shy. It isn't something within the darkness. It's part of it. *It is the darkness…*'

But there was something there. They'd seen it. Physical. Writhing. Tentacles. Claws. A slimmer of… slime, or shell. Something sluggish. Quivering. Stretching. Reaching.

'Why did we take so much…?' Cass asked. 'We were too greedy… we stole, stole too much…'

She was feeling it; the guilt and shame and sorrow.

'Kurt…' Shylee responded. 'We took it for…'

They both remembered at once. What they'd told Kurt. Made him remember. Now they remembered.

Cass gathered up the fire. All the beautiful firelight on the awful black. She skimmed the chrome copper and took a deep breath as The Fear itself rose before them like an unholy, almighty, incoming wave of –

TWENTY-THREE: DEAD

Davy was so pumped that he rushed right back into the thirtieth floor. Kelli was still on her back, on the desk, as though she didn't have the energy to get up, unless she absolutely had to.

'It's here, isn't it?'

'Kelli, we have to get out. It's killed a bum on the ground floor, and the mad woman with him is pointing the finger…'

'Killed…?'

'Melted him, sucked all the flesh off his bones, then sucked the bones dry. There's only goo left. Just shit and dust.'

Kelli sat up, like a vampire from an old horror movie.

'Are you sure?'

Davy wasn't listening. He went for the books in the corner and took the old rucksack he used as a pillow, and stuffed them in. The rest of what they owned was already in there; clean underwear, a second tee.

'Why?' Kelli whined. 'What have we done? Why is it coming after us?'

Davy stared into her eyes as he walked back to her.

She'd lost it.

'What's anyone done…?' Davy muttered to himself.

They heard a commotion downstairs, echoing up through the shaft and down the corridor. More cops had arrived. Then the building hummed. The power was back on.

'They're coming up in the…'

They could hear what sounded like a SWAT team coming up the stairs, too. Suddenly the elevator door at the end of the corridor dinged, and closed. The building seemed to roar as they heard all of the heavy doors beneath them close, almost all at once.

'The belly of the beast…' Kelli uttered, emotional. 'It's coming alive and we're inside it…'

Danny snapped.

'We exist. That's what we've done.'

Kelli smiled at him. 'You go.'

The footsteps on the stairs grew louder. The sound of the cables clattering, and gears changing, and wheels grinding, seemed insanely loud, and rude, and brutal. The sounds stopped. More clattering and rolling. The cage had reached the ground floor.

'We have to get out, Kelli. We have to rush.'

Kelli smiled, defeated, sympathetic.

'I can't, Davy. I'm half dead. I could barely walk to you from here, let alone…'

Davy grabbed her shoulders. He could feel, beneath, so thin and frail, and tiny.

He had failed; his one job was to protect her, and he had failed.

'We can go slow; double back, as soon as they come in…' He was thinking it through, desperately as he spoke. '…we go down three floors, then three, then three…'

'I can't…' A huge tear rolled down her cheek. Half as big as her eyeball. '…and even if I could, Davy… where to from there?'

He ignored her question. 'We can, Kelli! We can go! We can reach somewhere they won't find us!'

'Dammit, Davy…' Kelli rasped, trying to shout, but too weak. 'They have found us!'

He let go of her.

'Davy, this is supposed to be the place they can't find us!' She was broken, done. It was awful to see. 'It's over, Davy! We're dead!'

A man wearing a dusty tuxedo jacket and a fur top hat materialized at the end of the desk.

Davy stared at him, his mouth agape.

A man… no older than he was.

'I'm Crispin.'

TWENTY-FOUR: NO

Oh, *no*, Kelli sighed within.

She felt a second tear descend down the same cheek.

She hadn't known that there were any tears left.

She'd cried the first few nights Davy had gone out on his own, without her; not because of that, of being left here alone by the only person left in her life. Just because she had finally found herself alone. Alone, somewhere she could allow it all to come out without concerning him. Without anyone else hearing, anyone at all.

Then, after about five nights of crying, almost on command each time she sensed Davy was a good block away, the tears had stopped.

She had thought then that she'd never cry again.

She'd thought she'd burned that facility out, forever.

Still one of two left, apparently. Saved, for movements such as these; when she'd been ready to die, at her brother's side, having given it the best damn shot that she, that they, possibly damn well could have given. But knowing, always, the whole time, that eventually it would catch up with them. And now, right when she had made peace with the fact that this was the end, that this was it, that they were going to die, by either the Bureau, or The Fear, or his temper, or his libido; always one of these things had been going to kill them, and now it actually was, in effect, she suspected, all of those things, all of the above, about to kill them, no way out, and okay, okay, time to go now, time to sleep and…

She'd really thought this was it.

But no, a last minute reprieve.

She'd come from a death penalty state; she understood now how it could be torture, merciless, intolerable cruelty enough to drive you insane…

Back from the brink of acceptance and the abyss…

The dream last night, someone breaking in…

She'd sensed someone down there but had been too weak, too frightened to look properly.

She'd sensed the things closing in, down there.

The Fear.

But her Wrath was so weak as well, so faded and dull, almost chilly, that she was starting to think it had all been imaginary, a shared illusion from people equally as delusional, along the road.

A virus they all had, that made them all think they were…

Hyperpsychics, or…

…somethin'…

Davy just stood there, gaping at Crispin.

'Listen…' Crispin reached up and popped his hand upon the top of his hat, securing it one centimeter tighter on his head after the rush. It looked like an unconscious move, but a regular one, like nervous habit, and she… she liked him, immediately.

'Listen, it's the cops. Most of them aren't really expecting hyperpsychics, they're expecting a hyper-psycho. But there are at least a dozen coming up the stairs, and maybe a dozen more crammed into that lift, with another dozen waiting in the lobby. Some of them believe in us, some of them don't, that's just the way it is.'

He smiled.

God, such a knowing smile.

The kind of cunning you want on your side.

'This isn't the first body that's turned up like this.'

'Crispin?' Davy demanded.

'I know a way out.'

'What?'

'We can rush through the city.'

'But that's…'

'That would be breaking the golden rule, I know.'

'We all know that…' Kelli uttered. 'All of us…'

Crispin shrugged. 'We just have to go from building to building. I know a way, I've spent a long time, mapping pathways through the city, urban exploring, searching for safe stepping stones where no-one goes. Places where someone can appear out of nowhere and not be spotted, by people or cameras or satellites.'

Davy stepped forward, angry. Furious she saw, as his fist clenched, about to punch him.

Crispin didn't back off. He totally understood and just kept talking, calm and knowing.

'You know we can't go about in threes; you're new here, only a month, I've been watching you, and some of the others, to see, if you were okay. Not a lure…'

'A lure?'

'I heard some of us have gone over, and they're luring us in, to places like this. There are places like this, all over, too good to be true some of them, but they are true, as it happens, and they are real. Mostly. But you still have to be…' Crispin closed his eyes, tight. He had freckles across his nose, and long black eyelashes. He opened his eyes again. Blue, like the ocean on a sunny day. They looked completely out of place; here especially, but anywhere in this world. '…it's great, finally being here and introducing myself and talking to you…'

'Is this true?' Kelli demanded.

Davy snarled. 'You're Bureau!'

'…but this isn't the time for me to explain all of this, or who I am or…'

Crispin pointed out of the window, diagonally to the building to the right.

'From this block we can rush across the street to that building. The top six floors are vacant, locked off. Right across, even with this floor, straight line, across the open sky!'

Davy snarled again. 'I don't believe you!'

'Look, Davy Worth, you saw me. Before, I sensed it… right?'

Davy went to say something snarky, in denial.

But then Kelli saw his features drop; his whole angry façade vanish. Gone.

'I'm sorry,' Crispin continued. 'I've spent a few nights here myself before you guys moved in. But I am totally for real; from over there, we can go to the empty top floor of an old state government building another block west, and from there, sweet suburbia, if you want. But you don't have to; there are places here, safe places. I've been wanting to...' Crispin sighed suddenly, exasperated. 'Davy, we have seconds.'

Kelli chimed in. She thought it right. Davy was almost as beat as she was.

'Davy, I think he's for real.'

'What's wrong?' Crispin asked, sensing her despair. 'I know every route there is; more than that, I have a safe place, I think we call all stay there...'

'What?'

'I think we can all stay there, I just need to... look, *what is it?*'

Kelli almost tripped over herself as she walked to the window, one foot not rising properly and connecting with the back calf of the other leg. Then she steadied herself.

With one bound, Kelli was free...

Except...

She practically heard the penny drop in Crispin's head.

'Wait... how long since you guys had a Mac attack?'

Kelli stared across at the building.

So... God... damn... close.

'You need good concentration for a rush that long...'

Kelli heard Crispin sigh deeply.

Then she turned back and saw him look to Davy.

'That's true...' Crispin uttered. '...she's right. You do need solid energy. For the particularly scary ones.'

'Thirty story skylines...' Davy uttered. 'Two blocks distant...'

She saw the look on Crispin's face; pain.

Emotional pain. That he had... what?

Waited too long?

Watched too long? Been too cautious? Too paranoid?

All of the above.

But she was willing to bet all of that was what had kept him alive this long.

Then, he did something she so admired; something she found amazing. Crispin immediately changed gears, just as they heard the elevator crunch again. He found the positive, where there was none.

'Listen…' He looked back and forth, speaking more quickly in his deceptively easygoing Australian accent. '…this isn't so bad. Right? I mean, listen, there are things I know, about the Bureau, and if you're going to get caught by the cops, this is the best day for it…'

'What?'

'Listen, Dave, mate, I am *totally* serious.' The way he specifically pronounced the 't' on the end of mate. Clipped. He really was totally serious, somehow. 'I've been watching, for months. I was an actor. I did a movie about urban explorers.'

'You were an actor?'

'Sidekick, in a couple of low budget… look, that doesn't matter. I was ready, when this happened. It happens to actors, but I got lucky. It happens to people who…' He pulled himself together again; he was nice, she could see. He wanted to tell them things, help them, share, but there wasn't time. He was dealing with the fact that there wasn't time, just as much as they were.

Then she realized something else.

Like he'd said; he had been waiting for this.

He'd been lonely, and building up to it, trying to be sensible but fighting off the lonely. He squeezed his eyes shit. For some reason he'd stopped looking at her. '…look, you're going to escape and we can talk later, okay?'

Kelli shrugged, amazed at his confidence. 'Sure…'

He kept his eyes squeezed shut. 'Just *don't do anything* to make them *shoot you*, here, and now, okay?' He opened his eyes again, looked back and forth again. But he didn't really look, not at her. At Davy maybe, but not at her. 'Some of them will want to; if they're looking for an excuse, this will be where they find it. Don't give them one, don't give them *anything*. Just get down on the ground, hands behind your head, do as they say, and just stay still. Don't say anything…'

'Has this happened to you before?' Davy asked, his voice resigned and weary.

'I've seen it before…' Crispin confessed. 'But like I said, tonight it's okay; really. The people who run the Bureau, the worst one is having a day off. She's the one who's actually in charge. If she was here you'd be dead in half an hour, the Bureau would turn up and let you run, because you're weak, then they'd track you and chase you like animals…'

Davy snarled. 'We know…'

'But she's not here; she's gone, to the country, she does it at least once a fortnight. But the other thing is; the other one, the weird one, the one who thinks he's in charge, he's gone too, flew off somewhere for the night. They hate each other; they want to kill each other, so their personal war is getting in the way of their jobs, which is good for us; for you two, tonight, now.'

'I get it…' Davy uttered, hoarse. Maybe a shred of hope.

'The police…' Kelli understood as well. '…they think we're the Black Dog.'

Kelli looked to Crispin. He looked at her, a certain keenness in his eyes, then past her, across the skyline again.

She knew what he was thinking; what she was thinking herself.

Kelli looked back to the building and thought, thought hard.

Could she?

Just – once?

With everything she had?

Then she felt her knees give out. She was shocked, and threw her arms out to stop her face impacting the glass. She ended up on her side, sliding down, then with her arms out, up, pressed against the glass. She heard herself gasp, in a definitive tone of quiet surrender.

'We'll never make it…'

Crispin kept talking regardless. 'Then, there's no other way out for you. You have to let them take you.'

'Kelli,' Davy urged. 'It's okay. If it's just the cops, we can escape, *psyche them*, then we'll run and head north…'

Crispin looked to him and scoffed. 'North?'

'There's a colony there. Some place called Darwin. People like us.'

Kelli looked back and saw Crispin stare at Davy, pitiful. She saw, that Davy saw, in Crispin's eyes, that there was no colony. She saw him nudge his head to the side, toward Kelli. Crispin looked back at Kelli. She turned fully away from the view, her back, her black cape, against the tinted glass, and let go of everything.

She smiled at Crispin. She let him know it was okay.

'Stop lying to yourselves, to each other…' Crispin demanded, firmly but not unfairly. '…you need to believe this, what I say now, regardless of whatever you've been telling each other.' He looked from Kelli to Davy. 'There is no colony. Either we survive here, in the darkness, or we die. That's all there is.'

Then he looked out, across the skyline.

Kelli saw him… assess the rush.

She saw him look out.

He had a kind face, she could see. A buddy face, that could be in anything; comedy, drama, melancholy, any age, any style. He was a character actor, a good looking character actor, with strong dark eyebrows and sad eyes, an expressive mouth with a crooked smile, and a strong stance, like he knew himself.

Like he was solid, within.

As he assessed the gap, his fingers had curled in and were rolling, tapping the air, nervously. All the time, his hands had been moving, his eyes darting here and there… avoiding her.

Then Kelli knew.

He was not just one of them.

He was one for her.

He was one she could be with.

He didn't look at her, he looked to Davy.

Because he *couldn't look at her.*

'Play the undernourished card. Don't talk; can't talk. If you survive the next few minutes, the cops will feed you. They'll bring in a psychologist. A care worker. They'll talk. I've seen this before. Let the food digest before you run. Get coffee. Get a double shot. Then run. Look for me, Davy. Look for me and follow me when you see me, okay?'

Davy looked to her. She looked back from the floor, up into his eyes, and again let him know it was okay.

The elevator dinged.

'I have to –'

'*Go,*' Davy demanded.

Kelli watched him look back at the rush.

He did not even look at her.

He couldn't bear it, she knew.

'I'm sorry.'

And he was gone.

TO BE CONTINUED...

For the next book in this series
and other novels by Alex James...

www.GalexyTales.com

(OR SEARCH

"GALEXY TALES"

AT AMAZON...)

Novels by Alex James:

DARK STREETS:
Book One: Agents of Fear
Book Two: Avatars of Wrath (in 2019)

AMAZON SEVEN
VOLUME ONE
Book One: Mission Queen
Book Two: Queen Renegade
Book Three: Intergalactic Ingenue (Pre-order)
Book Four: Princess Executor (Pre-order)

SAGA OF THE URBAN SORCERERS:
Book One: The Summoning of Barker Moon
Book Two: The Reckoning of Emerald Tarragon
Book Three: The Shaping of Cheryl Equiniox (Pre-order)

THE CHRONICLES OF THE TERRAGUARD:
Book One: Maker of Rules

THE ASCENSION SEQUENCE:
VOLUME ONE
The Pandora Sequence
VOLUME TWO
Book One: The Pandora Inheritance
Book Two: The Pandora Arcana (Pre-order)
Book Three: The Daughters of Pandora (Pre-order)

www.GalexyTales.com

(or search "GALEXY TALES" at Amazon!)

Acknowledgements

Enormous thanks and much love to Melissa Sheldrick.

Endless kudos to Michal Dutkiewicz for the brilliant cover.

Huge thanks to Adam Dutkiewicz for the formatting.

Massive gratitude to Gretel Newman-Sugrue for her excellent suggestions.

Many thanks to all four for their patience, help and advice.

Thanks to Bronwyn Bean, Greg C. Grace, Pat McNamara, Dave Oz, Hamish Stokes, Melissa Stokes, and Francis White, for help, advice and encouragement.

And again just, thanks, really, to everyone who helped.

Thanks!

About the Author

Alex James is a writer who lives in and is inspired by Adelaide, South Australia.

Alex studied European History, Classical Mythology, Film Studies and Screenwriting under the Communications and Liberal Studies banners at the University of South Australia.

Between 1992 and 2005 he wrote many, many, many outlines, treatments, concept documents, bibles, pilots and screenplays, for just about every active Australian production company there was.

From 2008-2014 he was an in-house writer for Angel-Phoenix Media, who published his first two e-book novels, *The Pandora Sequence* and *Venus AI*, both of which were launched at the 2013 San Diego Comic-Con.

Alex's most recent works are epic novel sagas which include *The Saga of The Urban Sorcerers*, *Amazon Seven*, *Dark Streets*, *The Chronicles of The Terraguard*, and *The Ascension Sequence*.

He publishes via his own independent imprint, Galexy Tales.